JUSTICE POSTPONED

Recent Titles by Anthea Fraser from Severn House

The Rona Parish Mysteries
(in order of appearance)

BROUGHT TO BOOK
JIGSAW
PERSON OR PERSONS UNKNOWN
A FAMILY CONCERN
ROGUE IN PORCELAIN
NEXT DOOR TO MURDER
UNFINISHED PORTRAIT
A QUESTION OF IDENTITY
JUSTICE POSTPONED

Other Titles

PRESENCE OF MIND
THE MACBETH PROPHECY
BREATH OF BRIMSTONE
MOTIVE FOR MURDER
DANGEROUS DECEPTION
PAST SHADOWS
FATHERS AND DAUGHTERS
THICKER THAN WATER
SHIFTING SANDS
THE UNBURIED PAST

JUSTICE POSTPONED

Anthea Fraser

This first world edition published 2014
in Great Britain and the USA by
SEVERN HOUSE PUBLISHERS LTD of
19 Cedar Road, Sutton, Surrey, England, SM2 5DA.
Trade paperback edition first published
in Great Britain and the USA 2015 by
SEVERN HOUSE PUBLISHERS LTD.

British Library Cataloguing in Publication Data

Fraser, Anthea author.
    Justice postponed. – (The Rona Parish mysteries)
    1. Parish, Rona (Fictitious character)–Fiction. 2. Women
    authors–England–Fiction. 3. Chiltern Hills (England)–
    Fiction. 4. Detective and mystery stories.
    I. Title II. Series
    823.9'14-dc23

ISBN-13: 978-0-7278-8418-3 (cased)
ISBN-13: 978-1-84751-528-5 (trade paper)

All Severn House titles are printed on acid-free paper.

Severn House Publishers support the Forest Stewardship Council™ [FSC™],
the leading international forest certification organisation. All our titles that
are printed on FSC certified paper carry the FSC logo.

MIX
Paper from
responsible sources
FSC
www.fsc.org   FSC® C013056

Typeset by Palimpsest Book Production Ltd.,
Falkirk, Stirlingshire, Scotland.
Printed and bound in Great Britain by
TJ International, Padstow, Cornwall.

PROLOGUE

God, what had he *done*? This should never have happened – he couldn't believe that it had! In the cold light of dawn he sat on the edge of the bed, raking his fingers through his hair and thinking back over the evening behind him. It had started in the rush hour – she'd been lost and panicky and it was starting to rain, so after giving her directions he'd suggested they had a drink till the shower stopped. She agreed readily enough and it hadn't dawned on him that she wasn't used to alcohol till it became clear she'd had too much, by which stage he couldn't just abandon her.

So he'd followed his usual practice and taken her back to his flat. She'd seemed so impressed with it and with him that he assumed she was expecting him to make love to her – damn it, most girls did – and by the time he realized she wasn't just playing the tease it was too late to stop.

He groaned, putting his head in his hands. Because as she'd lain there sobbing he'd begun to suspect with dawning horror that, despite the heavy make-up, she was nowhere near the seventeen she'd claimed to be, and that realization coupled with the alcohol he'd consumed rose as vomit in his throat. He'd made a dash for the bathroom, and by the time he returned she had gone.

That was when the panic set in. He'd flung on some clothes and dashed into the street but there was no sign of her, and for the next few days he'd lived in dread of an official knock on the door. But none came and gradually the panic eased, if not the remorse. At least, thank God, he'd not used his real name, a ruse he always employed with one-night stands. But, oh, God, he would have given a great deal to be able to turn back the clock.

ONE

September already, Rona thought, flipping over the calendar. Where had the summer gone? Not, on reflection, that it had been uneventful; the Furness family, who owned the house next door, had, after a long sojourn overseas, returned to reclaim their extensively modernized and redecorated house, providing herself and Max with permanent rather than transitory neighbours – a very welcome move. Another major change was that her mother and her fiancé Guy Lacey had moved from the old Parish home in Belmont and installed themselves on the outskirts of town, and to celebrate there was to be a family lunch there today by way of a house-warming.

An *extended* family lunch, Rona reminded herself, since not only she, Max and Lindsey, but Guy's daughter Sarah and *her* fiancé, due to marry next month, would be there as well.

The family had also expanded in the other direction to include Catherine, who would marry Rona's father, Tom, when her parents' divorce was finalized, together with Catherine's son, daughter-in-law and baby granddaughter. After all those years of its being just Mum, Pops, her twin Lindsey and herself, it took a bit of getting used to.

The front door slammed as her husband returned from walking the dog, followed by a pattering as Gus, released from his lead, loped down the basement stairs and into the kitchen, making for his water bowl.

A moment later Max followed him. 'It looks like being a scorcher,' he commented. 'If we're going to be in the garden, I hope they've enough umbrellas.'

'There were a couple at home,' Rona said. 'Mum's sure to have taken them with her. It'll be odd, won't it, only having to drive ten minutes instead of twenty to visit them?'

Max slipped an arm round her. 'You miss the old home, don't you?'

'I suppose so, though it was never the same after Pops moved out. It'll seem strange seeing familiar furniture in a new setting.'

'Intermingled, no doubt, with Guy's. All things considered it's worked out well, the four of them each making a fresh start.' He glanced at her. 'The only one *not* doing so is Lindsey. Or rather, she's making too many.'

Rona frowned, moving away to fill the kettle. Implied criticism of her twin triggered defensiveness coupled with irritation, for there was no denying Lindsey *had* made mistakes, and though successful in her career – she was a partner in a firm of solicitors – her personal life had consisted of one disaster after another.

She had married and then divorced Hugh Cavendish but had continued to dally with him between affairs, one of which had been with a murderer from whom Hugh had had to rescue her. Other liaisons had involved Jonathan Hurst, a fellow partner at Chase Mortimer, and Dominic Frayne who, Rona suspected, was the love of her twin's life, but whose sleeping arrangements with his attractive assistant had led to what seemed to be a permanent break-up. Matters were further complicated by the fact that Hugh had recently acquired a girlfriend and was no longer at Lindsey's beck and call, and to Rona's disquiet she seemed to be drifting back to Jonathan, a married man with a family.

Max's voice broke into her thoughts. 'Have we got them a house-warming present?'

'Some coasters,' she replied, pushing her worries aside. 'Rather nice ones, with local views. It was hard to know what to go for when they already have the contents of two houses between them!'

'Good choice; you can't have too many coasters. What time are we due there?'

'Around twelve. I've been wondering what to do about Gus; I forgot to check, and as you know Mum wasn't too keen on having him at Maple Drive.'

'That was during her difficult stage,' Max reminded her. 'She's mellowed since Guy came on the scene.'

'All the same, I think on this first visit we should play safe.'

'Fair enough. At least he's had a good walk, which should last him till we get back.'

Once clear of the confines of town, Guild Street, Marsborough's main shopping centre, metamorphosed into Belmont Road, leading eventually to the suburb where Rona had grown up. Along the route were sporadic groups of houses, a couple of shopping parades and a school, and just beyond one of these clusters Max turned left into

Brindley Grove. It was a cul-de-sac of some twenty houses of varying designs and sizes, and Guy and Avril's was halfway down on the right, easily identified by the copper beeches either side of the gates, which now stood open.

They'd not been here since their initial visit soon after the previous owners moved out, when the house had been completely bare. Rona had mixed feelings about seeing it in its new guise as her mother's home in which she herself had no part – feelings she hastily dismissed as both Guy and Avril came hurrying out to meet them.

'Welcome to Tall Trees!' Avril cried gaily. 'Our very first visitors!'

'I hope we're not too early,' Rona said, returning her mother's kiss and receiving one from Guy.

'Not at all!' Avril assured her. 'Someone has to be first, but we'll wait till everyone's here before we do the grand tour. Now, come inside and have a drink.'

Guy peered into the back of the car. 'No Gus?'

'We weren't too sure he'd be welcome,' Max admitted.

'Nonsense, of course he would. We're thinking of getting a dog ourselves.'

Rona bit back an exclamation of surprise. Throughout their childhood Avril had withstood all her daughters' pleading for pets and once Rona was married with a home of her own, one of their first purchases had been the retriever puppy. Avril had taken her arm and was leading her up the path. 'It's an attractive-looking house, isn't it?' she said contentedly, and Rona had to agree with her. Like others in the road it was built of the local stone, with a bay window either side of the door and a steeply pitched roof. As they went inside her first impression was of light and space since the hallway, panelled in pale wood, was filled with sunshine flooding in from the open door and the window at the head of the stairs; but she'd barely had time to register it when Guy's voice reached them from outside.

'The others have arrived!' he called, and they went out again to see Sarah and her fiancé, Clive, emerging from a car and Lindsey coming through the gates, a sheaf of flowers in her hand.

There was initial awkwardness as they all greeted each other and moved en bloc into the house, talking and exclaiming at the same time. Rona had met Sarah only a few times, Clive even fewer, and Lindsey hardly knew them at all. They both taught at Belmont

Primary School, Clive as a PE instructor, and it was when Sarah, moving from her home in Stokely, had answered Avril's advertisement for a lodger that the Laceys had entered their lives.

'Now,' Avril said when everyone had a glass, 'we'll show you round the house, then we can all move outside.'

As Rona had foreseen, there was a pang in seeing well-loved furniture in these new surroundings, but as she had to admit it fitted admirably into its new location and, mixed with pieces from Guy's previous home, created an attractive and comfortable ambience. Even in the dining room, furnished with the suite from Stokely, the china and glasses on the table were those she'd known all her life.

The inspection duly completed they were led through the sitting room and out on to the terrace where, to Max's relief, two large umbrellas provided shade.

'Now,' Guy began, 'before I sit down, let me top up your drinks. Rona – sorry, Lindsey!' He gave an embarrassed laugh as he took her glass. 'I so seldom see you together I have difficulty telling you apart!'

Yet beneath the surface, Max thought privately, they could hardly be more different. He could not forget – though he'd tried often enough – that Lindsey had arrived at his studio one evening after her marriage broke up and begged him to make love to her. It was something he'd never told Rona and never would, but Lindsey hadn't forgiven him for sending her packing and relations between them had been strained ever since.

Having refreshed their drinks, Guy seated himself and raised his glass. 'Here's to Tall Trees, its residents and all who visit it!'

They joined in the toast and he sat back in his chair. 'Now, that's quite enough about us and our affairs. What have you all been up to? Rona? Any thoughts on your next project?'

Rona shook her head. 'I'm still coasting,' she said. With a difficult biography at last behind her, she had put on her other hat as occasional contributor to the prestigious monthly *Chiltern Life*, an altogether less demanding occupation. 'Max is the one with some news,' she added. 'He's been asked to do two portraits, of our new MP and of the principal of the art college.'

'I did suggest the head commission one of his students to do it,' Max remarked, breaking into the chorus of congratulations, 'but no one took me seriously.'

'And Lindsey?' Avril smiled encouragingly. 'What about you?'

'Nothing to report, I'm afraid.' Lindsey's voice was brittle. 'Just the same old, same old.'

Rona felt a quiver of unease. Her sister wasn't meeting her eyes, but now wasn't the time to probe. Guy, meanwhile, had turned to his own daughter.

'And you two, of course, are on the final countdown! Not long now!'

'Seven weeks and six days!' Clive supplied, and everyone laughed. He was a tall, broad-shouldered young man as befit his profession, his face and arms tanned and his fair hair bleached almost white by the summer sun. Little though she knew him, Rona felt more at ease with him than with Sarah, who could be somewhat prickly.

Avril glanced at her watch. 'Lunch in ten minutes,' she announced, 'so if any of you want to freshen up, now's your chance. The downstairs "facilities" are to the left of the stairs.'

As she went back into the house, Lindsey rose to her feet and followed her. The conversation round the table continued but Rona was only half-listening and, after a couple of minutes, she too went inside, hoping for a private word.

'Everything OK, sis?' she asked anxiously as Lindsey re-emerged into the hall.

'Not really.' Her cheeks were flushed. 'I just *hate* being odd man out on these occasions, when all the rest of you are in pairs.'

'Oh, Linz!' Rona said helplessly. 'It's only temporary, you'll soon—'

'—latch on to someone else unsuitable?' Lindsey cut in bitterly.

Rona studied her face. 'There's something else, isn't there?'

Lindsey hesitated.

'How about lunch tomorrow? We could talk it over.'

'All right, but it will have to be quick. Twelve fifteen at the Bacchus?'

'I'll be there.' And as Lindsey went to rejoin the others, Rona determinedly put her anxieties on hold.

The lunch was up to Avril's usual standard: cold watercress soup with swirls of cream served with home-made croutons, a side of salmon in aspic decorated with shrimps and circles of cucumber, a selection of British cheeses and a raspberry pavlova. By the time they returned to the patio the sun had moved off it and Guy closed the umbrellas.

'We haven't had a tour of the garden yet,' Max commented.

'It was too hot before lunch and you can see most of it from here. But we can wander round now if you like.'

So, with the afternoon sun warm on their backs, they strolled past sweet-smelling herbaceous borders, an ornamental pool and a neat vegetable patch screened by a hawthorn hedge, to the summer-house at the far end. Here, nature had been allowed to run wild and there were lush grasses, wild flowers and the murmur of bees.

'It's heavenly,' Lindsey said. 'Almost makes me wish I'd a garden at the flat!'

'"Almost" being the operative word,' Rona told her. 'Your idea of gardening is to sit in a deck chair and give orders!'

'It'll require a fair bit of work,' Max remarked, grateful for his own paved plot with its ornamental tubs and statues.

'I'll enjoy it,' Guy said. 'I'm hoping to take early retirement, and it'll give me something to do.'

Rona turned and looked back at the house, its patio doors standing open and the drooping umbrellas by the table where they'd had drinks. Sarah and Clive had stopped by the pool and were looking down into it, hand in hand.

'Love's young dream,' Lindsey remarked, following her gaze.

'Long may it last,' Guy said quietly, and Rona, seeing her mother slip her hand into his, felt a lump in her throat. It was a continuing wonder to her that this was the same woman who for years had taken no interest in her appearance, who had complained and criticized and generally made life difficult for everyone. Small wonder that her father had finally snapped and, on meeting the quiet, restful Catherine, decided to cut his losses. Had Avril's metamorphosis happened only months earlier, things could have been very different and family lunch might still have been held at Maple Drive.

'Nice house,' Max said noncommittally in the car on the way home. 'I wouldn't like to take on that garden, though, particularly at Guy's time of life.'

'They can find a gardener if it gets too much for him.'

'True. And I suppose, before we know it, we'll be shown round Tom and Catherine's new place! Have they started looking yet?'

'I don't think so, but in any case they wouldn't move in till they're married. Pops is insisting they stay under their own roofs to avoid gossip and protect Catherine's ex-headmistress reputation. Mind you . . .' She broke off with a smile.

'Quite!' said Max. He glanced at her. 'Lindsey was rather quiet, I thought. You went after her, didn't you, before lunch?'

'Yes, but she's fine. We've not seen each other for a while so we're meeting for lunch tomorrow. Sarah's a strange girl, isn't she?' she went on, adroitly changing the subject. 'Pretty unforthcoming. I remember Mum saying she had a difficult time with her when she first moved in, even before Mum and Guy started seeing each other.'

'Pampered only child, apple of her father's eye?'

'Perhaps.'

'She and Avril seem OK now.'

'Yes; meeting Clive probably made her less possessive of Guy. Which reminds me, we've not decided on a wedding present. I must have another look at the list, though they won't be short of the essentials; once Mum and Guy had taken what they wanted, Sarah had the pick of the Stokely house and a fair bit has gone into storage till they move to somewhere bigger.'

'House-moving seems on the agenda all round,' Max remarked. 'I'm just thankful we're exempt.'

A feature of the Bacchus wine bar was the individual booths that lined its walls, separated by shoulder-high divisions which gave the illusion of privacy. Rona, seated in one of them, saw her sister come in and raised her hand, watching her thread her way between the tables. It was another hot day, and as Lindsey sat down Rona poured glasses of ice-cold water from the jug on the table. They avoided wine with lunch when they were working, and though Rona would have been free to enjoy a glass, Lindsey was not. 'I'm opting for onion quiche and a side salad,' Rona said.

'Sounds good.' Lindsey drained her glass. 'God, it's hot out there.'

The waiter approached and they gave their order. Then Rona folded her hands on the table. 'Now,' she invited, 'tell me what's wrong.'

Lindsey shrugged. 'It's nothing desperate; sorry if I gave that impression.'

'But there is something, isn't there?'

She sighed resignedly. 'Well, if you must know, it's Jonathan. I didn't want to tell you because you don't approve anyway, but he's getting more and more demanding, and – even worse – he takes risks at work, coming into my office all the time and so on. It's as though he doesn't care who knows about us, but at a firm like Chase Mortimer affairs between partners are a definite no-no, particularly when one of them is married. If it came out, one of us would be expected to leave, and I'll give you three guesses who it would be.' She reached for the jug to refill her glass. 'Damn it, Ro, affairs are meant to be fun – the odd stolen night together, a discreet dinner out of town. Anything too routine spoils the concept.' She smiled fleetingly. 'Which is why I'm not good wife material!'

'And Jonathan's crowding you?'

'Exactly. He wants to see me almost every evening. It's getting altogether too heavy, not helped by the fact that he insists he's in love with me. That wasn't part of the deal.'

'Because he's not Dominic?'

Lindsey flushed. 'That was below the belt.'

'Sorry, but it's true, isn't it? I suppose there's no chance . . .?'

'Not as long as Bloody Carla's on the scene.' In the last year or so the adjective had become part of the assistant's name.

Rona sighed. 'So, to get back to Jonathan, what are you going to do? Warn him off? That could be tricky, when you have to work together.'

'Exactly,' Lindsey said again. 'Also, if you remember the last time I broke it off he was spiteful and malicious for months and made things really uncomfortable.'

Rona shook her head. 'You should never have restarted it.'

'Wise words, sister dear, but not much help now.'

The waiter materialized and laid their plates in front of them, placing crescent-shaped dishes of salad alongside.

'You were a bit evasive yourself when Guy asked you about work,' Lindsey commented, sprinkling vinaigrette over her salad. '*Have* you anything on at the moment?'

'Not really; I did a couple of articles on blue and white china, which Barnie seemed quite happy with.' Barnie Trent was the features editor at *Chiltern Life*. 'What he'd really like, though, is for me to embark on another series of some kind that could run for several months.'

'Like the one you did on the history of local firms?'

Rona nodded. 'I didn't want to go into it yesterday because I've not thought it through, but I'm toying with a similar idea, based on individuals this time rather than firms. Originally I'd thought of something along the lines of *Moments That Changed My Life* but there mightn't be enough of those for a series. On the other hand, there must be plenty of people whose lives have been a bit unusual, like our next-door neighbours who've spent a lot of time abroad. They should be good for a couple of articles if I can talk them into cooperating.'

'Sounds an excellent idea. Go for it.' Lindsey paused, her thoughts returning to the previous day. 'It was weird, wasn't it, seeing Mum in a new domestic set-up?'

'Yes, and as Max said, we'll soon have Pops following suit. It's amazing to think the decree absolute will be through in a few months.'

'Fresh starts all round.'

Remembering Max's comments on the subject, Rona merely nodded in reply.

Unaware that his daughters were discussing him, Tom Parish was also thinking about lunch. He'd spent the morning preparing a meal for Catherine that evening – an undertaking more complicated than he'd bargained for – and the thought of now having to produce something for himself was a step too far. What he needed, he told himself, was to get out of the kitchen for a while and enjoy a spot of fresh air followed by a pub lunch, after which he could return to his task with renewed vigour.

He therefore set off at a brisk walk for Guild Street, and had reached the doorway of the Five Feathers when he heard his name called and turned to see his old friend Frank Hathaway hurrying towards him.

'Tom! I thought it was you! Good to see you!'

Tom took his outstretched hand, guilt washing over him. 'Frank, how are you? I've been meaning—'

'If you're thinking of a pub lunch,' Frank interrupted, nodding at the door behind them, 'I'd be happy to join you, unless you're meeting someone?'

'No, no, I'd be delighted.'

When they were seated with glasses of beer in front of them, Tom took stock of the man opposite. Older and greyer was his immediate impression, and there were lines between the eyes he'd not noticed before – hardly surprising in the circumstances. They'd met at university and though never close had, over the years, managed to bump into one another without actively seeking each other out. The last time he'd seen Frank was at his wife's funeral almost two years ago, which he and Avril had attended shortly before they broke up. However, his guilt stemmed from the fact that in the interim Frank had been badly injured in a failed rescue attempt following a car crash and, though fully intending to, Tom had not contacted him.

'How are you getting on?' he asked now. 'I meant to phone after the accident, but—'

Frank dismissed his apology with a wave of his hand. 'At least I got out of it alive, unlike the other poor chap. As to life in general, I'm coping OK. My son and grandson are living with me at present, so I'm not rattling around so much.'

Tom stretched his memory. 'Wasn't your son working in the States?'

'That's right; he flew home for Ruth's funeral and I went back with him for a while. For two pins I'd have stayed there rather than face the empty house, but his contract was for a limited time and there was no point in uprooting myself when I'd have to come home again within a few months. As it happened it was extended, though only till last December, and since he'd rented out his home in Kent and the lease had a way to run, he and Luke came to me and, as I said, are still here. Luke has settled well at Marsborough Grammar and as Steve does most of his work on the phone or internet it doesn't matter where he's based.'

'Well, that's good.' Tom paused. 'Are you sure you're over your injuries, though? You still look a bit . . . drawn, if you don't mind my saying so.'

Frank swirled the beer round his glass, not meeting his friend's eyes. 'To tell you the truth,' he said after a moment, 'I'm a little concerned about Steve. Since he got back he's made no attempt at any kind of social life and resists all my efforts to introduce him to anyone, which is completely out of character. He seems to have no interests outside his work and, damn it, he's only forty-two.'

Again Tom struggled to retrieve barely registered facts. 'Didn't he . . .?'

'His wife – Ella – left him,' Frank said baldly. 'Seven years ago, when Luke was five. It was a body blow – he thought the world of her – but off she went with someone else and eventually married him. Naturally she took the boy and Steve was granted access, but it was never easy and Ruth and I hardly ever saw him.'

Frank shook his head sadly, remembering. 'That went on for several years, but then he was recommended for this secondment to the States, which put him in a quandary. If he turned it down it wouldn't look good on his CV. On the other hand, it would mean losing what little contact he had with Luke. And while he was agonizing over it, Ella was killed in a car crash.'

'Of course; I remember now.'

'She'd been drinking.' Frank's voice was expressionless. 'What's more, Luke was with her; it's a miracle he wasn't killed too. Anyway, the long and the short of it was there was nothing to keep Steve in the UK. He accepted the secondment and Luke went with him. Though it was a wrench for us, it was good for him to get away; he was grieving for Ella, having in effect lost her twice, and we assumed that given time he'd come out of it. It should only have been for twelve months, but the job proved more complicated than anticipated, so arrangements were made to lengthen it and in the end it was over two years.

'He met a girl over there – the boss's daughter, actually – and Ruth and I hoped it might come to something. She was still around when I was there after the funeral but she's not been mentioned since he came home – which could account for his unsociability – but since he blocks off any attempt at questioning I'm unable to help him.'

'You've a daughter too, haven't you?' Tom asked after a moment. 'Is she married?'

'Vanda? No, she's a career woman – jewellery designer, gold and silver mostly. She lives in London but she insisted on coming home after the accident and stayed till Steve came back, which was very good of her.' He picked up the menu on the table. 'What do you fancy?'

'Sausage and mash with onion gravy,' Tom said promptly. 'It's the house speciality.'

'Then I'll join you.'

Tom pushed back his chair. 'I'll order them.' He went to the bar and waited his turn, Frank's story circling in his head. He really should have contacted him, he chided himself; the accident coming relatively soon after Ruth's death would have been a double blow. At least he had family with him now, which would ease his loneliness, even if his son had brought more worries with him. Tom tried to picture him, but failed.

'They'll bring it over when it's ready,' he reported, reseating himself.

'What's the damage?'

'We can settle up later.'

Frank nodded. 'So . . . what have you been up to since I saw you? Avril keeping well?'

Tom's eyes widened; he hadn't realized quite how out of touch they were.

'She is, yes,' he answered carefully, 'but I'm afraid we're no longer together.'

Frank stared at him. 'What?'

'We separated nearly two years ago. It had been difficult for some time, rubbing each other up the wrong way and so on, and eventually we had to accept we'd be happier apart.'

Frank sat back in his chair, his eyes still on Tom's face. 'Well, you do surprise me! I thought your marriage was rock solid. So where are you living now? Still in Belmont?'

'No, I'm renting a flat in Talbot Road, but . . . it's temporary. We've both been lucky enough to find someone else, so once the divorce comes through there'll be a couple of weddings on the horizon.'

'Table six!' called the barman, and Tom turned and raised his hand. Two steaming plates were laid before them together with cutlery and condiments, and the interruption allowed both of them some breathing space.

'Well!' Frank said when they were alone again. 'I must say you're full of surprises!' He picked up his knife and fork. 'So, tell me more. Who is this new lady of yours and how did you meet?'

'She was a customer at the bank,' Tom answered. 'Still is, actually, though I've retired now. Her name is Catherine Bishop and she's a retired headmistress, a widow with a married son in Cricklehurst.'

Frank digested that for a moment. 'And Avril?'

'When I moved out she advertised for a lodger, and the young woman who applied was a teacher at Belmont Primary. Her father helped her move in, I gather one thing led to another, and he and Avril have just bought a house down the road in Brindley Grove.'

'You don't let the grass grow, do you, either of you? Have you met her new man?'

'A couple of times. I like him, and more importantly they're ideal for each other.'

'Well, I'm very glad for you both. If you're thinking of setting up a marriage bureau, bear Steve in mind!'

Tom laughed. 'I think first in the queue would be my daughter Lindsey.'

'Of course, your girls – I should have asked after them. Isn't one a writer?'

'A biographer, yes. She's happily settled, I'm glad to say, but Lindsey's divorced and as far as I know has no one on hand at the moment. I worry that she's unhappy.'

'Perhaps we should start our own bureau and bring her and Steve together.'

Tom smiled wryly. 'A potential pitfall if ever there was one! Much as I love her, Lindsey can be difficult and I'd say your son has had enough trauma in his life.'

'Let's hope they both sort themselves out, then, sooner rather than later.'

Their conversation drifted to mutual friends from the past and to Frank's previous peripatetic lifestyle. Working for an oil company, he and his wife had spent a large part of their lives overseas and in the process been involved in several precarious situations.

When they finally parted outside the pub, they resolved to keep in more regular touch.

'You must come for a meal and meet Catherine,' Tom said, which reminded him of the task awaiting him at home. Hurrying back down the road, he hoped fervently that his overly ambitious menu could be achieved without major disaster.

TWO

He hadn't been completely honest with Tom, Frank Hathaway reflected on his way home. It was true he was concerned about Steve, but if he was looking drawn, as Tom had said, it was down to the more urgent worry that was gnawing at him, a worry that, try as he might, he was unable to pinpoint.

All he knew was that on a crowded escalator at the station last week something had happened that brought him out in a cold sweat, reigniting the memory of the blazing car and leaving him so sick and shaken that when they reached street level he almost fell off and had to cling to the barrier until his panic subsided. And he still had no idea what it was! Had he subconsciously seen someone, heard something, smelt something that had triggered the memory? If so, who and what? Or, as seemed more than likely, was he being totally paranoid? He'd been warned there might be flashbacks, a symptom of post-traumatic stress, and been given hints on how to deal with them. But this was different from the others; this had seemed so *real*, so much in the here and now . . .

Impatiently he shook his head. It's over, he told himself, taking his front-door key from his pocket, and you're lucky to be alive. So pull yourself together and forget it.

Unfortunately, it was easier said than done.

It wasn't being a productive week; after lunch with Lindsey on Monday, there'd been a dental appointment on Tuesday and on Wednesday the car had to be taken in for its service. While none of these engagements had taken up much time, they'd served to distract Rona from settling down to plan her proposed new series. Now it was Thursday and she was still doodling at her desk, lost in thought, when the phone rang, identifying the caller as her father.

'Hi Pops! How are things?'

'Fine, sweetie, fine. I just happen to find myself in your vicinity with a giant-sized pizza in my carrier bag, still warm from the oven. Which is my less-than-subtle way of inviting myself to lunch.'

'Excellent! I'll put a couple of plates in the oven.'

She had just finished laying the table when the doorbell proclaimed his arrival, and Gus preceded her up the basement stairs, barking furiously.

'I *know* someone's there, you daft mutt!' Rona told him, taking hold of his collar before opening the door. 'Come in, Pops, and keep the carrier bag above nose level of the Hound of the Baskervilles.'

Obeying instructions, Tom kissed her cheek before turning to the dog jumping excitedly round his legs. 'Hello, Gus old man. Nothing here for you, I'm afraid.'

'Let's reheat it while we have a pre-prandial,' Rona suggested, leading the way back downstairs.

'Still not working then?'

'Afraid not. I'm mulling over a new series for Barnie, but I haven't sounded him out yet.'

Tom seated himself at the table, watching her slide the pizza into the oven. 'What is it this time?'

'Another local slant – interesting lives people have led. The Furnesses next door were abroad for years, which should be a good start.'

'Sounds a promising angle. Once it gets under way you'll be inundated with people eager for their fifteen minutes of fame!'

'Fine by me.' Rona took a bottle of Muscadet from the fridge. 'Provided their experiences are genuinely interesting, all contributions will be gratefully received.'

'Any news of the family?' Tom asked as she seated herself beside him.

'We had lunch at the new house last Sunday.'

'Ah, yes, you said you were going. What's it like?'

'Very nice; much the same size as Maple Drive, but with an extra room downstairs. There's a mixture of our furniture and Guy's, which felt a bit odd, but it goes well together. The garden's bigger and stretches back quite a way, and as Max pointed out will require a fair bit of attention.' She sipped her wine. 'We were wondering if you and Catherine had started looking for somewhere?'

'Not actively, no, though we glance in estate agents' windows as we pass, and if anything appealed we'd certainly take a look.'

'Any idea where you'd like to be?'

'Not really, as long as it's no more than half an hour out of town. We don't want to vegetate in our retirement!'

Rona laughed. 'Not much chance of that.'

'How's Lindsey?' Tom asked with assumed casualness.

'Fine. What with Sarah and Clive being there, we didn't get much chance to chat on Sunday so we met for lunch the next day.' Before he could enquire further, she added, 'What about you? Been hitting any high spots on the social scene?'

'Not that you'd notice. I did bump into Frank Hathaway the other day. Do you remember me speaking of him?'

'Vaguely.'

'He made the news last year when he pulled someone out of a crashed car which then tipped over, pinning them down, and burst into flames. God knows how he's still alive. Come to think of it, he'd be an ideal subject for your series: he and his wife lived abroad for years and had all manner of nerve-racking experiences. We never saw much of them, but every time we did they seemed to have been involved in some misadventure. Your mother commented that they were "incident-prone", which summed it up pretty neatly.'

'What kind of experiences?'

'Well, he was in Kuwait when Iraq invaded in 1990, and I remember him telling me he and Ruth were on that plane that was hijacked at Entebbe. How's that for starters?'

'Fantastic! Do you think he'd let me interview him?'

'I don't see why not. It might take his mind off his worries.'

'And what would they be?'

'Oh, he's a bit concerned about his son. He took off to the States after his wife's death, taking his young son with him, and worked there for a couple of years. They came back last December and for the moment they're living with Frank.'

'And that's what's worrying him?'

'No, no, he's glad to have them, but Steve seems to have become a bit introverted.'

'What about the boy? How old is he?'

'About twelve, I believe. He's seen a few changes in his life, poor kid,' Tom added reflectively. 'Ella took him when she left Steve to marry someone else, and he was in the car with her when she was killed.'

'So he was snatched from one father, presented with another, saw his mother die, was reclaimed by his real father, whisked off to another country, and is now living with his grandfather? It's a wonder *he's* not introverted! I hope he had counselling.'

Tom smiled wryly. 'They were in the States, remember, so I'd say you could bet on it!'

Rona pushed back her chair and went to retrieve the pizza, bringing it to the table together with the bowl of salad originally intended for her lunch. 'Well, I'd certainly like to talk to your friend, if you're sure he wouldn't mind. Could you put in a word for me?'

'Sure; we said we'd keep in touch. I'll mention it next time I see him.'

Tom had only just left when the phone rang, the caller this time being Rona's old school friend, Magda Ridgeway, who owned a string of fashion boutiques around the county.

'You *are* coming to my show next week?' she began, and before Rona could confirm it, added excitedly, 'We're featuring a few outfits from the Mackenzie autumn collection.'

'Yes, so I saw on the invitation. Is he the one who's been hitting the headlines?'

'That's right; he was awarded the MBE in the Birthday Honours last year. What's more, I met him in London two weeks ago, we got on really well, and I can hardly believe it but he's agreed to come to the show – which is especially good of him so close to Fashion Week. With luck, the fact that he's actually there should encourage customers to order.'

'That's really great, Magda, well done!'

'The reason I'm ringing is to invite you to a private supper afterwards. I doubt if it will be up Max's street – he'll be working anyway – but if Lindsey would like to come she'd be very welcome. There'll just be a dozen of us, all friends, since I couldn't show favour among customers.'

'We'd love to, thanks. With our cheque books, I presume?'

Magda laughed. 'It might be wise, but orders will be taken immediately after the show, as always. The supper will be purely social.'

'We'll look forward to it,' Rona said.

Lindsey was in bed with Jonathan when Rona phoned that evening.

'I've an invitation for you,' Rona began. 'Magda has asked us to a private supper after her show next week, to meet the designer Ross Mackenzie whom she's press-ganged into attending.'

'Good for her,' Lindsey said, struggling into a sitting position. 'Remind me what evening it is?'

'Tuesday. Seven o'clock at the Clarendon.'

Beside her, Jonathan sneezed suddenly and Lindsey threw him an irritated glance.

'Who's that?' Rona asked sharply.

'Only Jonathan. He came back after work to collect some files.'

Rona glanced at her watch. It was nine thirty. 'Sorry to have disturbed you,' she said drily.

'Oh, you haven't,' Lindsey assured her. 'See you Tuesday, then. Have a good weekend.' As she rang off Jonathan tried to pull her down again, but she resisted. 'I could have done without that,' she said, turning her face away. 'It's time you were going home, anyway. What excuse did you give this time?'

'A meeting with a client,' he said lazily, tracing the line of her jaw with one finger. She shook it away and turned to look at him, at his thick, over-long hair, his deep-set eyes, the cleft in his chin.

'One of these days,' she said slowly, 'Carol will check, and then what will happen?'

'I have contingency plans,' he said.

She felt a shaft of annoyance. 'You do realize that after all your fine words we're back exactly where we were last time – a hole-in-the-corner affair that was just what I wanted to avoid.'

He sat up and kissed her bare shoulder. 'I can't let you go, Lindsey. You know that.'

She swung herself out of bed and reached for her dressing gown. 'You've got it made, haven't you? A loving wife who's a social asset, bright kids, a respected position in the community – and a bit on the side to spice it all up. But what exactly do I get out of it?'

'Me!' said Jonathan.

'It's not enough,' she answered shortly.

He frowned at her tone of voice. 'What brought this on? You weren't complaining half an hour ago. Did your strait-laced sister prick your conscience?'

'This has nothing to do with Rona.'

'Then what is it? The way things are, we have time together without hurting anyone. What's wrong with that?'

'A great deal, as you well know.'

She could feel him looking at her but wouldn't meet his eyes, and a minute later he too got out of bed.

'There's not much point in my staying when you're in this mood,' he said shortly.

'No point at all,' she agreed.

He started to dress while she sat with her back to him, her heart pounding. This was the nearest they'd come to a row since they'd resumed their affair last spring. She should have known better than to let it start again, but as she'd told Rona more than once she needed a man in her life and, even more importantly, she'd needed to show Dominic she could manage without him. Which had got her precisely nowhere.

Dressed once more in his office suit, Jonathan moved into her line of vision. He paused for a moment but she refused to look up.

'See you tomorrow, then,' he said gruffly.

She nodded and sat motionless, listening to his feet running down the stairs and the slam of the front door. Oh, God, she thought wearily, where do we go from here?

*   *   *

As well as being features editor of *Chiltern Life*, Barnie Trent and his wife had become personal friends, and he greeted Rona enthusiastically when she phoned the next morning.

'How's my favourite contributor?'

'Funny you should say that; I'd like to sound you out on an idea for a series.'

'Brilliant! The answer to my prayers!'

'Not sure about that, but I was thinking there must be a lot of people around who've had interesting or unusual experiences they'd be willing to recount. People who've been there when something momentous happened such as the Berlin Wall coming down.'

'No doubt you're right; how do you propose to dig them out?'

'We could put a piece in the mag asking for contributions. I reckon we should get at least half a dozen we could use, and I've a couple of ideas to start it off; my next-door neighbours were ex-pats for years, and my father knows someone who's had an interesting life.'

'Then by all means go for it. Limit it to six to start with, and we'll see how it goes.'

'Thanks, Barnie.'

'Incidentally, your ears must have been burning: Dinah was asking after you only yesterday. No doubt she has a stack of baby photos to show you!' The Trents' daughter, who lived in the States, had had her third baby in June. 'Mel and the kids are coming over for two weeks in December, Mitch will join us for Christmas, and they'll all go back after New Year.'

'We'd love to see them while they're here, and meet the new baby. What was it they called him?'

'Silas,' supplied Barnie without expression.

'Oh, yes.' She paused. 'Different!'

'You should hear Dinah on the subject. Rona, someone's on the other line. Let me know how you get on with your project.' And he rang off.

As the call ended, a plaintive bark from the foot of the stairs reminded her that Gus's walk was overdue and Rona, who, now she had the go-ahead, would have preferred to settle down and plan the series, reluctantly responded to his summons.

Fortunately, however, as they reached the gate Monica Furness drew into the kerb and wound down her car window.

'Just the person I wanted to see!' Rona exclaimed.

'Likewise! I've been meaning to pop round all week to invite you for a meal. I'm ashamed how long we've been here without getting round to it – I don't know where the time's gone. Are you by any chance free tomorrow? Short notice, I know, but nothing formal. We'd love to see you if you'll take pot luck.'

'Thanks, Monica, that would be great.'

'About seven thirty, then?' She'd started to close the window when she paused. 'Did you say you wanted to speak to me?'

'Yes, but it'll keep till tomorrow.'

And Rona, setting out on her walk, reflected with satisfaction that she had, after all, taken the first steps on her new project.

Rented out as it had been during the years its owners were abroad, the house next door had harboured many residents during the time Rona and Max lived at number nineteen, most of whom had merged into an indistinct blur in their memories. An exception was the last tenants, whom Rona was still trying strenuously to consign to oblivion, murder not having made a comfortable neighbour. She was inordinately grateful that before returning to the UK Charles and Monica had had their home completely renovated, leaving no trace of what had been.

From the outside, the four-storey Georgian house was a twin of their own, but once through the front door all similarity disappeared. Rona and Max had removed the wall between the two rooms on the ground floor, making one large sitting room and limiting their eating facilities to the kitchen table, while here the original layout had been retained. In addition several pieces of furniture from their Hong Kong house lent an oriental flavour, accentuated by pictures and ornaments the Furnesses had collected on their travels, and Rona examined them with interest.

'Every picture tells a story!' Monica said laughingly, handing her a drink.

'I'm glad to hear it, because that's what I wanted to talk to you about.' Quickly she outlined her proposed series.

'Goodness!' Monica exclaimed. 'But we didn't do anything exciting – it was just day-to-day living.'

'It doesn't have to be exciting, just different. I for one should be fascinated to hear about it, and I'm sure the readers of *Chiltern Life* would, too. And we needn't confine it to Hong Kong.' She glanced at the wooden toucan on the mantelpiece. 'You were in South America, weren't you, before that?'

'Oh, we've been around, admittedly, and if you really think people would be interested, I don't mind describing it. There's a boxful of photo albums upstairs which might be useful.'

Before Rona could reply, Charles called across the room. 'If I could interrupt for a moment, Monica and I have a confession to make. When we were in the flat waiting for the furniture to arrive, we discovered an excellent Chinese restaurant in Alban Road, and it helped to tide us over our withdrawal symptoms. Since then we've had the occasional takeaway, and we wondered if you'd be insulted if we ordered one in this evening? Their food really is good.'

'We'd love it!' Rona declared. 'It's some time since we had Chinese, and with your recommendation it must be great. Monica did say it would be pot luck.'

'Just not our pot! I know it's cheating, but this evening was spur of the moment because we wanted to see you. So, any particular favourites? We have their takeaway menu, if you'd like to look at it?'

'We're more than happy to leave it to you,' Max assured him.

'Very well, then we'll order what we consider the perfect Chinese banquet. And since it's a lovely evening, I propose we eat outdoors while we still can. In fact, why don't you all take your drinks out while I phone through the order.'

The back gardens in Lightbourne Avenue were not large, but as they were separated by high brick walls did at least have the advantage of privacy. Rona and Max had paved over theirs, decorating it with Italianate statues and terracotta pots and urns, the contents of which Rona changed according to the season. This garden, like the house, had been completely done over, and despite its size now contained a built-in barbecue, an area of decking and a small pond with goldfish. All that remained of its previous incarnation was the apple tree, under which Rona had sat drinking lemonade with a murderer. Monica led the way to the decking, where a table and chairs had been set up and where they were shortly joined by the Furness children.

'Dad's staying indoors so he can hear the doorbell,' fifteen-year-old Harriet reported, lounging in one of the chairs. 'He'll give us a shout when he wants help with the serving.'

Rona leaned back contentedly, watching the sky redden in the sunset. 'Pity the summer's nearly over,' she commented. 'When do you go back to school?'

'We already have,' Giles told her. 'Term started yesterday.'

'Having been there for the summer term they at least know everyone,' Monica said. 'It was a bit strange at first.'

'It must have been, after being abroad for so long.' A thought struck her and she turned to Giles. 'Do you by any chance know a boy called Hathaway? I don't know his first name, but he lived in America for a while and I should think he's about your age.'

'Luke Hathaway, yeah. We sometimes hang out at break.'

'Really? My father and his grandfather are friends. Has he . . . settled in OK?'

'He got teased at first because of his accent, but he's lost most of it now.'

'And he seems quite . . . happy?'

Too searching a question, perhaps, for a twelve-year-old boy. Giles frowned, nodded and fidgeted uncomfortably in his chair, and, aware both of his embarrassment and the curious glances of the others, Rona let the subject drop.

As dusk fell lights had come on around the garden and a slight breeze rustled the leaves.

'Let me know if you feel cool,' Charles said, passing Max the last prawn cracker, 'and we can go back indoors.' The children had already done so and two windows at the top of the house flowered with yellow light.

'No, it's fine,' Rona said. 'I have my pashmina, and there won't be many more evenings we can eat outside; let's make the most of it.' She laid down the ivory chopsticks. 'That was wonderful! What restaurant did you say it was?'

'The Lotus Flower, in Alban Road. I'll let you have a copy of the menu; we have several.'

'My wife lives on takeaways when I'm not home,' Max said drily. 'She has a pathological dislike of cooking!'

'You're still away during the week?'

Max nodded. 'It works very well. I have classes at my studio across town three evenings a week and, since early morning is my best time for painting, it makes sense to spend the night there ready to start at first light. On Wednesdays when I have afternoon classes I come home, and of course I'm here from Friday till Monday.'

'It all started,' Rona explained, 'because Max likes loud music while he's painting and I need complete quiet in which to write. Our marriage mightn't have survived if we'd continued to work under the same roof, and we do speak on the phone at least twice a day.'

'Sounds an admirable arrangement,' Monica said. 'I sympathize with the noise angle; the children seem to need continuous music while they do their homework – heaven knows why – but life has become more bearable since we issued them with headphones.'

Talk drifted on for another half hour, then Max glanced at his watch. 'Time we were making a move. The pooch will be wanting his bedtime walk.'

'It's been lovely,' Rona said. 'Thank you so much. And if it's OK, Monica, I'll give you a ring to fix a time for our first talk.'

Charles raised an enquiring eyebrow. 'First talk? What have you been doing all evening?'

Monica smiled. 'I'll explain later. Right, Rona, I'll wait to hear from you.'

'Good to have them home again,' Max commented as they strolled out of one gateway and in at the next. 'We've never had time to get to know them properly, but they're good value, aren't they?'

'Yes, they're a great addition to our social circle. We must introduce them to Gavin and Magda, I'm sure they'd get on together.'

Max put his key in the door. 'Prepare for the onslaught,' he warned, and inched it open as Gus's nose forced its way through the gap. 'All right, all right, boy, give me a chance to get your lead!'

Rona stretched sleepily. 'I think I'll go straight up,' she said. 'Enjoy your walk. I might be asleep by the time you get back.'

Max bent and kissed her. Though he'd not betrayed the fact, he was thankful that their first social visit to the house next door was safely behind them. 'Pleasant dreams,' he said, and felt reasonably certain that they would be.

THREE

L indsey saw Hugh the moment she came up the stairs into the café. He was sitting at a window table studying the menu, and before her courage failed her she walked straight over and slid into the seat opposite him.

'Lindsey!' The word seemed to be jolted out of him.

'Hello, Hugh.'

'Look, I'm sorry, but I'm . . . meeting someone.'

'That's all right; I'll keep you company till she arrives.'

He didn't correct the pronoun, and her fingernails dug into her palms.

'This really isn't a good idea.'

'I haven't seen you for a while,' she said breezily. 'How are things?'

He had coloured, the painful flush staining his pale face, and she wondered briefly if he was going to make a scene. The tension between them was, as always, tangible; ridiculous that five years after their divorce they should still be so strongly attracted to each other.

'I hear you played golf with David at the weekend. Nicole says you were on top form.'

'Don't do this, Lindsey,' he said in a low voice.

The waitress, for whom they usually had to wait at least ten minutes, materialized promptly beside them. Hugh said in a strangled voice, 'I'm waiting for a friend,' and Lindsey simultaneously, 'Cheese omelette and a side salad, please.'

As she moved away Hugh said sharply, 'When it comes, you'll have to move to another table.'

Lindsey didn't reply. Her eyes passed slowly over him: long nose, blue eyes fringed with short, sandy lashes, sleeked-back red hair – and the rush of desire took her breath away. Their eyes met and his almost imperceptible shudder proved that he'd shared it. She experienced a surge of triumph: Mia Campbell or no Mia Campbell, she hadn't after all lost her hold over him.

The thought must have conjured her up, as Hugh's change of expression signified. Even as Lindsey turned to look, registering her first sight of her replacement, he pushed back his chair, snatched up his briefcase and went to join Mia in the doorway, taking her arm and steering her quickly back down the stairs.

Slowly Lindsey turned back to the table, aware of interested glances and discreetly hidden smiles. Cheeks flaming, she took a ten-pound note out of her purse for the uneaten omelette and, looking neither to left nor right, hurriedly left the café.

'I swear we hadn't arranged to meet,' Hugh said forcibly as they walked quickly up Guild Street in the direction of the Bacchus, their alternative choice for lunch. 'She just came and plonked herself down at my table. I *told* her I was meeting someone.'

'It's all right, Hugh, it's no big deal.'

As always, Mia was completely unruffled, and Hugh found himself wishing she *had* minded just a little. He was quite unaware that she thought he still loved his ex-wife, whether or not he admitted it, and the fact didn't concern her unduly; if anything, it made him more interesting.

Mia had noticed Hugh Cavendish as soon as she joined Hesketh, Weaver & Bright seven months earlier – principally because, like her, he was red-haired – and had known from day one that she would sleep with him. This awareness, coming totally out of the blue, had caused her some surprise, as she'd been careful to steer clear of involvement since her marriage broke down three years previously.

It was hard to pinpoint what it was about Hugh that she found intriguing. In appearance he was as unlike her ex as it was possible to be – tall and pale, while Ewan was dark and stocky. And she suspected the differences were more than skin-deep: with Ewan, what you saw was what you got, but in Hugh she sensed an intense nervous energy, at present contained but liable to explode at any moment.

That brief glance across the café was, in fact, the first time she'd seen Lindsey Parish in the flesh, though there was a photo of her in Hugh's wallet and she had briefly met her sister, marvelling at how alike they were. She found it interesting that Rona, though married to the artist Max Allerdyce, had kept her maiden name, while after her divorce Lindsey had reverted to hers. A show of independence, perhaps, by both of them, but more understandable in Rona's case, since it was the name she used professionally.

For herself, she'd kept her married name, partly for their son Colin's sake, but mainly because it hadn't occurred to her to discard it. In the eighteen-odd years of her marriage she'd *become* Mia Campbell, and, Ewan or no Ewan, was happy to remain so. She'd also continued to live in the marital home until, the previous year, two separate events had occurred within months of each other.

The first was the retirement of the senior partner in the firm where she worked, to be succeeded by a man who, from the first, had tried to undermine her, possibly seeing her as a threat. Within weeks she'd realized she'd be unable to continue working there and had begun looking for an alternative, preferably out of the Stokely area.

Before she'd found one, however, her father, her sole remaining parent who'd been in a care home suffering from dementia, had finally died, leaving her a surprisingly large legacy. And one week later she saw the advertisement for a senior accountant in the Marsborough firm of Hesketh, Weaver & Bright. Within what seemed a remarkably short space of time, she had applied for the position and been accepted, sold her home and bought an attractive house on an executive development in Marsborough, within walking distance of work. And the rest, she thought with a touch of self-mockery, was history.

She glanced sideways at Hugh's worried face and slipped a hand through his arm. 'As it happens,' she said rallyingly as they turned into the doorway of the Bacchus, 'I'd prefer tapas to a quiche, so it's worked out for the best!' And as he smiled in response, she felt his tension ease.

The Clarendon Hotel, situated on the corner of Guild Street and Alban Road, was Marsborough's premier hotel and a popular venue for local functions. It was owned and run by the Fairfax family, who had had traumas of their own with which Rona had reluctantly become involved. She'd known the hotel all her life; childhood parties had been held there, as had post-pantomime teas and special family meals. Dinner in its Grill Room had been her first date with Max and they'd chosen it for their wedding reception.

Twice a year Magda held a fashion show in its Albany Suite, to preview the clothes her boutiques would be stocking for the coming season. Her database was widespread and well-known faces from stage and screen could be spotted among the clientele. As always, drinks and canapés were served in the anteroom, and a buzz of excited conversation met the Parish sisters on their arrival. Magda was standing in the doorway to welcome her guests, and at her side was a man who, resplendent in black velvet jacket and tartan trews, could only be the star of the show. Next to him was a tall, slim woman, elegant in a black dress – his wife, Rona surmised, but was proved wrong.

'Rona and Lindsey, lovely to see you!' Magda exclaimed. 'May I introduce you to Ross Mackenzie and his sister, Isobel Firth?' She turned to the couple beside her. 'My very good friends, Rona and Lindsey Parish.'

Ross Mackenzie was tall and broad-shouldered with narrow hips which, Rona found herself thinking, would have looked good in a kilt had he gone one step further in proclaiming his nationality. He had fair to sandy hair, blue-grey eyes under straight brows and a disconcertingly direct gaze.

'My pleasure,' he said, gripping her hand. Then, turning to Lindsey, who was awaiting her turn, 'God, I'm seeing double!' He gave a short laugh. 'Sorry, that was unpardonably rude, except that it's a compliment to both of you that you look so alike! *My* sister's just thankful we don't!'

And indeed, though there was a slight family resemblance, the woman beside him seemed more sharply defined, her features finer than her brother's, her hair more gold – though possibly with help – and her eyes more blue. Conscious of the queue forming behind them, Rona and Lindsey quickly shook her hand and, moving into the room, took glasses of wine from the proffered tray and joined a group of their friends.

'What do you think of our eminent guest?' Georgia Kingston greeted them. 'Quite a coup for Magda to have him here.'

'I was just saying,' Hilary Grant put in, 'that apart from the velvet jacket he's not my idea of a fashion designer. His hair's not long enough and he's altogether too rugged; looks as though he should be striding over the heather, not closeted in a studio somewhere!'

Rona smiled, sipping her wine. 'Is his sister connected with the business?'

Louise Dawson nodded. 'Yes, I read in an article that she's his stylist – coordinates jewellery and accessories for fashion photographs and the catwalk. They work as a team.'

'Presumably she's married, since her name's not the same?'

'Divorced, I think.'

Other friends came up to join them, and shortly after they were directed into the main room where the fashion show was ready to begin.

As usual, there were several outfits Rona coveted but though, like Lindsey and her friends, she made notes on her programme, she wasn't actually intending to buy. Anticipation had been mounting, and as the first Mackenzie outfit appeared it elicited a burst of applause which Rona, aware of unexpected disappointment, uncharitably put down to the designer's presence.

Though she was uncertain what she'd been expecting, it wasn't the muted fawns, greens and mauves that now paraded before her. Admittedly there was a distinctiveness of style that marked all the garments as being from the same collection, but their impact was considerably less than she'd anticipated.

'Attractive enough,' Louise conceded in a whisper, 'though hardly setting the world on fire. If these are from his autumn collection, I'll be surprised if it generates as much interest as his spring one.'

'Magda's chosen wisely, all the same,' Lindsey remarked. 'Those outfits will appeal to the majority of her customers, if not the high-fliers. They look chic and easy to wear, and at least they have a designer label!'

The show ended with the usual display of wedding gowns, which were duly applauded, after which there was a rush to the desks at either end of the room, where Magda's staff were taking orders. To Rona's relief, Ross Mackenzie and his sister had been escorted from the room; it would have been embarrassing had they known that the majority of those joining them for supper were not among the buyers.

The Fairfax Room was a small dining room on the first floor, available for hire by private parties. A table laid for twelve stood in the centre, and at one end a temporary bar had been set up dispensing glasses of champagne.

Ross and Isobel were at the centre of a small group, and Rona noticed that while most of the questions and comments were being directed to her brother, it was Isobel who answered them while Ross himself stared moodily into his glass, taking no active part in the conversation. Was this simply reaction, she wondered, or, despite the applause, was he less than satisfied with the reception of his designs?

When, minutes later, they were called to table, Rona found that as Magda's closest friend she'd been placed next to him. She could only hope he'd snap out of whatever was worrying him, or she was in for a difficult meal. However, as she cast around for a way to open a conversation, he pre-empted her with the abrupt comment, 'Magda tells me you write.'

'I do, yes,' she replied, slightly taken aback.

'Articles for the local glossy?'

'Under one of my hats, yes.'

'I suppose I couldn't twist your arm and persuade you to interview me?'

Rona turned to stare at him. 'I don't think you'd have to twist too hard.'

'I could do with some positive publicity at the moment.'

She said carefully, 'I should have thought you'd have all you could handle, with the collection just out.'

He played with his fork, not looking at her. 'What did you think of it?'

God, she should have prepared for this! 'It was . . . great. I particularly liked—'

He waved a dismissive hand. 'No, it wasn't, though I'm not supposed to admit it. Izzie says I must believe in myself or no one else will, but the truth is the whole collection's jinxed – was from the outset. All manner of things went wrong while I was working on it, and to crown it all I went down with a particularly nasty illness which held me back for months.'

'I'm . . . sorry to hear that.'

'Oh, it's no excuse, I should have snapped out of it. It wouldn't have been so bad if the last collection hadn't attracted so much notice. It was a lot to live up to, and as things were I should have skipped this one and concentrated on next spring's.'

Magda leant forward. 'Ross, Nicole was asking . . .'

And as his attention was diverted, Rona breathed a sigh of relief. But was he serious about an interview for *Chiltern Life*? Barnie would fall on her neck if she pulled that off.

Nothing more was said on the subject, but as they were leaving Ross asked Rona for her card, much to Lindsey's astonishment.

'What was that all about?' she demanded as they went down the stairs.

'He wants me to interview him for *Chiltern Life*.'

Lindsey snorted. 'You mean you asked if you could.'

'No, it was his idea; it wouldn't have entered my head. He says he needs some positive publicity.'

'God, you have all the luck, don't you? Sitting next to him at supper, and now this! What a waste, when you've a perfectly satisfactory man of your own!'

'Lindsey, for heaven's sake!'

They reached the foyer and paused for a word with Dorothy Fairfax, the doyenne of the establishment, but as they walked to the car park Lindsey returned to the subject.

'The first attractive man I've seen in ages, and my sister snaffles him! The least you can do is let me know when the interview is, so I can casually drop in.'

'It probably won't come to anything.'

'I tell you one thing,' Lindsey said as they reached their separate cars. 'If *I'd* been sitting next to him, he wouldn't have had to ask for *my* card!'

Steven Hathaway lay on his bed fully clothed, his arms behind his head, staring up at the ceiling. He'd been back in the UK for nine months now, yet each night, alone in his room with nothing to distract him, his mind invariably turned to the States and the Van Olsen family.

Why had he become so involved with them? Better by far to have kept things on a business footing, but the old man had taken a liking to him, which inevitably led to a closer connection with the family.

Inga Van Olsen was, like her father and brother, on the board of directors of Van Olsen Enterprises, a cool, blue-eyed blonde whose level gaze gave warning that she was not to be trifled with. Steve had learned during his first week that she had a brief, unsuccessful marriage behind her, the reason for the divorce being, in his informant's words, another man – her father, Henrik. She was clearly devoted both to him and the company, and though Steve found her attractive, it had never occurred to him that there could be any romantic connection between them.

He had not lived a monastic existence since Ella's departure, but nor had there been anyone special in his life. He'd been content enough with what female companionship he had, and even before her death had been careful that none of it should impinge on Luke. He was aware that his arrival in the States opened the possibility of embarking on a new relationship, but the embargo held even more strongly now his son was in his sole care.

During his first few weeks there he'd met several women, usually through the offices of Chuck Jeffries, the colleague who'd imparted the family history, but no fires had been lit. It was at that point that Henrik, a previously somewhat distant figure, began to take an interest in him and took to inviting him to the family home at weekends, bringing him into contact with Inga, her brother Dirk and Dirk's ambitious wife, Madison.

At first Steve had felt awkward, sensing that the rest of the family resented the intrusion of a stranger, and Dirk and Madison had continued to keep him at a distance. Inga, however, perhaps in the first instance feeling sorry for him, made an effort to be friendly, and over the following weeks they had begun, cautiously at first, to meet for a drink after work. And the attraction between them steadily grew. A few weeks more, and they were sleeping together. But even in the heat of his infatuation, Steve had acknowledged it was a no-win situation. Inga would never leave her father and the company, and he had no wish to settle permanently in the States, even if that were possible. He had tried – and failed – to regard it as a pleasant interlude, and when the time finally came for him to return home they'd agreed it was better not to keep in touch.

Now, the only news of the firm and the family came via intermittent emails from Chuck, and lying on his bed with the Atlantic Ocean between them, Steve acknowledged that they increased rather than lessened his sense of loss.

'Why did you ask that woman for her card?' Isobel asked as she and Ross drove home the next day.

'She's a journalist; she might be useful.'

'But we have publicity agents; we mustn't tread on their toes.'

'I'm assuming this would be more of a profile – how I came to be in the business, where I get my ideas and so on, rather than just comments on the collection. Magda says that's Rona's style – understandably, since she also writes biographies.

'Amazing, wasn't it,' he added, 'how alike they were, she and her sister? Too bad they're not models; it would add a new dimension to the catwalk.' He paused, considering. 'We might persuade them to be photographed in some of the lines for Rona's glossy. Informally, of course,' he added quickly, as Isobel opened her mouth to protest. 'No fees or anything that could cause problems.'

Isobel's heart sank; she'd been aware that Ross had found the Parish sisters attractive and his weakness for a pretty face had landed him in trouble before.

'I'd be much happier,' she said tightly, 'if you'd tear up that card and forget all about it. You've attended the show, as you rather ill-advisedly promised Magda. Now it's time to step back.'

'Oh, I don't know,' he said lightly. 'The extra publicity would be a bonus.'

Isobel glanced at him sharply but held her tongue. If necessary

she could stress the potential conflict with their publicity agents –
who certainly wouldn't welcome any trespassing on what they
considered their ground – but for the moment she'd let it ride. Her
brother had these fancies from time to time and would usually forget
about them by the next day. With luck that's what would happen
in this case.

FOUR

T he following week the October edition of *Chiltern Life* came
out and, as Barney had promised, a piece had been inserted
asking for contributions for the new series. It was headed
Has some event or experience changed your life? and Rona read it
eagerly.

*Have you ever been present as history was being made? Were
you in London for a royal wedding or Princess Diana's funeral or
the bombings in July 2005? Or perhaps you've a more personal
story, such as living as an ex-pat in a totally different culture? If
you would like to share these experiences, Rona Parish would be
pleased to hear from you for a new series she's planning. Replies,
limited to 250 words, should be typed and sent to these offices (for
address see Letters page) together with a contact number or email
address and an s.a.e. if you wish your entries to be returned.*

'Prepare to be inundated,' Max prophesied, reading over her
shoulder. '"My friend's auntie—"'

'No,' Rona interrupted, 'I'm not going down that path; it will be
first-hand accounts only. And I might as well make a start with
Pops's friend, who sounds to have had more than his share of
adventures. I'd better check first, though, to make sure he's been
forewarned.'

Tom, however, had not contacted Frank in the interim. 'I didn't
think there was any hurry,' he protested in answer to Rona's query.
'It's only ten days since I saw him – too soon to arrange another
meeting. But you don't need a go-between. Give him a ring, say
who you are and that I suggested he'd be a good subject for your
project. He can only say no.'

Rona sighed. 'OK; what did you say his surname is?'

'Hathaway, and he lives in Alban Road. He'll be in the phone book. Good luck, and let me know how you get on.'

'It'll be a cold call,' Rona reported gloomily to Max. 'He doesn't know me from Adam, so I'll just have to hope Pops's name will open doors.'

Frank Hathaway sounded considerably surprised to hear from her. 'But I don't understand,' he said. 'I thought you were a biographer.'

'I am, but I also write for *Chiltern Life* between "lives". I'm sorry, I thought Pops might have explained. The point is I'm hoping to start a new series . . .' And she outlined what she planned. 'I believe you not only lived abroad for a number of years but became involved in various dangerous situations.' She gave a little laugh. 'In fact, it sounds as though you could fill the whole series single-handed!'

'I fear your father was exaggerating,' Frank demurred.

'But you *were* in Kuwait when Iraq invaded, and you *were* involved in that plane hijacking?'

'True. I suppose, looking back . . .'

'That's exactly what I want you to do – look back over your life.' She paused. 'May I at least come and discuss it with you?'

'Yes, yes, of course, though it might not be as highly coloured as Tom led you to expect.'

'I'll take a chance on that! When would it be convenient to call?'

'More or less anytime. How about tomorrow, around three o'clock?'

'Perfect – thank you. I look forward to meeting you.'

'And I you. It's number four-two-seven Alban Road, on the left just past the turning for Barrington Road.'

'Thanks, I'll find it,' Rona said.

In the past Alban Road, which ran across the top end of Guild Street, had been one of Marsborough's prime residential areas featuring large houses standing in their own grounds, but over the years the road had gradually split into two halves with Guild Street being the crossover point. The greatest change lay to the south, where virtually all the original houses had been pulled down and commercial buildings erected in their place, among them the town hall, the Royal County Hospital, office blocks, restaurants, and, farther along past the railway station, the boys' and girls' grammar schools.

By contrast, to the north of Guild Street the road remained residential; though some of the houses had been pulled down to make way for new ones, others had mutated into flats and three had become hotels, one of which, Springfield Lodge, had loomed large in Rona's last investigation.

Despite all this diversification, number four-two-seven, though smaller than its neighbours and somewhat dwarfed by them, had clung to its original incarnation and remained a private house – though still over-large, Rona considered, for one elderly gentleman. Turning into the gateway, she wondered why he'd not sold it when his wife died and moved into something more manageable.

Frank Hathaway had the door open before she could ring. 'Well, well, Tom's daughter!' he greeted her. 'Yes, I can see the resemblance, particularly around the eyes. But you don't want to hear all that – come in, come in.'

The hall, like the exterior, appeared to have had little done by way of modernization, the red Turkey carpet and dark wooden door frames being in keeping with the age of the house. But when Frank opened the door to the sitting room, Rona gave a gasp of surprise. Although the basic furniture – three-piece suite, piano and bookcase – continued the nineteenth-century theme, the room was highly individualized by its ornaments and pictures which, like those she'd seen in the Furness house, spoke of a life largely spent abroad. There were carved African figures, Chinese ginger jars in vibrant yellows and blues, Aztec paintings and rich Persian rugs.

Frank, noting her reaction, smiled self-deprecatingly. 'I hope you don't feel you're being shown into a museum,' he said.

'It's wonderful! We could make a start by your telling me the story behind each of those artefacts.'

As he poured the tea Rona surreptitiously studied him. He must be roughly the same age as Pops since they were contemporaries at uni, but he seemed considerably older, his face more lined and his hair, though still plentiful, an almost startling white. There was a faint scar down one cheek and more noticeable ones on his hands, and as he'd shown her in she'd noticed he walked with a pronounced limp – all legacies, presumably, of that burning car.

'We've met before, you know,' he said smilingly, handing her a bone-china cup and saucer, and, at her confusion, added hastily, 'Oh, I don't expect you to remember! You would have been three or four at the time – Ruth and I ran into you and your family in the gardens of some stately home. I remember two little girls in pink dresses, as alike as peas in a pod.'

'Quite a while ago!' Rona said. 'You have family of your own, I believe?'

'That's right – a son, a daughter and a grandson. As Tom might have told you, Steve and Luke are living with me at the moment. You'll probably meet them when Luke comes home from school. He gets the bus almost at the door and it takes him straight down Alban Road to the grammar school. He was quite intrigued when he learned that his school and his temporary home were in the same road, even though there's quite a distance between them.'

'And your son's carrying on the family tradition by working abroad?'

'Not to the same extent; in fact, though he's travelled quite extensively, those years in America were the only time he's been based outside the UK.'

'Is he likely to be again?'

Frank shrugged. 'I can't help hoping not. Luke needs stability in his life – he has no mother, as you probably know – and moving schools and homes repeatedly, particularly now that he's older, would do nothing to provide it. With Ruth and I abroad, Steve and his sister spent most of their adolescence at boarding school, but having lost Luke once due to divorce, Steve's anxious they shouldn't be separated.'

Rona nodded. 'Understandably. Is your daughter married?'

'No, she's too independent by half! She lives for her work, and is making a very good niche for herself as a jewellery designer.'

'How fascinating!' Rona exclaimed. 'I'd love to see something she's done.'

'I'm afraid I haven't anything; although she does design men's jewellery, she's given up on me since I didn't even have a wedding ring! The only item I wear is my watch, and even that is too old-fashioned for her liking! I believe Tarltons in Guild Street have several of her pieces, though, if you're interested.'

'Thanks, I'll go and have a look.'

He put down his teacup. 'So tell me, Rona, what exactly do you want of me?'

'Just your reminiscences really, about what it was like being caught in dangerous situations.'

'Frightening!' said Frank.

She smiled. 'That's not quite enough for an article!'

'Ruth would have been so much better at this.' He broke off, frowning. 'Hold on a minute; she kept diaries all the time we were abroad. At least, she called them diaries though they were actually exercise books in which she kept notes about holidays or places we visited. I know she wrote reams after the hijacking, principally so the children, as they then were, would understand what had happened.'

Hardly daring to hope, Rona asked, 'Do you still have them, the diaries?'

'Well, I'm sure neither of us would have thrown them out so I suppose we must have, probably buried somewhere in the attic.'

'They might act as an aide-memoire,' Rona said eagerly. 'We could go through them together and you could . . . enlarge on them as we went. If you wouldn't mind my seeing them, that is,' she added hastily.

'Of course not, but it's a question of finding them. That's the trouble with these big old houses – there are plenty of places to salt things away and then you forget where you put them. Wait a minute, though.' He stood up. 'There's just a chance they could be in her desk in the bedroom. If you'll excuse me a moment, I'll go and have a look.'

And before she could protest that there was no hurry, he'd gone. Left to her own devices, Rona went to look more closely at the pictures, intrigued by their vibrant splashes of colour. She was studying a particularly intricate one when the door behind her opened and a voice said, 'Dad, you haven't come across my pen, have you? I had it last night—'

She turned and found herself face-to-face with a tall, dark-haired man who was staring at her in surprise.

'I'm so sorry!' he said. 'I'd no idea my father had company. I'm Steven Hathaway.'

'Rona Parish. I—'

'Of course, I remember now, Dad did mention you. Something about an article on ex-pats?'

'Not exactly, but close enough,' Rona said.

He smiled and came forward with his hand out. 'I'm delighted to meet you. Sorry to burst in like that, but what was Dad thinking of, leaving you alone?'

'He's gone to look for the diaries your mother used to keep.'

'God, yes, the famous diaries! I'd forgotten all about them.'

Out in the hall the front door opened and slammed.

'That, no doubt, is my son home from school,' said Steven Hathaway. He raised his voice. 'In here, Luke.'

Luke came into the room followed by his grandfather, and Rona noted that Frank was empty-handed.

'Ah, I see you two have met,' he commented. 'And this is Luke, Rona. Say hello to Miss Parish, Luke. Or rather – I'm sorry, I don't know your married name?'

'Rona will be fine,' she said, smiling at the boy who stood regarding her. 'I think you know Giles Furness? He lives next door to us.'

Steve nudged his son. 'Well? Cat got your tongue?'

Luke said shyly, 'Yeah, I know Giles.'

'OK, then, go and change out of your school clothes.' And Luke thankfully escaped.

'The diaries aren't in the desk,' Frank told Rona. 'I thought that would be too easy. I've not seen them since we came home all those years ago.'

'They'll be in one of those boxes you brought back,' Steve said. 'I'll help you look at the weekend.'

'I don't want to put you to any trouble,' Rona apologized. 'I'm sure we could manage without them.'

'No, no, they'll be just what you want. There'll be photograph albums too. Could you make use of those?'

'It depends how clear they are; I'd have to leave that to the editor.'

Frank nodded. 'They'll probably have faded by now. No digital cameras in those days.'

'Well, thank you for the tea and for agreeing to be interviewed. I won't hold you up any longer.' She smiled at Steve. 'Nice to have met you.'

'Likewise!'

Frank went with her to the front door. 'If you give me your phone number, I'll let you know the result of our search.'

'Thank you, that would be great.' Rona handed him one of her cards. 'I look forward to hearing from you.'

So that was the introverted Steve Hathaway, she thought, backing her car out of the drive. He didn't seem to have any hang-ups that she could see. True, his face, though attractive, was rather gaunt but it lit up considerably when he smiled. Perhaps Pops had the wrong end of the stick. Anyway, the interview with Frank had been interesting and promised well – particularly if the elusive diaries could be found.

Pleased with her afternoon encounter, Rona drove home.

Mia had just returned from work when her phone rang, and she was startled to find her ex-husband on the line.

'Ewan! This is a surprise.'

'How are you, Mia?'

'Well, thank you. And you?'

'Worried.'

She frowned. 'What about?'

'Not what, who. It's Colin, Mia. I'm very much afraid he's in some kind of trouble.'

She went cold, acknowledging that this was news she'd been dreading for some time. In his teens, their son had changed overnight from an affectionate, biddable child to a morose and awkward youth who seemed to delight in baiting his parents. Par for the course, they'd told each other, but the fact that their marriage was coming under strain did nothing to help the situation and the gulf between parents and son had widened. They'd no longer known who his friends were, and more than once he had spent a night in a police cell after disturbances in some pub or other. The one bright spot was that despite their embarking on divorce proceedings during his last year at school, his exam results had qualified him for a place at Farnborough University to study economics. Both she and Ewan had hoped that, away from home and with a new life opening for him, he would find his feet.

Now, her mind spun as she frantically tried to remember when she'd last spoken to him. 'What do you mean? What kind of trouble?'

'I can't discuss it over the phone. Would it be all right if I came to see you?'

'Of course, but . . . it's not serious, is it?'

'I think it might be, which is why we should talk as soon as possible. Are you in this evening?'

She and Hugh had arranged to see an amateur production of *Waiting for Godot* at the local theatre. When she didn't immediately reply, Ewan added, 'I've been in Marsborough all day on business, but I'm due back in Stokely tonight.'

'Then of course we must meet.' Hugh would understand, but if he didn't it was too bad; he came far below her son in her list of priorities.

'Seven thirty at your place?'

Mia glanced at her watch. It was six fifteen. Mentally she reviewed the contents of her fridge. 'Fine, come for supper,' she said, reckoning there might be less awkwardness if they had something to occupy them.

'You're sure? I could eat first if that would be easier.'

'No, come here. I promise not to poison you!'

There was a pause, then he gave a short laugh. 'OK. Piper's Way, isn't it? How do I get there?'

'Turn up Windsor Way off Guild Street and follow it round. Piper's Way is the third turning on the left – it's a so-called executive development.'

'Is it, indeed?'

'See you then,' she said and switched off before he could make any further comment.

For a moment she stood motionless, the phone in her hand, waiting for her heartbeat to steady, unsure whether its agitation was at the prospect of seeing her ex-husband or hearing what he had to say.

She and Ewan had married, against family advice, when they were both twenty. Bright and ambitious, it had seemed the world was their oyster, that, together, there was nothing they couldn't achieve, but Colin's unplanned arrival ten months later had put a brake on their plans. Money became tight with Mia off work, and though she went back sooner than she'd have liked, they never regained their momentum. Ewan settled for a humdrum, nine-to-five job in local government, while Mia, tied by child-minding and, later, school hours and holidays, was reduced to temporary work well below her capabilities.

In the evenings she'd studied for her accountancy exams, and although she passed them with flying colours it was only when Colin started secondary school that she was able to put them to good use. Meanwhile, sadly, she and Ewan had drifted apart, each silently regretting lost opportunities and in part blaming the other.

It had come to a head three years ago. Ewan had had a brief, unsatisfactory affair with someone in his office and Mia, on learning of it, realized it was her pride rather than her heart that was bruised. She'd suggested, calmly and rationally, that they'd be happier apart, and though Ewan had protested for a while, insisting he'd made a foolish mistake that would not be repeated, he eventually came round to her way of thinking.

She gave herself a little shake. This was not the time for reflection; she had barely an hour in which to prepare for his arrival. Hurrying through to her small but state-of-the-art kitchen, she checked what vegetables were to hand and unwrapped two chicken breasts which, fortuitously, were in the fridge. For the next forty-five minutes she worked quickly and efficiently, holding her worries in abeyance, and by the time Ewan arrived, promptly at seven thirty, the table was attractively laid, she'd changed into a silk trouser suit, and there was a dish of tarragon chicken ready in the oven, together with creamed potatoes and Vichy carrots. Since she never ate desserts, this would be followed by a selection of cheeses and a bowl of fresh fruit. He couldn't, she told herself, expect a three-course meal at the drop of a hat.

Her heart gave a painful little twist on seeing him on her step and for a heartbeat they stood and looked at each other. Then he stepped forward, kissed her cheek and handed over a bottle of wine.

'Well,' he said, looking about him as he came into the hall, 'you've done well for yourself.'

She flushed, remembering the unassuming little house that had been their home throughout eighteen years of marriage. 'Thanks to Father's legacy,' she said.

He went ahead of her into the open-plan living space, with its white carpet and glass wall overlooking the back garden.

'Wow!' he said. His eyes narrowed as they lit on a painting and he moved swiftly to examine it. 'God, is that an original Allerdyce?'

'Yes; you know I've always admired his work, and now I'm lucky enough to be in a position to treat myself. He lives locally – and actually,' she added, remembering an exchanged word in the Bacchus on an early date with Hugh, 'I met him briefly. He's the ex-brother-in-law of a colleague at work.'

'What exalted circles you move in,' he said.

Without enquiring his preference she handed him a glass of whisky and water which he took without comment. 'Now, tell me about Colin.'

Ewan seated himself gingerly on the oatmeal sofa and took a sip of his drink. He'd put on weight, Mia noticed; his jawline was less defined and there were flecks of grey in his black hair.

'When did you last see him?' he asked, throwing the question back to her.

'I've been trying to remember. I've invited him several times, but he's always had something else on. Only to be expected, I suppose, at his age. He did come for Christmas lunch with a couple of friends whose parents were abroad, but we didn't have a chance to talk.'

'How did he seem?'

She shrugged. 'Much as usual. There was a lot of banter and they all drank too much. It wasn't exactly a family occasion.'

'Since when have we been a family?' Ewan asked bitterly.

'Look, it's no use castigating me. I accept that perhaps I should have made more effort to keep in touch, but you know how aloof he can be and I didn't want to appear the clinging mother. Now for God's sake, tell me what you know.'

Ewan swirled the whisky in his glass, his eyes following its movement. 'It's been going on for a while,' he said. 'I thought at first it would blow over, but it seems it hasn't.'

'*What* hasn't?' Mia demanded impatiently.

He looked up. 'That's the hell of it – *I don't know!*'

She took a deep breath. 'Suppose you start at the beginning.'

He sat back, squaring his shoulders as though bracing himself for what was to follow. 'I first noticed it last summer, when we met for our usual lunch.'

'Your *usual* lunch?'

He looked surprised. 'Yes, I go over about once a month. Didn't you know?'

She hadn't, and felt a twinge of jealousy mixed with guilt. Avoiding the question, she said, 'By "last summer", you mean a month or two ago?'

'No,' he said heavily, 'I mean last *year.*'

'God, Ewan, and you're only telling me *now*?'

'I assumed you'd either have noticed yourself and dismissed it as nothing serious, or he'd confided in you and you were helping him deal with it.'

Since when had Colin confided in her? Mia said steadily, 'And what exactly happened at that lunch?'

'Nothing concrete, he just wasn't himself – flushed, distracted, not seeming to listen to what I was saying. And, most unusually, he hardly touched his food. I asked what was wrong, but he shrugged it off and I assumed it was just a tiff with the latest girlfriend. I forgot about it till we met again.'

'A month later?'

'About that. And by then it was more noticeable – bags under his eyes, still no appetite, and he'd lost weight.'

'And you *still* didn't contact me?'

'I tried to have it out with him but he swore there was nothing wrong, adding that if I was going to give him the third degree every time I saw him, I needn't bother coming again. He actually said, "And *don't* go worrying Mum; I'm perfectly OK."'

'And then?' Mia asked aridly.

'Well, after that he seemed to perk up a bit, and I assumed he'd got over it. Then it was Christmas, which he said he'd spent with you, so—'

'A very small part of it.'

'He didn't mention that, nor that he'd had friends with him. I thought you'd have had time together and if anything *was* wrong it would either have been ironed out or you'd have been in touch.'

'Even so, that's nine months ago! What's happened in the interim?'

Ewan shrugged. 'We've continued to meet but less regularly, though he's always had a good reason for cancelling. But last week he called me out of the blue and asked if he could come over for the weekend.'

Again that shaft of jealousy. 'To your flat?'

'Yes.' Ewan wasn't meeting her eyes. 'I don't know if you're aware of it but I'm living with someone – have been for a while. She knew I'd been worried about Colin, so she offered to go and stay with her sister and let us have the flat to ourselves. Which she did.'

'And?'

'On Saturday evening we went for a pub meal and he'd a fair bit to drink, and when we got home he suddenly broke into some story I was telling and said, "Dad, suppose someone saw something suspicious, something *wrong*, ought they to report it?"'

Mia moistened suddenly dry lips. 'What did you say?'

'Well, as you can imagine he'd taken me completely by surprise. I asked what kind of thing, but he just repeated, "something wrong". So of course I said yes, it was always best to report anything suspicious. Then – and this is what really threw me – he said, "Even if it might get the person reporting it into trouble?"'

Mia stared at him wide-eyed and he drained the last of his whisky.

'Naturally he wouldn't explain what *kind* of trouble,' he continued, 'and when I tried to press him he shook his head and said, "Forget it, Dad; it happened some time ago, so it would be too late anyway". I tried to get more out of him but he wouldn't be drawn and soon afterwards he went to bed.'

Ewan ran a frustrated hand through his hair. 'I was hoping to bring it up again the next morning, but at breakfast he announced he must get back to uni to do some work, and left more or less straight away. It was obvious he regretted having said anything.'

Mia said slowly, 'And you think what happened "some time ago" dates from summer last year?'

'That was my conclusion, yes.'

'You've no idea what it could possibly be?'

'None whatsoever.'

'Do you think he was actually *involved* in whatever it was, or simply . . . witnessed it?'

'God knows.'

She stood up abruptly, 'If you're driving back to Stokely this evening, we'd better eat.'

In fact, she needed a few minutes alone to try to digest what she'd heard. What could Colin possibly have seen that was still having this effect on him all these months later? But by the time she'd brought the meal through and served it and poured the wine, no answer had suggested itself.

As they started to eat, Ewan said dully, 'What do you think we should do?'

'Might it help if we saw him together? Convinced him that whatever was troubling him, we were right behind him?'

'It might,' he said doubtfully.

'Is there no one at Farnbridge, a tutor or someone, whom he respects and trusts and might confide in?'

'Rather than his own father?'

She said gently, 'It might be easier if it was less personal.'

'But bear in mind he said reporting it could get this hypothetical witness – and three guesses as to who that might be – into trouble. So he's obviously been up to something shady himself.'

'Then God help me, I hope he *doesn't* report it,' she said.

For the rest of the meal they went over and over such facts as they had, but no solution occurred to them. Finally, as Ewan was leaving, Mia said, 'See how he is when you meet. If, please God, he seems better we'll let sleeping dogs lie; but if he's still uptight we'll think again, and perhaps I could go with you the next time.'

'Fair enough.' At the door he hesitated. 'Thanks for the meal – quite up to your usual standards!'

She forced a smile, and was taken by surprise when he suddenly bent forward and kissed her cheek. 'I feel better for having talked it over with you,' he said.

Hugh had been at the Gallery Café having a pre-theatre snack when Mia's phone call came, and was not at all pleased by this last-minute cancellation. Dumped in favour of her ex, for God's sake. Why the hell, if she *had* to see him, must it be this evening? It wasn't as if he lived at the other end of the country. But when he'd tried to argue the point she'd cut him off, saying she was short of time and would speak to him tomorrow.

It was a let-down on two fronts, since he'd been counting on going back to spend the night with her. Obviously that was off, but he'd also been looking forward to the show and he was damned if he was going to waste both tickets. Accordingly, when he finished his meal he set off at a brisk walk along Guild Street and nearly cannoned into Lindsey as she came hurrying out of Chase Mortimer's doorway. As they simultaneously apologized, an idea struck him and without pausing to consider the wisdom of it, he said impulsively, 'Are you doing anything this evening?'

Her eyes widened. 'No,' she admitted cautiously. 'Why?'

'Mia's just cried off a visit to the Darcy; she's spending the evening with her ex.'

Lindsey said slowly, 'So you're wondering whether to follow suit?'

He held her gaze. 'Purely as a no-strings one-off, so as not to waste the ticket.'

Lindsey smiled wryly. 'I've had more flattering invitations, but why the hell not?'

He smiled back. 'And I've had more flattering acceptances. Right, let's go.' And, linking arms, they set off towards the theatre.

FIVE

'Guess who I spent the evening with?'

Rona sighed. 'Linz, couldn't this have waited till morning? I was almost asleep.'

'Hugh!' Lindsey announced triumphantly.

Rona frowned, settling the cordless phone under her chin. 'Don't for pity's sake tell me—'

'We literally bumped into each other as I was coming out of the office and he was en route to the Darcy; he'd arranged to go with his lady-love, but she dumped him at the last minute because her ex was over, so on the spur of the moment he asked me.'

'I hope this doesn't mean—'

'It means nothing, sister mine. Or rather, it means whatever you want it to mean.'

'You sound on a high,' Rona said grumpily. 'Have you been drinking?'

'Actually I'm in the middle of a stiff gin. I felt in need of it after that play – *Waiting for Godot*, if you please! I might have thought twice if I'd known what we were going to see!'

'No you wouldn't, not if it was Hugh doing the asking.' Rona paused, pulling the duvet over her bare shoulder. 'How did you get on?'

'Oh, the old chemistry was there, but we kept it pretty well in check,' Lindsey replied blithely. 'It was agreed at the outset to be a no-strings one-off.'

'Hm!'

Lindsey laughed, a low, throaty sound down the phone. 'Anyway, I thought you'd like to know. You can go back to sleep now. Sweet dreams!' And she rang off.

Rona reached out to replace the phone on its stand. One of these days, she told herself, firmly closing her eyes, she'd be able to stop worrying about her twin.

The next phone call came at breakfast time, from her father.

'Just wondering how you got on with old Frank,' he said.

'It was only a get-to-know-you meeting, but he's going to look out some diaries his wife kept, which could be really useful. I met his son while I was there,' she added, 'and he didn't seem at all introverted to me.'

Tom laughed. 'I'd defy anyone to be introverted around you!'

'Seriously, Pops, he was fine, relaxed and at his ease. I liked him.'

'I don't think I've met him; he always seemed to be away at school when we bumped into his parents.'

'The grandson also appeared briefly. He knows Monica and Charles's son at school, and he – Giles – said Luke had settled well.'

'That's good to hear. As you said, he's had a chequered life, poor kid.' He paused. 'Catherine tells me your request's in the mag. I hope you get a decent number of replies.'

'Max is convinced I'll spend all my time sorting the wheat from the chaff. I'll have to make a chart listing them in order of interest, with murder and mayhem at the top!'

'I sincerely trust there'll be none of those!' Tom said.

Lindsey sat staring at her computer, her mind on the previous evening, and started guiltily at the knock on her door. She was not reassured when Jonathan came in, his face tight.

'I'm busy,' she said tentatively.

'Really?' He stared pointedly at her blank screen. 'Well, I won't keep you. I was just wondering how you enjoyed the play.'

Her eyes flew to his face and her cheeks grew hot. Though why, she thought, as indignation swiftly followed embarrassment, should she feel guilty?

'A bit beyond me, I'm afraid,' she said.

'But no doubt the company made up for it.'

She turned purposefully to her computer and logged on. 'Don't be childish, Jonathan. Hugh had a spare ticket, we happened to bump into each other and he suggested I make use of it.'

'Very opportune.'

'No doubt you were there with *your wife*?'

He leaned forward, his palms flat on her desk. 'Are you getting back with him, Lindsey? Is this what it's all about?'

'I don't know what you mean by *all*, but I'd remind you that our relationship wasn't supposed to be total immersion. You have your family life and I have . . . interests of my own.'

'Including Hugh Cavendish?'

'Well, he *is* my ex-husband, and since we live in the same town we're bound to come across each other.'

'Which doesn't necessarily entail spending an evening *à deux* in a darkened theatre.'

She clicked on a client's file and opened it. 'If there's nothing else, perhaps you'd allow me to get on with my work.'

He straightened. '*Something's* up. You've been getting more and more distant over the last few weeks.'

'Only because you've been more and more pressing. You don't *own* me, Jonathan, and I'm not answerable to you. The sooner you realize this, the better it will be.'

Before he could reply there was a quick knock and Lindsey's secretary put her head round the door. 'Just to remind you Mr Reynold's due in five minutes.'

'Thanks, Susie; I'm just checking his file.'

Aware that Jonathan was staring down at her, Lindsey kept her eyes firmly on the screen, and after a moment he turned on his heel and left the room. She leaned back in her chair and drew a deep breath. It was, she knew, only a temporary reprieve, but things couldn't continue like this. It was time to end the relationship, and all that held her back was anxiety as to Jonathan's reaction and the threat it might pose to her career.

'So you took Lindsey?'

Hugh and Mia were sitting in the Five Feathers over a pub lunch.

He threw her an anxious glance. 'You don't mind, do you? It seemed a pity to waste the ticket.'

'My dear Hugh, why should I mind? I let you down at the last minute.' All the same, she thought privately, his action did rather smack of tit-for-tat, even if it had been coincidental. Not that it concerned her; she was too worried about what Ewan had told her to bother about Hugh and his motives. 'How was the play?' she added after a minute.

'Well acted but a bit obtuse.'

'I'm sorry to have missed it.'

He could no longer hold in his curiosity. 'So, how was your ex? It must be some time since you saw him?'

'Well over a year, yes, at one of Colin's uni dos.' She paused.

'Actually, it was Colin he wanted to speak to me about. He seems a bit . . . down.'

For no reason he could explain, Hugh always felt uncomfortable on being reminded Mia had a grown-up son. 'How old is he?' he asked diffidently.

'Twenty.'

'Probably exams,' he offered after a moment.

Mia nodded. 'Probably.' She'd no intention of discussing the real reason for Ewan's anxiety.

Briefly Hugh tried to imagine himself with an adult son, and hastily abandoned the attempt. One day, perhaps, he told himself vaguely, and was relieved when she changed the subject.

That weekend, as promised, Steve helped his father search for his mother's diaries. In fact, with the narrow attic stairs in mind, plus all the bending and stooping, he'd have preferred to do it alone, but Frank would have none of it. 'Nonsense!' he'd declared roundly. 'I trust I'm still capable of getting about in my own home!'

The attics at the top of the house, originally servants' bedrooms, had over the years accumulated the discarded relics of a peripatetic life. Among them lay broken skis, ancient tennis rackets in wooden frames, boxes of clothes from warmer climes, suitcases and piles of mouldering books and papers.

But despite their diligence, Saturday's search proved unfruitful and they returned downstairs despondent and covered in dust.

'I'm quite sure we wouldn't have thrown them out,' Frank kept saying.

'Well,' Steve commented, handing him a beer, 'tomorrow is another day.'

'I can't expect you to give up your entire weekend,' Frank protested. 'Now we've broken the back of it, I can continue looking on my own.'

Steve shook his head. 'Certainly not. I'm enjoying unearthing things I'd forgotten about, and it's not as though I'd anything else on.'

And as it happened it was he who, the following day, pushed aside a crumbling tarpaulin to reveal a tea chest that had been packed by a removals firm and apparently never emptied. Inside it, buried among piles of photograph albums, lay the exercise books in which Ruth had recorded happenings in their lives.

He called to his father in the adjoining room. 'I've found them, Dad!'

Frank came hurrying through. 'Oh, well done! I was beginning to think it was a lost cause!' He glanced at the faded covers in his son's hands. 'Yes, I recognize those. How many are there?'

'Half a dozen or so.' Steve flicked through the pages of fading ink. 'This one dates from the sixties. It was on top, but they mightn't be in order.'

'Well, let's take them downstairs and have a look at them. That'll give us a better idea of whether they'll be any use to Rona Parish.'

It took several journeys to and from the attic to transport all the contents of the tea chest downstairs, after which Steve covered the dining table with sheets of newspaper and spread them out. It proved to be a motley collection: letters bound by disintegrating elastic bands which Frank, with a catch in this throat, thought he recognized as his love letters, postcards, invitations, school reports, childish artwork and, of course, the photo albums and exercise books.

'I'd no idea she'd kept so much,' he said wonderingly. He picked up a notebook and started to leaf through it, but it was clear that the fading ink and Ruth's uneven scribbles would require time to decipher.

Steve had opened one of the albums and was flicking through the pages of browning photographs. 'Gosh, this takes me back! Look at the length of my hair! It must be that holiday we spent in Bali . . . Yes, isn't that the café we always went to? This is turning into a real nostalgia trip!'

They were still going through the albums when Luke came downstairs for a Coke and stayed to listen to the reminiscences, asking questions about his father's youth that had previously never occurred to him.

'Is that Auntie Vanda with *plaits*?' he asked incredulously, pointing to one of the photos, and the two men laughed. It was admittedly hard to reconcile the young girl in the snap with Vanda as she was today, hair neatly sculpted to her skull.

In this sharing of old memories and anecdotes Frank felt closer to his son than he had since Steve's return from the States, and later that evening, when Luke was in bed, he again tried to voice his concerns.

'You've been more relaxed this weekend than I've seen you for a while,' he began cautiously.

Steve, who'd been reaching for the TV remote, paused. 'Sorry, have I been taciturn?'

'Not that exactly, but you never make the effort to go out and meet people. Heaven knows, I'm no company for a man of your age, week after week.'

Steve smiled. 'You're excellent company, Dad.'

Frank waited a minute, and when he did not go on, prompted, 'So you're not going to tell me what's troubling you?'

Steve made an impatient gesture. 'Nothing's *troubling* me exactly, I'm just . . . being a bit juvenile, I'm afraid. I fell rather heavily for a girl over there, and I suppose I'm . . . pining. Pathetic, isn't it?'

'That girl I met – Ingrid, was it?'

'Inga, yes.'

This was like pulling teeth, Frank reflected. 'And she didn't reciprocate?'

Steve sighed. 'On the contrary, she did – that was partly the trouble. But basically she'd never leave the States and I'd never leave the UK. Not permanently.'

'Have you been in touch since you came home?'

'No; we decided a clean break was the only way.' He paused, staring into space. 'Luke didn't care for her.'

'Did he say so?'

'Not in so many words, bless him. He just . . . went quiet every time she was around.'

'Probably on Ella's behalf,' Frank suggested.

'Perhaps, but rumour has it Inga's first marriage ended because of her commitment to the firm, which doesn't bode well for another attempt. And Luke, after all, is my main concern. I've no intention of laying him open to the possibility of another failed marriage.'

'He's only a boy, Steven; he might have come round.'

'Well, as I said, there were other reasons. I'm well aware I should have got over it by now, but I stupidly keep twisting the knife.'

'You'd get over it more quickly if you met someone else,' Frank said firmly, 'and you're not going to do that if you spend every evening and weekend at home.'

'True. Sorry if I've been a pain. I will make an effort, I promise.'

Frank nodded, accepting that the conversation had ended. After a minute he got up and, to Steve's surprise, went to the bar unit and poured out two glasses of whisky.

'As a matter of fact,' he said as he handed his son a glass and seated himself again, 'I've also had something on my mind for the last couple of weeks or so.'

Steve looked up enquiringly. 'Oh?'

Frank raised his glass in a silent toast before drinking from it. 'It harks back to the accident.'

'Dad, you're not still getting flashbacks? Surely—'

Frank shook his head. 'This wasn't the same; it was the day I'd been to London, and I arrived home in the middle of the rush hour. The station was going like a fair and we were jammed on the escalators like sardines in a tin – and as you know, I don't like those things at the best of times.' He paused, staring down into his drink. 'And the hell of it is I don't know what happened, but I was suddenly transported straight back to that poor chap in the car crash. Whether this was caused by something I saw, or heard, or – for God's sake – *smelled*, I've no idea, but it was the most vivid experience I've had, as though I was actually reliving it.'

Into the brief silence Steve said, 'Have you seen the doctor?'

Frank shook his head impatiently. 'And that's not all; as you know, I've never been too clear on the sequence of events, what with concussion and the burns and smoke inhalation, but during that flash he was *saying* something. Or at least trying to.'

Steve leaned forward, his eyes fixed on his father. 'Go on.'

'He was clutching my arm and I could see his eyes staring up at me, willing me to listen as he struggled to speak.' Frank paused, looking inwards at the searing memory. 'Finally he did manage to whisper a couple of words. Then he . . . was gone.'

There was a long silence. Steve cleared his throat. 'I suppose it's no use asking what they were?'

Frank shook his head. 'I've been going over and over it in my head, willing myself to remember, but it's no use.' He paused. 'However, all that brain-racking wasn't entirely in vain, because something else has belatedly come back to me, something from minutes *before* the crash. It was dark, of course, on that country road, well past midnight, and suddenly out of nowhere two sets of headlamps appeared in my rear-view mirror. They were approaching at a fair lick as though they were racing each other, and the one behind was leaning on the horn. It struck me at the time they were playing a dangerous game on such a twisting road. Then they'd passed me and were out of sight.'

'And you think there might be a connection?'

'Seems likely, wouldn't you say? Those were the only cars I'd seen for miles; it stands to reason it was one of them that crashed. So where was the other? And that led me to thinking that the only point a dying man would be so desperate to get across was . . . an accusation. Suppose he was trying to tell me it wasn't an accident – that he'd been forced off the road?'

Steve whistled. 'You mean it was deliberate, and the other car just drove off?'

Frank shrugged. 'If it wasn't, why didn't he stop?'

'But wouldn't you have seen him?'

'No; there were two hairpin bends within a hundred yards of each other. I didn't see it happen, remember, just heard a tremendous crash as I approached, which must have been the car slamming into a tree, ricocheting off it and bouncing down the slope. When I rounded the corner all I was concerned about was getting to the driver and dragging him clear before the petrol ignited. But it had only just happened, and no one else had overtaken me.'

Steve thought for a moment. 'And you think it was those words – the words he was trying to say – that you might have heard again on the escalator?'

Frank moistened his lips. 'Possibly.'

'What we don't know,' Steve said reflectively, 'is which car went over.'

'Does it matter?'

'It might. But either way, if it wasn't an accident it sounds as though the victim *knew* who ran him off – and presumably meant to kill him. I remember you saying that if that another tree hadn't been in the way the car would have plunged right down to the bottom of the hill.' He stared into his glass. 'How much did you tell the police at the time?'

'Everything I could, but I was in hospital feeling pretty woozy and there were large gaps in my memory. I do recall wondering if they thought it was me who'd caused the accident; they kept going on and on about how I'd come on the scene. According to Vanda they arranged for a recovery agent to collect my car, and I'm willing to bet they had a good look at it. But all I knew at that stage – until a couple of weeks ago, for God's sake – was that I heard a crash as I was approaching the corner, saw that a car had gone off the road and dialled nine-nine-nine on my mobile. Then I scrambled down to it, but as I was trying to drag the driver out it shifted, pinning us down.'

'You've not contacted them again, since this happened?'

Frank shook his head. 'To be honest, I'm still not sure I wasn't hallucinating. Anyway, after all this time what can they do?'

'God knows, but we'll get on to them tomorrow.' Steve paused. 'He was a reporter, wasn't he, for one of the red-tops?'

'So I believe.'

'It opens up all sorts of possibilities, doesn't it? But the fact remains that if you're right, and he tried to tell you the name of whoever forced him over, we're looking at a case of murder. By person or persons unknown.'

SIX

Lindsey glanced at her mobile as it juddered into life. Text from Jonathan. This just had to stop, she thought irritably; she couldn't cope with it any more.

Dinner tonight. Rendezvous Nettleton 8.30, she read. *Collect you 8.10. Great surprise in store!*

The Rendezvous. Ironically enough, that was where she'd had a disastrous dinner with Hugh a few months ago. Though her immediate instinct was to opt out, she hesitated, considering. Why keep postponing the inevitable? This might provide just the right opportunity to end things once and for all, and with luck the fact that they were in public might restrain Jonathan's inevitable outburst. She could only hope so.

'Rona? This is Frank Hathaway.'

'Oh – hello!'

'I'm ringing to let you know that we've found the diaries.' He cut short her exclamation. 'However, thanks to the ink having faded and Ruth's scribbling being almost illegible at the best of times, they'll take a fair bit of deciphering.' He paused. 'I know you suggested we go through them together, but I hope you won't mind if I do this myself in the first instance. They'll inevitably bring back memories, and it's possible I might not want to share all of them.'

'Of course. I understand completely.'

'I appreciate that you're anxious to see them—'

'When I contacted you, I didn't even know of their existence,' Rona reminded him. 'If you'd prefer we could make a start on your own memories, but it's entirely up to you.'

He considered for a moment. 'Give me a week. I promise to come back to you then.'

'Fine. Thanks for letting me know.'

A pity, Rona thought as he rang off. The prospect of the diaries had whetted her appetite. However, replies to the magazine request had already started to trickle in with each post. Some, inevitably, were very similar: sleeping in the street prior to a royal wedding, a few memories of World War II, meeting so-called celebrities – nothing very promising so far. Just as well she had Monica and Frank Hathaway in reserve, she thought. If the need arose, they'd both be good for several articles.

The phone again interrupted her reflections; Max this time – a surprise, since it was barely an hour since he'd returned to the studio.

'Sweetie, I'm sorry,' he began. 'Would you mind looking on the side in the kitchen and see if I left a large envelope there?'

'Hang on.' She ran down the two flights of stairs, past the sleeping dog in the hallway, to the basement. 'Yes, it's here,' she reported.

'Damn! Those are the photos I took of Crawford last week. I'd intended to look at them over the weekend but never got round to it, and now I need them to work on.' He paused. 'You're not by any chance coming up this way?'

'I wasn't,' Rona said. Dean's Crescent North, where the studio was located, was on the far side of Guild Street, in the opposite direction from her normal shopping or dog-walking circuit. However, the offices of *Chiltern Life* were in Dean's Crescent – she could kill two birds with one stone. 'OK,' she relented. 'I need to see Barnie anyway, so I can come on from there.'

'You're an angel,' he said gratefully, 'and you'd be even more of one if you could see Barnie on the way back! I really need those photos; Crawford's due in for another sitting before he returns to London and I've a lot to do before he gets here. I'd come back for them myself, but I really can't spare the time.'

'You've made your point,' Rona told him. 'Gus and I will be with you in twenty minutes.'

The day had clouded over and there was a hint of autumn in the air. When they reached the corner of Lightbourne Avenue the dog turned expectantly in the direction of Charlton Road and the slipway to the park, but Rona gently steered him to the left.

'Sorry, you won't be off your lead till this afternoon,' she told him. 'We're having an urban walk this morning.'

Dean's Crescent, as well as housing *Chiltern Life*, was home to Rona's favourite Italian restaurant, Dino's. There was much speculation in the town as to whether the proprietor had taken his name from his address, but none of his many satisfied customers had been brave enough to ask him. With Gus trotting contentedly at her side, Rona followed the crescent round, past a cluster of antique shops, an old-fashioned barber's shop where you could look through the window and see work in progress, and the substantial building that contained *Chiltern Life*. Then they were across Guild Street and turning into the northern end of the crescent.

Farthings was a small, white-washed cottage whose upper floor had been converted into Max's studio. Its ground floor comprised a bedroom he slept in three nights a week following evening classes, a living room, a kitchen and, beyond it, a shower-room extension. The open staircase led directly into the studio, and as Rona opened the front door she was met with a blast of music, a reminder of why they needed separate spaces in which to work.

As at home, Gus was not allowed above the ground floor, so she let him into the postage-stamp garden before going up to the studio where she found Max at his easel.

'Personal delivery,' she said, raising her voice to make herself heard.

'Thanks, love.' While he slid the photos out of the envelope, she studied the strong face on the canvas, already, though not much more than a sketch, recognizable as that of the Right Honourable George Crawford.

'I'm surprised you agreed to do another MP,' she commented. The last one he'd painted had proved to be a murderer.

'I'd never earn a living if I painted only upright citizens,' Max returned, studying the photos in his hand.

Rona laughed. 'Fair enough. OK, I'll leave you to it. Speak to you this evening.'

Polly, the receptionist at *Chiltern Life*, made the usual fuss of Gus, whom she always looked after while Rona saw Barnie.

'How's married life?' Rona asked her. 'I don't think I've seen you since the wedding.'

'Oh, it's great, thanks. We're gradually getting the flat in order. Thanks so much for the lovely little butter dish. Tony laughs at me, but I always take the butter out of its wrapping and put it in. It makes the meal more special somehow.'

'I'm glad you're finding it useful,' Rona said. 'Was there any post for me today?'

''Fraid not. They've been tailing off over the last few days.'

'I'll have to make the best of what I've got, then.'

Leaving Gus in Polly's charge, Rona went up the stairs to Barnie's small, untidy office. He rose from behind his desk to greet her, a bear of a man well over six feet tall with a voice that could stop traffic.

'Rona! Brenda's bringing coffee. Sit down.'

A tap on the door heralded its arrival, and Rona thankfully took a mug.

'Now, any progress on the new project? I hear mail's been coming in for you.'

'There's not much of interest, to be honest. However, there's a handful of possibilities, so I'll go through them again and arrange to see the most hopeful.'

'I was thinking about that; instead of your trailing all over the county, why not interview them here? I could let you have a room for the duration.'

'Thanks, Barnie, that would be great. I doubt if we'll have any more now, but I should be able to make up the half-dozen we agreed on. I've already spoken to a friend of my father's who's had an exciting life, and he's found some diaries his wife wrote while they were abroad. With luck they could be gold dust, but he wants to vet them first.'

'Can't say I blame him. Don't know that I'd like anyone reading Dinah's diaries – too many home truths in them! When do you reckon the first could be ready?'

'It shouldn't take long so the next edition, all being well. Oh, and Barnie, there's something else I wanted to run past you: have you heard of the fashion designer Ross Mackenzie?'

Barnie tapped his pen against his teeth. 'The one who turned up at the Clarendon show?'

'That's right; I met him there, and when he heard I do articles for *Chiltern Life*, he asked if we'd interview him.'

Barnie's bushy eyebrows shot up. 'That'd be quite a scoop.'

'Mind you, that was a couple of weeks ago and I've heard nothing since. It might just have been spur of the moment and he's forgotten about it.'

'Any chance of jogging his memory?'

'I've no contact details but Magda will have, or at least know how to get in touch with him.'

'Then go for it, girl. Strike while the iron's at least tepid, and if he's still game get straight on to him and put the series on hold.' He drained his coffee. 'So, how are things otherwise? Max OK?'

'Yes, he has two commissioned portraits on the go, on top of everything else.' In addition to his classes and his own work, Max taught at the local art school once a week.

'And your folks? I hear there'll be a couple of weddings when the divorce goes through.'

Rona smiled. 'That's right, and by way of a dummy run, my soon-to-be stepsister is getting married next month.'

'Sounds like you should start saving up.' The phone clarioned on Barnie's desk and he reached for it. 'Right, let me know when you're ready for an office. See you.'

Hastily finishing her own coffee, Rona left him to his call.

Having reclaimed Gus and set off towards home, it occurred to Rona that while she was in town she should take the opportunity to look at Vanda Hathaway's jewellery. Tarlton's was one of Marsborough's oldest family firms and Rona had researched them for a series on local companies, a series that had proved far more traumatic than anyone had anticipated.

Kate Tarlton was in the shop when Rona went in, and came forward to greet her. 'Rona! Haven't seen you in ages! How are things?'

'Fine. I'm only window-shopping, I'm afraid.'

'Pity!' Kate said with a smile. 'Anything I can help with?'

'I've been speaking to Vanda Hathaway's father and he says you sell her jewellery.'

'Vanda? Yes indeed; we have a showcase of her work.' Kate led the way to one of the display cabinets and Rona leant forward with interest. Inside was a striking and distinctive array of jewellery – chunky rings and necklaces, some with multifaceted stones, a range of earrings that hung in tassels or coiled like shells or had tiny figures suspended from them, chains interlinked with gold and silver, minute watches with jewelled bracelets. Yet despite the diversity there was an underlying signature to all the items and Rona guessed that a professional eye would instantly identify the designer.

'And this is only a selection!' Kate said. 'She's a very versatile lady.'

'I suppose, since you're a buyer, you know her personally?'

'Oh, yes. She was up here for a while last year after her father's accident.'

'What's she like?'

'Quirky and intelligent but a bit abrasive till you get to know her.' Kate paused. 'You know her father, then?'

'Pops does, and put me in touch with him for a new series I'm doing for *Chiltern Life*.'

Kate sobered. 'What's the theme this time?'

'Interesting or unusual experiences – *Moments That Changed My Life* kind of thing.'

'Well, I hope he has an easier ride than we did; he was in a pretty bad way and Vanda was quite concerned about him. She stayed until Christmas, when his son came back from the States.'

Rona nodded, but she'd picked up on Kate's first comment. 'Things are all right now, though? In the family?'

'Yes, of course. I didn't mean to imply you were to blame for everything that came out. It had been festering for years, as you know, and it's largely thanks to you that we're back on an even keel.' She glanced at her watch. 'I'm due my lunch break. Any chance of your joining me?'

'Love to,' Rona said promptly; any opportunity to avoid having to prepare a meal for herself was welcome. Having untied Gus from the post outside the shop, she and Kate made their way through the lunchtime crowds to the Gallery Café.

'Now,' Kate instructed when they were settled at a table and had given their order, 'fill me in on what you've been doing since we last met.' She smiled. 'I have, of course, read about some of your wilder exploits in the *Gazette*.'

'I do seem to attract trouble,' Rona admitted, 'but it's all grist to my writing mill.'

'How's the family? The last time we really spoke your father had just moved out. Were they able to sort themselves out?'

'Not in the way you mean. The divorce goes through in December, after which they'll both be remarrying.'

Kate stared at her in astonishment. '*Both* of them?'

Rona nodded. 'Mum to the father of her ex-lodger, Pops to a client at the bank. It's been a terrific upheaval but they both seem ridiculously happy so no doubt it's worked out for the best.'

Kate digested that for a moment. 'Well, good for them,' she said then. 'And Lindsey? Is Hugh still on the scene?'

'He's around, but they're not together.'

Kate waited for more details but none seemed forthcoming, and she reflected that Rona had always been uncommunicative about her twin, even when they were at school. Resignedly she moved the conversation on to her own family, and the rest of the meal was spent exchanging news of old friends.

'Tell Max Vanda makes jewellery to order,' Kate said as they parted on the pavement. 'That would be a Christmas present to remember!'

Rona smiled. 'I'll tell him, but I don't hold out much hope!'

'It's been good to see you, Rona. We mustn't leave it so long next time. Love to the family.'

'And mine to yours.'

Then Kate turned left to return to the shop and Rona turned right towards home. It hadn't been the morning she'd planned, but it had been enjoyable and now she must get down to work. Once she'd been through the day's replies, she might have some idea of the shape the series would take.

As the day wore on Lindsey's anxiety level increased, and with it a growing dread of the evening ahead. Jonathan was bound to react badly to her decision. Why oh why had she let herself become involved with him again? Wasn't the last time warning enough? But of course she knew the answer: it had been intended as a slap in the face for Dominic. As if he either knew or cared.

It was now nearly six months since she'd stormed out of his

flat having learned he'd spent the night before their trip to France with Carla. Since then she'd seen him precisely three times – once when she and Jonathan were dining with a client at the Clarendon and he'd paused at their table to speak to their companion; once when they'd come face-to-face on Guild Street and he'd given her a cool nod and walked on; and the third time at the theatre. He'd been seated a few rows in front of her but they'd managed to avoid acknowledging each other. She wondered wistfully if he ever thought of her; she still dreamt of him most nights.

Lindsey gave herself a little shake. This was no time to reminisce over Dominic; she should be planning her strategy for the evening ahead. But once she'd ditched Jonathan, she thought bleakly, there was no reserve waiting in the wings and, as she'd told Rona repeatedly, she needed a man in her life. Was she just cutting off her nose to spite her face?

At exactly ten past eight there was a tooting from the gravel that fronted the flats, a summons that never failed to annoy her though until now she'd not commented on it. With a last quick check in the mirror, she went downstairs and out on to the forecourt. Jonathan leant across to open the passenger door.

'It wouldn't hurt you to get out and ring the bell like everyone else,' she said tartly.

Unabashed, he kissed her cheek. 'Hoity-toity!' he said, and started the car with a characteristic flourish that set the gravel flying. They were on their way and there was no going back. Like a lamb to the slaughter, Lindsey resigned herself to the inevitable.

'I've finished with Jonathan.'

Rona, befuddled with sleep, peered at the bedside clock. It was a quarter to seven.

'Lindsey, do you know what time it is?'

'Be thankful I didn't ring you at five. And is that all you've got to say?'

'Well, I'm glad, of course. Well done.'

'Ro, it was horrendous. Worse than I ever imagined. We were at the Rendezvous in Nettleton and he stormed out without paying the bill and drove off, leaving me stranded.'

Rona struggled up on to one elbow. 'Oh, Linz, I'm so sorry.'

'I thought it might be better to tell him in public, that he wouldn't make a scene. How wrong I was!'

'What brought it to a head?'

'I'd decided to end it anyway, but he announced that he'd booked us into a Paris hotel for the weekend. There was no way I could have gone.' She paused. 'And now I've got to face him at the office.'

'Like to come round after work? We could eat at Dino's.'

'That'd be great, Ro. Thanks.'

'In the meantime, treat him like a potentially dangerous animal: keep your head down and don't make eye contact.'

Lindsey gave a choked laugh. 'Good advice. See you about six.'

As she rang off, Rona lay back again, staring up at the ceiling. Though Lindsey had laughed as she'd intended, her advice had been half-serious. Jonathan Hurst was unpredictable; his male pride had been badly dented and there was no saying how he'd react. This was the second time her twin had dumped him; she could only hope he wouldn't cause her any lasting damage.

SEVEN

There was one other task to complete before embarking on the interviews, and later that morning Rona phoned Magda on her mobile.

'Where are you today?' she asked when they'd exchanged greetings. Magda had eight boutiques scattered around the county and made a point of visiting them all on a regular basis.

'Chilswood,' Magda replied. 'This is the last to open a café and I'm checking on the initial takings.'

'Excellent! Now I can have lunch or tea wherever I visit you.'

'As you decide how many outfits you're going to buy!' Magda supplied.

Rona laughed. 'Talking of outfits, the reason I'm phoning is to ask if you've a contact number for Ross Mackenzie. He suggested *Chiltern Life* do a profile of him and I'd like to take him up on it.'

'I'll have it somewhere. Hang on.' There was a pause while she scrolled through her contact list. 'It's for the studio, not his mobile.'

'If he's not there, no doubt someone could put me on to him.'
Rona noted it down. 'How are his clothes selling?'

'Steadily rather than spectacularly,' Magda replied. 'But that's
between us! I'm counting on the fact that being the autumn collection they're mainly warmer clothes and as the colder weather kicks
in sales will improve.'

'Sure to. Thanks, Magda. We must arrange dinner sometime.'

'Definitely. See you.' And she rang off.

Rona promptly dialled the number she'd been given and a crisp
voice said, 'Ross Mackenzie's studio.'

'May I have a word with him, please? It's Rona Parish speaking.'

There was a brief pause, then, 'Ah, Miss Parish. Isobel Firth here.
I'm afraid my brother isn't in today. Perhaps I can help?'

'Could you give me a number where I can reach him? We
discussed the possibility of featuring him in our magazine and I'd
like to arrange a meeting.'

'I'm not sure that he'd welcome an interruption. He's visiting
textile manufacturers with a view to his next collection.'

'I shan't keep him long.' Aware of the battle of wills, Rona waited
for Isobel's next move. Fortunately she capitulated.

'Very well. But I suggest you wait till nearer lunchtime before
contacting him.'

'Certainly. Thank you very much, Ms Firth.'

The dragon at the gate! Rona thought, as she added his mobile
number to her own contacts. It was ten thirty; she had a couple of
hours before she could call him, during which she would start to
arrange interviews. She'd been disappointed by both the number
and quality of the replies she'd received, hoping for more from
Chiltern Life's wide circulation. Perhaps the majority of their readers
lived ordinary, humdrum lives and relied on books and drama series
for their excitement. Far from having to restrict herself to the
maximum Barnie had set, it had been difficult to reach it. The
remainder – those recounting having sat next to a 'celebrity' in a
restaurant and such-like – she would thank for replying and return
the synopses where self-addressed envelopes had been supplied.

By twelve fifteen she'd arranged to see four of those selected,
and phoned Barnie to request use of the promised office.

'I've arranged the first interviews for Thursday,' she said. 'Two
in the morning and two in the afternoon. That leaves two whom
I've been unable to contact, possibly because they're at work. I've

left messages, and if they agree I could see them at the Clarendon on Saturday morning; I've done interviews there before.'

'Do those six include your neighbour and your father's friend?'

'Not at this point – I'm holding them in reserve. I suspect Frank Hathaway in particular will be more of a long-term project. It's always possible, though, that those I'm seeing won't be what I want after all – they could have exaggerated or not been directly involved or whatever – in which case I'd have something to fall back on.'

'Right. Let me know how it goes.'

'And now,' she ended, 'I'm about to phone Ross Mackenzie, so I'll report back on that too.'

He picked up after the first ring. 'Ross Mackenzie.'

'This is Rona Parish, Mr Mackenzie.'

He immediately dispensed with formality. 'Ah, Rona! Isobel said you'd be phoning.'

So she hadn't herself waited till lunchtime, Rona noted. 'I was wondering if you're still interested in doing a profile for us?'

'Certainly I am.' His Scottish accent was more noticeable over the phone.

'Then perhaps we could meet?'

'Of course. I've no plans to be up your way, but I presume you can come to London? Not the studio, though. No privacy there, and Isobel might cramp my style!' A smile had crept into his voice.

'Where would you suggest?'

'Do you know the Argyll Hotel in Mayfair?'

'I do, yes.' She and Max had spent the occasional night there after the theatre.

'What's today – Tuesday? I'm tied up for most of the week, but I could meet you at about five o'clock on Friday. How would that suit?'

Not well, since it would interrupt Max's evening at home. 'Fine,' she said diplomatically.

'In the bar lounge, then. See you there.'

She told Max of the appointment when he phoned as usual around six.

'I'm so sorry,' she apologized, 'especially as in all likelihood I'll be interviewing on Saturday morning. But I have to see him, and if that's the only time . . .'

'Tell you what; I need to see my specialist paint supplier – the local chap can't get quite what I want. Suppose I take the train down, visit him, then meet you at the Argyll after your interview and we'll treat ourselves to a meal before coming home?'

Friday was the one day in the week when Max had no commitments other than his own work.

'That would be great!' She paused. 'By the way, Lindsey has given Jonathan the chop. They had a dramatic confrontation last night, and she's going to tell me about it over a meal at Dino's.'

'Let's hope she sticks to her guns this time. You won't be home much before eleven, so I'll phone then.' Although they exchanged the news of the day before Max's evening classes, he invariably rang back at bedtime to say goodnight.

'I'll make sure to be back by then,' she said.

Tom said, 'I was wondering if we could invite Frank Hathaway and his son round to dinner?'

'The man you had lunch with a few weeks ago?' Catherine asked.

'Yes; I'd like you to meet him. I've known him most of my life and I gather he's been at rather a loose end since his wife died.' Tom grimaced. 'When we met, he asked after Avril.'

'Oh dear! I hope I'm not too much of a disappointment!'

'He's been having a rough time all round, but he's agreed to help Rona with her project on interesting lives, which is good of him.'

'In that case perhaps we should invite her too?'

Tom hesitated. 'But that would involve asking Max – though admittedly he's usually busy in the evenings – and perhaps Lindsey, which would make it all more of an event than I intended.'

'An event?' Catherine queried with a laugh.

'You know what I mean. Top-heavy. I was envisaging a more casual affair.'

'Right, let's leave it as just the four of us then. When were you thinking of?'

'We'd better give them a bit of notice. Next week sometime?'

'A week today?'

Tom checked his diary. 'That'll be the first of October. Where's the year gone? Right, let's see if they can make it for Tuesday the first. I'll give him a ring this evening.'

Rona, at her usual table at Dino's, awaited her sister's arrival with some trepidation, but when Lindsey arrived she brought a sense of anticlimax.

'I didn't see him,' she said at once as she seated herself. 'Either he was out with clients or just lying low. So I'll have to brace myself all over again tomorrow.'

'He'll have had more time to calm down,' Rona suggested.

'Or to fuel his rage. I shan't escape unscathed, I'm sure of that.'

Dino materialized at Rona's elbow. '*Buona sera, signoras,*' he greeted them, presenting them each with a menu. 'This evening I have the most delectable fish to offer you – *pesce gratinato*, cooked with the egg yolks, butter and rice. Or perhaps the red mullet marinated in white wine? Of if meat is your preference, we have—'

'The gratin sounds gorgeous, Dino,' Rona said. 'I'll have that, please.'

'And I'll try the red mullet,' added Lindsey.

The wine and accompanying vegetables having been ordered, Rona instructed, 'Now, tell me all.'

'He'd told me he had a surprise for me but he wouldn't say what it was until the dessert arrived – Floating Islands, which he knows is my favourite – and stuck into each of them was a tiny French flag.'

'You have to give him marks for originality,' Rona remarked, dipping her bread into the dish of olive oil.

'That's when he said he'd booked this Paris hotel for the weekend; he knew things had been "a bit sticky lately", as he put, and he thought we needed some time alone to talk things through.' She bit her lip, staring down at the table. 'Which is when I told him I couldn't go.'

'And he blew his top?'

'At first he thought I meant I'd something else on, but once he realized I was ending it the sparks started to fly. His voice got louder and louder and people were beginning to look at us. In the end he pushed back his chair, flung his napkin on the table – knocking off one of the French flags – and stormed out of the restaurant. It was all highly embarrassing. I was sure he'd come back but he didn't, so after about five minutes I called for the bill and asked them to order me a taxi, while ears were flapping at all the nearby tables.'

'Poor you,' Rona sympathized. 'He could at least have waited for you in the car.'

'But can you imagine what the atmosphere would have been like on the drive home? On reflection I can't say I blame him.'

They waited while a waiter filled their glasses and set the bottle in a bucket of ice alongside the table. 'Anyway,' Lindsey added, 'we're here to enjoy ourselves so let's change the subject. What have you been up to in the last two weeks?'

'Trying to get organized on the new series,' Rona replied, sipping her wine. 'I've made the first appointments, so we'll see how it goes. Oh, and we're going ahead with the Ross Mackenzie profile. I'm meeting him at the Argyll on Friday afternoon.'

'Are you indeed? Some people have all the luck! Afternoon tea at the Argyll!'

'More likely to be drinks; we're meeting in the bar lounge at five.'

'Even better!'

'Max is coming in to see his paint man and we'll have a meal after, which will be good.'

'Will you concentrate on the design angle or his personal life?'

'Both, with luck, but he might be a bit cagey about his ideas.'

'So you'll find out if he is or has been married?'

Rona shook her head despairingly. 'No doubt that would be your first question!'

'I can't believe a man that attractive hasn't been snapped up.'

'Unless his preferences lie elsewhere.'

Lindsey shook her head decidedly. 'No, I'm sure not.'

'Well, it's immaterial either way, but it will be interesting to know when and why he decided to be a fashion designer.'

Their food arrived, and by the time it was served the conversation had moved in other directions. It was only as they parted after their meal that Lindsey said, 'Be sure to phone with all the gen on Ross. I'll be waiting with bated breath!'

'You'll be the first to know,' Rona said drily.

Frank took a long time to go to sleep that night. For what seemed like hours he lay on his back staring into the dark as memories that had reawakened after reading the diaries returned to torment him – of Ruth twenty and thirty years ago, as she'd been when she was writing them and Vanda and Steve had still been children.

At what point he dropped off he couldn't be sure, but all at once he was wide awake – or thought he was – and back at the scene of the car crash, trying frantically to extract the driver without doing him further damage. Suddenly the man gripped his arm, and as

Frank paused to look down at him he seemed to be making efforts to speak, his lips repeatedly shaping a soundless word Frank wasn't able to interpret.

He heard his own voice say, 'It's all right, lad, I'm not going to leave you. But don't try to talk – conserve your strength.'

The driver shook his head, his eyes fixed wildly on Frank's as with increasing desperation he tried yet again to articulate, and seeing his obvious distress Frank bent closer.

'What is it, son?' he asked gently.

And then on a breath the words came, and whatever Frank had been expecting – his wife's name perhaps, or, more simply, just 'help me' – the only one he could make out sounded like *'frenzy'*.

He drew back, frowning slightly. 'You were in a frenzy?' he asked, puzzled. But there was no reply and at that moment, with a terrifying whoosh, the car burst into flames.

Then he was back in his bedroom, shaking and soaked with sweat. He reached urgently for the light switch and as the room leapt into clarity, lay back on his pillows, breathing heavily. Was that a genuine flashback, an expansion of the one he'd had previously, or simply a nightmare? *Had* the driver finally managed to communicate with him? And if so, how could a word such as 'frenzy' be so important that he should have spent the last of his dying strength to enunciate it?

It was no use going back to bed; he would simply lie awake going over and over the dream or whatever it was with no hope of coming up with an answer. Still shaky, he reached for his dressing gown and slippers and quietly opened his bedroom door. The stillness of the house lapped over him as he stole softly downstairs, refraining from putting on a light in case it seeped through Luke's open door and woke him. A streetlamp shining through the glass of the front door guided him to the sitting room, which seemed oddly alien at this unaccustomed time of the morning.

He poured himself a stiff whisky, put on one of his classical CDs turned down low, and prepared to await the dawn.

Finally he must have nodded off, because Steve found him still in his armchair when he came looking in the morning.

'I do wish you'd see the doctor, Dad,' he said worriedly, when Frank had recounted his experience. 'It's not good for you, being subjected to these nightmares or whatever they are.'

Frank shook his head. 'Don't worry, I'm not losing my marbles,' he said with a bleak smile. 'I'm convinced now that last night was just one more strand of memory breaking through the amnesia. There were details that hadn't been in the first flashback. For instance, the moon must have broken through the clouds, because I could see his face quite clearly. He had that scruffy look that seems so fashionable now – designer stubble, do they call it? His eyelashes were surprisingly long for a man, and his eyes – Steve, the expression in them! Intense pain and desperation to make himself understood. I can't help feeling I failed him.'

Steve leaned forward, putting his hand on Frank's. 'You mustn't think that. What could you have possibly done with the word "frenzy"?' He helped his father gently to his feet. 'Now, go and have a shower and try to put it out of your mind.'

'Easier said than done,' Frank returned. 'But you're right – worrying when there's nothing you can do is a pointless exercise and I feel better having talked it through with you. We'll just have to see if there are any further developments.'

Ten o'clock on Thursday morning. Rona rose to her feet as her first interviewee was shown into the office Barnie had assigned to her.

'Mrs Williams – do please sit down. Thank you so much for coming.'

As the woman seated herself, Rona took quick stock. Aged about fifty, she guessed, small and neat. No discernible make-up, noticeably nervous, but Rona hoped the coffee she'd requested would break the ice, and during the few minutes it took to offer sugar and biscuits her visitor did indeed begin to relax.

Rona indicated the recorder on her desk. 'I hope you won't mind if I use this? It provides an accurate record of our conversation and means I don't have to spend my time taking notes.'

Mrs Williams surveyed the instrument a little dubiously, but nodded. 'It was my husband who said I should write in,' she began half-apologetically. 'I wasn't sure it was what you were looking for, but he kept on at me.'

'I'm glad he did!' Rona said. 'There can't be many people in Buckfordshire who've lived through an uprising like that. Could we start with how you came to be nanny to the Sheik of Al Whari's children in the first place?'

Once she'd started on her story Mrs Williams lost her

nervousness, and her description of her charges – six children aged from ten years to a few months – the daily routine of life in the royal palace and the first indications of unrest, was fascinating, rising in tension as she recounted their night flight to a neighbouring country seeking asylum. If all her respondents proved of this standard, Rona thought, she'd be on to a winner.

Coincidentally, it appeared that she also owed the presence of her second interviewee to marital pressure, though she suspected Charles Conway might not have needed as much persuading as Amy Williams. He'd been serving in the Royal Navy at the time of the Falklands conflict and was on HMS *Sheffield* when she came under attack. His graphic account of the wounded ship, the dead and injured crew and the eventual abandonment of the vessel left Rona in sombre mood and she was grateful for the lunch break she'd slotted into her timetable. Two down, she thought, four to go.

It was during her break that one of those four, whom she'd been unable to contact, returned her call and agreed to meet her at eleven o'clock on Saturday morning in the lounge at the Clarendon.

The afternoon sessions were not as productive as the morning's: the first, Stan Lewis, had indicated that he'd been a television presenter and interviewed many prominent figures. In the event he proved to have been a chat-show host for a local station and immediately embarked on a series of scurrilous stories about the rich and famous. Rona, gaining the impression he'd a chip on his shoulder and was exacting some kind of revenge, stopped him in mid-flow, thanked him for coming and promised to contact him if, after interviewing others on her list, she wanted to take it further.

The final interview of the day was with a young woman called Sally Short, who had claimed to be the understudy for an actress in a West End musical. However, it was soon evident that her claims had been considerably exaggerated – she had not met half the people she'd named, and had never been called on to take the starring role. Which, Rona thought, slipping her recorder into her bag at the end of the afternoon, left her with only a fifty per cent success rate for the day.

'It looks as though I shall be calling on Monica and Frank Hathaway sooner rather than later,' she told Max when he phoned that evening.

'Any chance of going back to some you initially discarded?'

'Not a hope. I'm just crossing my fingers that the two I'm seeing on Saturday fit the bill. They've both come back to me now.'

'And if they don't?'

'It'll be a shorter series than anticipated.'

'Well, it's not the end of the world, is it? There was no fixed number you had to produce – and there's still a chance you could get more than one article out of Monica and What's-his-name.'

'Yes, there is that.'

'So cheer up, my love, all is not lost, and in the meantime you have the big interview with His Nibs tomorrow. I'll see you in the foyer of the Argyll around six, but don't worry if it goes on longer; I'll be quite happy relaxing and watching the world go by.'

'See you there,' Rona said.

Ross Mackenzie had arrived ahead of her and rose to his feet as she appeared in the doorway. He was dressed more conventionally than at the fashion show, in fawn trousers and jacket and a blue open-neck shirt.

'Good to see you again,' he said, taking her hand. 'Before we start on business, what can I get you to drink?'

'Vodka and Russchian if they have it; otherwise with tonic, please.'

'You were in luck,' he informed her, returning with their glasses and settling himself in his chair. 'I hope you don't mind my railroading you like this,' he added, 'but it seemed too good an opportunity to miss. I'm anxious to widen my clientele in Buckfordshire and an article in a magazine such as yours could do a lot to promote interest. I'd be most grateful for any publicity you could give me.'

'I'd be delighted to help, and so would our features editor.' She took her recorder out of her bag. 'Is it OK if I use this?'

'Go ahead. So, what do you want to know?'

'Let's start at the beginning, with your family. Where were you born?'

'Inverness. I lived there till I was eighteen. Both my parents were school teachers.'

'How many were in the family?'

'Just Isobel and myself. She was the brainy one, while I, according to my parents, had my head in the clouds.'

'Which of you is the elder?'

'Isobel, by two years, which is why she's so bossy!'

'And were you always interested in women's clothes?'

'I was, yes. My mother had a good dress sense which I greatly admired. I spent a lot of time sketching designs when I should have been studying. Eventually my father, who was somewhat macho, stopped trying to interest me in more "manly" subjects and accepted this was what I wanted to do. They bought me a sewing machine for my sixteenth birthday, and I remember swearing Isobel to secrecy; I'd never have lived it down if it had got out.'

'Did you study design at university?'

Ross took a long drink of his whisky. 'Not university, but I was lucky enough to win a place on the Fashion and Textiles course at Central St Martin's College of Art and Design here in London. That was invaluable but it was still a slog for the first few years, particularly as I'd met a girl at college, and against all advice we married. We stayed together for five years, but it was a rocky passage and my designing suffered in consequence.'

A nugget for Lindsey, Rona thought. 'Your sister seems very involved in your business. Have you always worked together?'

'No, as I said, she was on a totally different track. She went to uni, got a good degree and joined an accountancy firm. But sadly she too had a disastrous marriage – worse than mine as her husband was abusive – and it took her a long time to get over it. She gave up accountancy, and since I was still struggling, decided I needed a more business-like approach. She offered to come in with me for a while, we managed to turn things round, and though it was supposed to be temporary, she stayed on and is now indispensable in keeping things ticking over – diary engagements, photographic sessions, accessories and the running of the various fashion shows.'

'So where do you get your inspiration?'

He smiled. 'The million-dollar question! It sounds trite to say "from life", but that's the answer. Unusual colour combinations in a flowerbed, the sweep of a woman's skirt as she gets into a taxi, historical dramas on TV. When I'm lucky, something explodes in my head and I reach feverishly for pencil and paper. When I'm not, the idea fades before I can grasp it.'

Rona raised her eyebrows. 'Pencil and paper? In this day and age?'

'Indeed; most of us still do our initial designs by hand. I keep all my old sketchbooks and every now and then I refer back to see if something I abandoned as unworkable could be rethought and brought to fruition.'

'So what comes after the sketching?'

'The next stage is tracking down the right fabric, which is both exciting and frustrating and can take quite a while. And when I've found it, I spend hours draping it over a dress form to achieve the effect I want. Only when I'm satisfied do I hand over to my pattern and sample makers to do the technical stuff, after which it's made up in a cheaper material to see if it works.'

'What a time-consuming process! So how long does it take from your initial idea to the finished product?'

He shrugged. 'Anything from eighteen months to two years.'

'You mentioned over supper that you had trouble with this last collection and felt it was jinxed. Why was that?'

To her surprise he flushed, moved uncomfortably in his chair and took a long drink of whisky before replying. When he did so his tone was brusque. 'Sorry, I must have been waffling. Put it down to the booze.'

Since he was obviously not going to discuss it, Rona continued with her questions, gratified that he didn't dodge any others and marvelling at the intricacies of the fashion business.

'So, do you think you have enough to go on?' he asked, when at last she came to a halt.

'Yes, thanks, that was great.' She switched off the recorder and slipped it back in her bag. 'It should make a fascinating profile.'

'I hope so.' He reached for his wallet. 'Last time we met I asked for your card and failed to make use of it. Here's mine, and do please call if there's anything else you need.'

'Thank you, I will. And thanks so much for—' She broke off, staring towards the entrance to the bar.

Ross turned to follow her gaze and a smile spread over his face. 'Double vision again! How splendid!' he said, and rose to his feet as Lindsey walked towards them.

'Hope I'm not interrupting anything,' she said airily. 'I knew you were meeting, and as I happened to be passing I thought I'd drop in.'

Happened to be passing, indeed! Rona thought, but Ross was saying, 'We've just finished our business talk so let me get you a drink.' He pulled out a chair and Lindsey sat down, avoiding her sister's accusing gaze.

Rona, however, came to her feet. 'I'm sorry but I must go – I'm meeting my husband. Thank you so much, Ross, for the drink and for the interview. I'll be in touch if I need anything else.' And with a cool nod in Lindsey's direction, she left the room.

Max was just coming through the swing doors into the foyer. 'Ah, good timing!' He frowned at her flushed cheeks. 'Anything wrong?'

'Lindsey has just arrived,' Rona said tightly.

'*Lindsey?* But—'

'She just "happened to be passing".'

'Like hell she was! But how did she know you were meeting him?'

'*Mea culpa.* I mentioned it when we had dinner.'

He snorted. 'Well, it makes sense; she's finished with Jonathan so she's on the prowl.'

'But I worry about her, Max,' Rona said as he led her back through the swing doors. 'One of these days she'll find herself out of her depth.'

'She's old enough to know what she's doing.' He'd no sympathy for Lindsey Parish.

Rona glanced at his face, realized it was pointless to prolong the discussion, and asked instead, 'So where are we going to eat?'

'I thought we might try that new place in Covent Garden.'

And Rona, her thoughts turning to the meal ahead, reluctantly abandoned her sister to her fate.

EIGHT

That same evening Mia had another phone call from Ewan. In the week since they'd met she had several times been on the point of contacting him but had resisted, partly because she knew he'd call if there was further news of Colin, and partly so as to play down her own anxiety. Now, hearing his voice, her hand tightened on the phone.

'I'm going over to Farnbridge tomorrow,' he began, 'and was wondering if you'd like to come along?'

'Has he been in touch again?' she asked quickly.

'No, it was I who contacted him; in view of our last meeting I'm bringing my regular visit forward a little.'

Mia bit her lip, acknowledging that her ex-husband made more of an effort to keep in touch with their son than she did. 'Thank you, I'd like to come very much.'

'We meet at the Walnut Tree pub on the Buckford road. Do you know it?'

'I'll find it. What time?'

'He'll be coming at twelve thirty, so I suggest you make it a bit earlier, so we can present a united front when he arrives.'

She gave a breathless little laugh. 'I trust that won't put him off!'

'No, I have the feeling he'd welcome a bit of solidarity.'

'Let's hope, then, that he feels he can confide in us,' she said, and wondered even as she spoke if that was really what she was hoping for, or whether in truth she'd rather not know.

Rona had been half-expecting one of Lindsey's early morning calls to report on her meeting with Ross, but the phone remained blessedly silent – probably, she reasoned, because her twin knew Max was around. When, however, they'd finished breakfast and he went out with the dog, she phoned Lindsey's flat, preparing some sarcastic comment on her sister's unexpected and unwarranted arrival. To her surprise, though, the call went to answerphone. Frowning, Rona tried her mobile, only to be directed to voicemail. What the hell was she up to? she wondered, now slightly anxious. She redialled both numbers, leaving a message on each to call her, and, dismissing the matter from her mind, prepared for her first interview at the Clarendon.

When submitting her précis Melanie Bates had identified herself as a reporter for a national newspaper, and one of the assignments she'd covered was the London Olympics. Rona listened with interest as she described interviewing the medal winners and sympathizing with the losers, travelling from one sports venue to another on double-decker buses masquerading as 'games vehicles', and making full use of the facilities at the Olympic Village, which had its own bank, post office, pharmacy and launderette. She'd been present at both the opening and closing ceremonies and, despite the passage of time, looked back on the experience as one of the highlights of her career. Furthermore, she was fairly confident that her newspaper might give permission for the use of some of their photographs to illustrate the article, providing they received due acknowledgment.

There was a fifteen-minute break between the end of that interview and the start of the next, and as Rona went in search of more coffee, Dominic Frayne came through the swing doors. There was no way they could avoid each other and, smooth as always, he came up to her with his hand outstretched.

'Rona! This is a pleasant surprise! Is Max with you?'

'No; actually I'm between interviews for a new series I'm working on.'

'Wearing your other hat? I read your Elspeth Wilding biography; interesting and informative, as always.'

'Thank you,' she said awkwardly.

'Ah, here comes my companion. Well, good luck with your interviewing. Nice to have seen you.' And with a smile and a nod, he moved away and she watched as he kissed the cheek of a tall, dark woman who had just entered, and, putting a hand under her elbow, guided her into the small bar on the other side of the foyer.

Rona drew a deep breath. Well, well! Business or pleasure? And should she, or should she not, report back to Lindsey? She had still not decided when her last interviewee arrived.

Harold Hargreaves was a tall, silver-haired man in his late eighties, and his claim to fame, as he smilingly referred to it, was that as a boy chorister he had sung in the choir of Westminster Abbey during the coronation of King George VI in 1937. Age did not appear to have dimmed his memory, and he described the pageantry in detail, listing the names of foreign dignitaries, minor royalty and ex-prime ministers with a fluency Rona could only envy. In particular he recalled 'the little princesses' Elizabeth and Margaret Rose, wide-eyed with excitement, and the imposing presence of Queen Mary who, in a break with tradition, had attended the ceremony to support her son, unexpectedly called on to accept the burden of kingship.

'He made it all come alive,' Rona reported to Max over a late lunch. 'You'd have thought from the way he spoke that it had taken place only yesterday. Oh, and talking of memory, I nearly forgot! You'll never guess who came into the foyer while I was there – Dominic! What's more, he was joined by an attractive woman whom he conducted into the bar.'

'Well, time moves on and no doubt he does too. Did he speak to you?'

'Just a few words, before his lady friend arrived.'

'Will you tell Lindsey?'

'I haven't decided yet.'

Max gave an enigmatic grunt and returned to what interested him. 'So – how many of these stories can you use?'

'Those I saw today, definitely, and the two from Thursday morning – all widely differing experiences. I'll make up the six with Monica and Frank Hathaway – it shouldn't be a problem.'

What *was* a problem was that she had still not been able to contact Lindsey, but she kept her increasing anxiety to herself. Max, she knew, would only offer a caustic comment in reply, and that she could do without.

Ewan was already in the pub when Mia arrived. She was more nervous than she'd expected, and requested a gin and tonic rather than her usual pub choice of lager. A tankard of beer was already on the table awaiting their son's arrival.

'Did you tell him I was coming?' she asked, as Ewan returned with her drink.

'No, I've not spoken to him since I phoned you.' He raised his tankard. 'Cheers!'

She nodded, returning the toast before taking a restorative sip. 'I don't know if I want to hear what's troubling him or not,' she confessed.

'Well, you'd better make up your mind, because here he is.' Ewan raised his arm as Colin appeared in the doorway, and Mia saw his momentary hesitation on catching sight of her. Then he came towards them and bent to kiss her cheek.

'Hello, Mum! Didn't know you'd be here.'

'It seemed a long time since I'd seen you,' she said feebly.

The initial awkwardness was smoothed by production of the menu and a discussion about what to order. While his attention was engaged Mia took the opportunity to study her son and felt a stab of unease: his face was certainly thinner and there were dark smudges under his eyes. Her reservations melted like snow and she accepted that whatever trouble he was in, she would move heaven and earth to help him. Over his bent head Ewan caught her eye, lifting an enquiring eyebrow, and she nodded agreement.

He wasted no time. Having ordered their meal, he leant back in his chair and said without preamble, 'We're worried about you, son. Tell us what's wrong and we'll do all we can to help.'

Colin looked up quickly, his eyes darting from one to the other as colour suffused his face. 'I'm OK really – just a few late nights when I should have been studying.'

Ewan shook his head. 'Sorry, that's not good enough.' And as Colin remained silent, he added bluntly, 'Exactly what happened last summer?'

Colin caught his breath, his colour fading as rapidly as it had come. 'Last . . . summer?' he echoed, playing for time.

'When you saw something suspicious and were afraid to report it.'

'Dad, I—' He broke off and Mia saw to her distress that tears had come into his eyes. She leant forward impulsively, putting her hand on his.

'Darling, we're on your side, whatever it is. Please tell us so we can help.'

There was a silence while she held her breath, wondering whether they'd got through to him. Then he said dully, 'It's too late.'

'Let us be the judge of that,' Ewan instructed. 'Come on, boy, you can't go on like this. Much better to get it off your chest, whatever it is.'

Another pause while Colin wrestled with himself, trying to evaluate the pros and cons of finally admitting what he'd seen. Then, having apparently reached a decision, he looked up, straightening his shoulders.

'Very well, but I'm afraid you won't like it.' He drew a deep breath. 'To start at the beginning, I didn't tell you at the time – you'd enough on your plate – but my first year at uni wasn't particularly great.'

Mia and Ewan exchanged guilty glances; the trouble at home couldn't have helped.

'There was no one I particularly gelled with,' Colin was continuing, 'and I felt very much on the fringe of things. I didn't get invited to parties or outings and I was pretty miserable, to be honest. There was a particular group of guys I really wanted to get in with; they were super-cool – had the best girls, gave the best parties, you know the sort of thing.' He smiled ruefully. 'Well, I could hardly believe it, but towards the end of the summer term one of them approached me and casually asked if I'd like to join them. You can imagine how I felt but, as I should have known, there was a catch: before you could be accepted into their crowd you had to perform a dare.'

'Table four!' called the barman for the second time, and, recalling their surroundings with a start, Ewan signalled their whereabouts and they waited in silence while their food was brought to the table.

Mia feared the interruption might throw Colin off his stride, that he might even now decide not to continue, but to her intense relief he took up the story again.

'Well, it sounded harmless enough. I thought I might have to shin up a lamppost and hang a pair of knickers from it – that kind of thing.' He paused, staring down at the plate in front of him but making no attempt to eat. 'But it was a lot more complicated. I was told to drive to the woods just out of town and retrieve a packet from a hollow tree. It would have to be after dark – and this was June, so that meant pretty late. The college gates are locked at eleven and as there was no way I could have extracted my car without the porter noticing, I was handed the keys to another car and told to collect it from behind a pub on the edge of town. It was also stressed that since a stationary car in the woods might attract attention I must drive off the road into the trees before collecting the package.'

'How would you know whereabouts to look?' Mia interrupted.

'There'd be a large boulder positioned on the roadside as a marker. God, it sounds like something out of *Midsomer Murders*, doesn't it? I thought it was a joke at first, but they insisted it was for real.

'Well, somehow or other I managed to slip off campus without anyone noticing, collected the car from the pub and drove out to the woods. It was pretty creepy at that time of night but the boulder showed up at once in my headlights, so I swerved off the road and drove in a little way so I wouldn't be visible. Then I had to find the hollow tree, which took time.'

He paused, taking a deep breath and not looking at them. 'But when I drew the package out of the hidey-hole I got one hell of a shock. It was pretty obvious it contained drugs.'

'Colin!' Mia breathed.

'I was in a right state by then, as you can imagine, and I couldn't wait to get the hell out of there. I fell into the car, started it up and was about to emerge on to the road when two cars came hurtling round a corner, their headlights only just missing me. Then everything happened at once: I slammed on my brakes; the second car started to overtake the first one and to my horror deliberately swerved into it. It was only a nudge but at that speed it was enough to send it careering over the edge. It crashed into a tree, bounced off, then rolled out of sight down the hill.'

'God, yes!' Mia exclaimed. 'I read about it in the paper.'

Colin nodded, picked up his knife and fork and took a mouthful of food. His parents, unable to eat, sat motionless, watching him.

'What did the other driver do?' Ewan prompted.

'He jammed on his brakes and I assumed he was going to help – but instead he suddenly accelerated and disappeared round the next bend. I'd instinctively jumped out of the car, but then – and I'll never forgive myself – I began to wonder what would happen if I got mixed up in it while I had the drugs on me. And how could I explain being out in the woods at midnight? I was still dithering when another car came round the corner and swerved to a halt – he must have heard the crash – and that driver *did* get out and started to run downhill after the car. That solved my problem, and as soon as he dropped below eye level I shot out of cover and drove like a maniac back to Farnbridge. It wasn't till the next morning that I heard the car had burst into flames, the driver was killed and his would-be rescuer seriously injured.' There was a pause, then he added flatly, 'And the police treated it as an accident. No one knew he'd been deliberately forced off the road.'

Belatedly aware of his cooling lunch, Ewan reluctantly picked up his own knife and fork. 'Could you describe either of the cars?'

'Not really. It was all over in a matter of seconds, though I think the front one had a broad stripe of some kind along the roof and down the bonnet.'

'Make?'

'Not a clue.'

'You could have made an anonymous call,' Mia said quietly.

'I know, I know. But it wouldn't have been much help, would it?' he added pleadingly. 'No make or colour of the offending car, let alone registration. All I could have said was that one car had a stripe, and since that was the one that crashed they'd have known that already.' He looked from one parent to the other but neither was meeting his eye.

'What did you do with the package?' Ewan asked.

'I considered ditching it but I hadn't the nerve. I handed it over, but about a week later when they invited me to a party I declined and they didn't ask again. They knew I wouldn't dare report them, so they weren't bothered. Then one of the girls in my year had a birthday and invited me along for drinks and suddenly I was in with a really good crowd. If only I'd been more patient.'

There was a brief silence, then Ewan said, 'You'll have to report it, you know.'

Colin stiffened. 'But how could I explain being there?'

His father shrugged. 'You could make up some cock-and-bull story about meeting a girl in the woods. They'll be far more interested in why you waited so long to come forward. Obviously they've much less chance of tracing him than if you'd contacted them straight away.'

'That's what I've been blaming myself for,' Colin said miserably. 'I let him get away with it.'

On the Sunday, Avril phoned.

'Sorry not to have been in touch,' she began, 'but it's been all systems go for Sarah's wedding – only four weeks now! I'd forgotten how much there is to arrange – marquee, flowers, cars, service sheets. You've received your invitation?'

'Yes, thanks, Mum, it came last week. Afraid I've not replied yet.'

The service was to be in the couple's local church in Belmont where both Rona and Lindsey had been married, and the reception in the garden at Tall Trees.

'We're hoping for a fine day, of course, but there'll be a covered way leading from the house to the marquee, just in case. And on top of all that, I've had to settle on my outfit; I hadn't expected to be mother of the bride again!'

Which reminded Rona that she'd not thought what to wear herself, belatedly realizing that as part of the bridal party she'd be expected to have something new. Better phone Magda in the morning.

'I've been trying to get hold of Lindsey,' Avril finished. 'Is she away this weekend?'

Would that she knew! She'd left enough messages on her phone. 'I think so, yes.'

'Well, I'll try again tomorrow. 'Bye for now, darling.'

Lindsey herself phoned a couple of hours later, while Max was watching rugby on TV. Rona took the call in the kitchen.

'Well?' Lindsey demanded belligerently. 'Why all the messages to call you? Has World War Three broken out?'

'Where have you *been*, Linz? And what was the idea of turning up out of the blue like that on Friday?'

'I wanted to see Ross. I told you, I didn't see why you should have all the luck.'

'And?'

'And,' Lindsey said calmly, 'I spent the weekend with him.'

Rona gasped. 'I must say you're a quick worker. Off with the old on Monday, on with the new on Friday! Shades of Solomon Grundy!'

'Except that he isn't.'

'Isn't what?'

'The new. Oh, the weekend was fine, but I doubt if we'll see each other again.'

'A one, or rather *two*-night stand?'

'Something like that.' Lindsey's voice was brittle.

'What went wrong, Linz?' Rona asked more gently.

Lindsey sighed. 'I found I didn't like him very much. Oh, he was a great lover and all that, but he's obsessed with himself and his work, which gets boring after a while.'

'He doesn't live with his sister, then?'

'No, he has a flat in the Barbican. Isobel's living with some actor in Mayfair. Actually,' a peevish note crept into her voice, 'he seemed more interested in you than me.'

'*Me?*'

'Yes, going on about how clever you are, with all your writing and everything, and how he's sure you'll do a brilliant job on him for *Chiltern Life.*'

Rona gave a half-laugh. 'I'm surprised you stuck it out for the weekend!'

'Oh, it wasn't all bad. We wined and dined in style both evenings and he presented me with an attractive silk scarf from his collection. I intend to write it down to experience.'

'And if he does contact you?'

'He won't.'

'But if he does?'

'I'll be otherwise engaged.'

It was *not*, Rona decided, the time to tell her about seeing Dominic.

Having ascertained that Magda was spending the day at the Marsborough boutique, Rona went straight there on Monday morning.

'I've been looking out a few ideas for you,' Magda greeted her. 'They're in the fitting room – see what you think of them.'

Obediently Rona moved along the rail, admiring the soft colours and fabrics. 'I'm going to be spoilt for choice!' she said.

'Well, you won't know till you try them on. Take your time. We have matching hats, bags and shoes for all these outfits, so it's a one-stop shop.'

'You're a wonder, Mags.'

'I'll leave you to it. Let me know if you want any help.' She paused in the act of drawing the curtain across. 'Were you able to get hold of Ross Mackenzie?'

'Oh, yes, thanks. I went to London on Friday and we conducted our interview over drinks at the Argyll.'

'Very civilized!'

'I'll probably work on that before getting down to the series.'

Magda raised an enquiring eyebrow. 'You're back on the *Chiltern Life* payroll, then?'

Rona smiled wryly. 'As you know, it takes time to recover from a biography, especially the ones I seem to become involved in.'

'So what is it this time?'

'It'll be about people whose lives have been unusual in some way. I've not decided on the final title, but something on the lines of *Moments That Changed My Life* or *Unforgettable Experiences*. We put in a piece asking if anyone had attended a spectacular event or been present when something out of the ordinary happened.'

'And had anyone?'

'One or two, yes. We had quite a varied response.'

'I'll look forward to reading them,' Magda said and, pulling the curtain across, left Rona to make her choice.

After some deliberation she eventually settled on a dress and jacket in chestnut brown, one of Magda's autumn collection that was not attributed to Ross Mackenzie.

'Excellent choice,' Magda approved as they selected accessories. 'The end of October can be unpredictable weather-wise; if it's warm you can remove the jacket, if it's cold add a wrap.'

Business satisfactorily completed, they had a quick coffee in the boutique café.

'I was saying to Max that you must come to dinner,' Rona said. 'I'd like you to meet our next-door neighbours; they're home permanently after living abroad for years – in fact, I'm interviewing Monica for the series. They're a great pair – I think you'd like them.'

'We'd love to come,' Magda replied. 'Give me a ring at home when I have the kitchen diary to hand.'

*   *   *

Rona arrived home to find a message from Frank Hathaway asking her to call him, and she eagerly clicked on his number. Perhaps at last she'd get her hands on those diaries. However, her hopes were immediately dashed.

'Rona, I'm so sorry,' he began. 'I'll have to ask you to be patient a little longer – the journals are proving more difficult than expected. Ruth's writing was always erratic, especially when in a hurry, added to which she wrote quite a lot in pencil and in places it's almost smudged away. Even when a pen was used the ink has faded or moisture has got at it and it's run.

'My son's better at deciphering than I am, but with a full-time job he has limited time at his disposal. We've managed to go through a couple, but they're really just holiday diaries and there's little that would be of interest to you.'

Rona held down her disappointment. 'Are they dated?' she asked. 'Could you perhaps look at those for specific years when you know something happened – the invasion of Kuwait, for instance?'

'We've been going through them chronologically,' he admitted, 'but we could try that, yes. I do hope we're not holding you up on your project.'

'Don't worry about that,' Rona assured him, 'I've plenty to be getting on with.'

'I really do apologize, but we'll try going for significant dates as you suggest, and perhaps we'll have better luck.'

Which, Rona thought philosophically, left Monica. However, as she'd told Magda, she had Ross Mackenzie's interview to write up first. For the moment the unforgettable experiences would have to be put on hold.

NINE

It had taken Frank some time to persuade Steve to accompany him to the dinner.

'They're your friends, Dad, not mine,' he'd protested.

'He, not they. It was Tom and his wife Ruth whom we knew. Like you, I've never met Catherine.'

'Nevertheless, you'll be wanting to talk over old times, and frankly that's of no interest to me. It'll be much better if I stay here with Luke; we can't go off and leave him, and we haven't any sitters we can call on.'

'That's all been taken care of,' Frank said calmly. 'He's having a sleepover at Ollie's.'

Steve eyed him suspiciously. 'On a week night? First I've heard of it.'

'His mother promised me they'd do their homework and not have a late night.'

'And since when have you been so pally with Ollie's mother?'

'Since I realized this was an opportunity to drag you out of your shell to meet people, and that you'd try to use Luke as an excuse to get out of it.'

Steve sighed. 'So there's no escape clause?'

'None.'

As it happened, Steve was after all grateful to have something to occupy him that evening. An email from Chuck on Tuesday morning brought the heart-stopping news that Inga Van Olsen was to marry again, and all day in the intervals between conference calls he kept coming back to it, like prodding an aching tooth to check if it still hurt.

From a positive angle the news at least drew a firm line under their affair, putting an end to his tentative if unacknowledged hopes that they might still get back together. He was hurt she'd not told him herself, but admittedly they'd agreed there should be no contact and after ten months of silence it would have been a difficult conversation. The fact that he'd liked her fiancé when they met at an office party made it no easier and he instinctively closed his mind on images of them together. Should he write and congratulate them, or would that only stir up old memories?

Closing his mind to all the ramifications, Steve took his next call.

It transpired that Catherine's bungalow in Willow Crescent was less than a five-minute drive from their own house, and both their hosts came out to meet them.

Tom Parish was tall with steel-grey hair and an easy manner, and his brown eyes reminded Steve of Rona. Catherine, however, was not at first glance as attractive as he'd expected, her pale face virtually untouched by make-up and her hair, light brown fading to grey, simply styled. However, as the evening progressed he revised his opinion. There was an air of stillness about her that was very restful and her voice, quiet and low-pitched, was a pleasure to listen to. He decided there was more to Mrs Bishop than met the eye, and his liking for her increased.

Conversation was wide-ranging throughout the meal, and although Steve had feared a re-hashing of old times there was actually very little reference to them, probably out of consideration for Catherine and himself. Tom was particularly interested in his time in the States and asked if he'd consider going back.

This seemed as good a time as any to break today's news to his father, and Steve braced himself. 'I don't think so,' he replied. 'I enjoyed my time there, but it ran its course and I'd done what I was sent out to do. Oh, and by the way, Dad' – he hoped his tone was sufficiently casual – 'I heard this morning that Inga Van Olsen's getting married again. The daughter of the firm I was working for,' he added to his hosts.

Frank's eyes widened in concern but, unable to ask the questions that urgently sprang to mind, he made what he hoped passed for an appropriate reply.

Remembering Frank's mention of a possible romance, Tom adroitly changed the subject. 'It's good of you to help Rona with her project, Frank,' he said easily. 'I hope I didn't land you in it by putting your name forward!'

Frank smiled, wresting his thoughts from the Van Olsens. 'Not at all, but I've not been much help so far. Ruth's diaries are proving more difficult to read than I expected; she always wrote as she spoke, and whereas this adds spontaneity it also causes problems in deciphering.'

'My heart sinks when Rona embarks on one of her series,' Catherine commented. 'They always seem to land her in trouble.'

'What kind of trouble?' Steve asked curiously.

'Murder!' Tom said, and laughed as both the Hathaways stared at him in disbelief. 'Oh, it's true. What's more she's managed to unearth several criminals – God knows how. She maintains that people talk to her more freely than to the police, but you have to know who to speak to in the first place. As Catherine says, it worries the hell out of us when she embarks on one of her investigations.'

Steve frowned in bewilderment. 'I understood from Dad that she wrote biographies?'

Catherine gave a short laugh. 'They're not exempt either; the last two also brought unsuspected murders to light.'

'Then since she's doing an article on me,' Frank remarked humorously, 'all I can say is I'm glad I haven't murdered anyone!'

'Though you might have been involved in the aftermath,' Steve said.

Frank made a protesting movement then, with a resigned shrug, sat back as his son told of his recent recollections of the car crash and its sinister implications.

'We went to the police after the first one,' Steve ended, 'and updated them after the second. They said they'd look into it, but I don't think they're too hopeful after all this time.'

'But why were you up there anyway, at that time of night?' Catherine asked.

It was Tom who replied. 'It was Reunion Weekend at uni, darling. If you remember I had to cancel because it coincided with Jenny's birthday party.' He turned to Frank. 'I know it's ridiculous, but I've always thought that if I *had* been there this would never have happened. We'd probably have driven up together, for one thing.'

Frank gave a twisted smile. 'Don't worry, I don't hold you responsible! I was later leaving than I should have been; I ran into Peter Sheldon at the last minute – remember him? We got talking, and when I looked at my watch it was eleven thirty.'

'Resulting in your being in the wrong place at the wrong time,' Steve said grimly.

There was a moment's reflective silence, then Tom pushed his chair back. 'I suggest we have coffee in the sitting room, where we can relax in more comfort.'

'I must say I envy you the compactness of your home,' Frank remarked as they returned to their previous seats. 'Makes me realize what a barn of a place we live in!'

'Actually I shan't be here much longer,' Catherine told him. 'We want our married home to be new to both of us, and we think we've just found it.'

'We've been keeping an eye open for some time,' Tom added, 'and at the weekend we happened to drive past an interesting-looking house with a For Sale notice. We asked if we could look round, fell for it and made an offer on the spot, subject to surveyor's report and so on.'

'Well done!' Frank said. 'Where is it?'

'Not far away; between Hollybush Lane and Fairhaven – which means I'll be nearer Lindsey than Rona in future. It's quite a small house but there's plenty of room for the two of us, and a pretty little garden that won't be too much to manage when we reach our dotage! Actually, you're the first we've told. We were going to keep it quiet till we'd signed the contract.'

'We won't say a word,' Steve promised for both of them.

'Well, are you glad you came?' Frank asked as they drove out of the crescent.

'I am, yes. They're a great couple, aren't they?'

'And very well suited. I was most impressed with Catherine.' He glanced at his son. 'Bit of a bombshell about Inga.'

Steve's jaw tensed but his voice remained level. 'Yep, but we're both free agents.'

'You're OK with it?'

He smiled grimly. 'I have to be, don't I? Seriously though, once the shock wore off I wasn't as cut up as I'd have expected. My feelings must have faded a bit over the months without my realizing it.'

'Excellent,' said Frank, much relieved. 'That's just as it should be.'

It was ridiculous, Rona told herself, that Lindsey's brief liaison with Ross should make her reluctant to write his profile. It made not the slightest difference to either his skill or his previous life, which was all that need concern her; but her twin's dismissive judgement – *obsessed with himself and his work* – somehow diminished him in her own eyes which, again, was totally illogical. Mightn't the same be said of many successful people? It didn't lessen their talent. She regretted now having nagged Lindsey into telling her about the affair. Damn it – she herself had quite liked him!

With a muttered expletive she switched on the recorder. Barnie wanted this profile ahead of the series, and to make the next edition of *Chiltern Life*, reservations or no reservations, she needed to get down to it.

Hugh glanced irritably round the crowded pub. It was the nearest eating place to their office but service at lunchtime could be slow. He wished now they'd gone farther afield, but Mia had an appointment at two and was reluctant to come out at all, which had annoyed him. Was she, he wondered uneasily, beginning to distance herself? A possible explanation occurred to him.

'You seem to be seeing a lot of your ex these days,' he remarked, breaking the lengthening silence between them.

Mia, whose mind had been on the client she was due to meet, refocused on her companion. 'I told you, we went to visit our son.'

'You don't usually go together.'

She shrugged. 'It just depends. We're divorced from each other, Hugh, not from Colin. Any time he needs us, we're both there for him.'

'Of course,' Hugh muttered, vaguely ashamed of himself. 'Still having problems, is he?'

She glanced at him, trying to remember what she'd told him. 'He's dealing with them.'

Ewan and Colin had seen the police on Monday, and after a lecture on the duties of a citizen and the public's responsibility to help the police he'd been dismissed with his tail between his legs – a great relief, though Ewan reported he was still blaming himself for the miscreant's escape.

But Hugh's less-than-subtle quizzing on the state of play between herself and Ewan was beginning to irritate her. She had no intention of becoming answerable to him, and the sooner he realized that the better for their relationship.

'If our food doesn't come soon I'll have to leave you to it,' she commented. 'I can't interview an important client while suffering from indigestion.'

'Well, you won't have to suffer from starvation either,' Hugh replied. 'They're bringing it now.'

'Hi, Magda,' Rona began, tucking the phone under her chin as she tipped dog biscuits into Gus's bowl. 'Is your kitchen diary to hand? I'd like to fix a date for you to come for dinner and meet our neighbours.'

'That sounds good. Yes, it's on the wall in front of me. When were you thinking of?'

'How about Friday next week, the eleventh?'

'It's clear so far, unless Gavin has arranged something without telling me.'

'Could you pencil it in then while I check the date's OK with

Monica? I'll come back to you and either confirm it or suggest
another.'

'Will do,' Magda said.

Rona had a guilty conscience about Monica. It was nearly a month
since their Chinese supper when she'd been full of plans to interview
her about her ex-pat life, and she'd done nothing to follow it up.
First there had been the replies to *Chiltern Life* to sort through,
followed by the interviews themselves, then both Ross Mackenzie
and Frank Hathaway had claimed her attention.

Monica, however, was unfazed by the delay. 'I'm not going
anywhere,' she said. 'The eleventh, was it, a week tomorrow? Thank
you, that would be great.'

'We're also inviting some old friends of ours, Gavin and
Magda Ridgeway. I think you'll like them; Magda and I were
at school together and she owns a number of boutiques around
the county.'

'Very opportune!' Monica said with a laugh. 'I'll need some
warm clothes for our first winter back in the UK, though I'll have
to limit my designer labels!'

Duty done, thought Rona with satisfaction as she confirmed the
date with Magda. Now she could sit back and let Max plan one of
his special menus while she concentrated on her postponed profile.

Putting her resolution into effect, she was at her desk at nine the
next morning when the phone rang.

'Barnie here, Rona. About that Mackenzie piece—'

'I'm working on it now,' she broke in guiltily.

'Well, this is to say the pressure's off. We've had to reschedule
and there won't be space for it in next month's edition. The initial
urgency was in pinning him down for an interview; now it's safely
on tape, if necessary we can hold it for a month or two. Happy with
that?'

'Perfectly!' Rona said with a sigh of relief. 'What about the series
interviews?'

'No panic there either. Let me have them as and when; I'm planning to space them out rather than run in consecutive months,
keeping some in hand for when copy's scarce. Remind me – how
many will there be?'

'About half a dozen.'

'OK. Once I receive them and the Mackenzie piece I can slot them into the schedule, but as I said there's no panic.'

As the call ended Rona thankfully removed the cassette she'd been working on and, dropping it back in the storage container, flicked through the others filed there. She'd do a couple for the series first, she decided. Barnie would choose what order they'd appear in, but presumably he'd separate the ex-pat ones, especially since both contributors might supply more than one article. It would also be wise not to run those concerning war or terrorism too close together – Charles Conway in the Falklands and Frank's escape from Kuwait, for instance. She'd start with the coronation of George VI, then, after next week's dinner party, she'd make a point of recording some of Monica's experiences. And perhaps by the time she'd done both those, she'd have distanced herself from Ross Mackenzie's link with her sister and could settle down to finish his profile.

An hour later she was engrossed in paraphrasing Harold Hargreave's description of Queen Mary's gown when the phone again interrupted her.

'Is that Rona Parish?'

'Yes?' It was a voice she didn't recognize.

'This is Steven Hathaway. We . . . met at my father's house.'

'Of course, I remember. How are you?'

'Fine thanks.' He hesitated. 'Look, this is going to sound rather strange, but I have a dental appointment in about an hour's time in Fuller's Walk, which I believe is just round the corner from you. And I was wondering if I could possibly call round afterwards? There's something I'd like to discuss with you.'

'Well, I—'

'Will you be home? I promise not to take up too much of your time.'

'I'll be in, yes. Will you be bringing the diaries?' she added hopefully.

'Afraid not, we're still going through them.' A pause, while she waited. Then, 'You're number nineteen Lightbourne Avenue, is that right?'

'That's right.'

'About eleven thirty, then? It's only a check-up at the dentist's.'

'OK. See you then.'

Curiouser and curiouser, Rona thought. What could Steve

Hathaway possibly want to talk to her about if it wasn't the diaries? And those, surely, would be Frank's prerogative.

By eleven thirty Rona was waiting in the sitting room with the coffee tray, and minutes later the doorbell rang. Gus, who'd been asleep on the rug, jumped up and rushed into the hall, barking loudly. Rona followed him more leisurely and opened the door to her visitor.

'I hope I'm not intruding too much,' he said apologetically.

'Of course not. Come in.'

She led the way into the sitting room and he paused on the threshold, looking about him. 'What a fabulous house!' he said. 'Georgian, isn't it?'

'That's right. We've tried to keep any alterations within the spirit of the period. The fireplace was rescued from a builder's yard but is genuine Regency and the small tables came from antique fairs.'

'The result's charming. Are those your husband's paintings? My father said he was an artist.'

'He is, but that's his collection of modern art.' She smiled. 'Max is ambivalent about displaying his own work, so they're confined to upstairs!'

'Pity, I'd have liked to see them.'

At her invitation he seated himself on one of the sofas and accepted a cup of coffee, declining both milk and sugar. 'You must be wondering why I'm here, and it's a bit tricky to explain.'

He took a sip of coffee and patted Gus, who was nosing at his trouser leg. 'I don't know if you've heard, but my father and I went to dinner at Catherine Bishop's on Tuesday, and the conversation turned to your success in tracking down villains.'

'Oh dear! Don't tell me you've a murderer you want me to catch!'

'I just might have.'

Her eyes widened. 'You're not serious?'

He stared down into his coffee cup. 'It's Dad's overseas experiences you're interested in, isn't it?'

She nodded.

'I suppose he didn't mention his accident last year?'

'No, but I think my father did, in passing. Something about being pinned under a car?'

'That's right. He tried to pull the driver free – he was still wearing his seatbelt – but the man died virtually in his arms. Dad was in

hospital quite a while with burns and concussion, and has been
suffering from periodic flashbacks ever since.'

'How dreadful for him.'

'The point is,' Steve went on slowly, 'he'd never been able to
remember the period immediately before or after the crash – traumatic stress or something – but a week or two ago his memory started
to come back and he recalled that minutes before two cars, one with
its horn blaring, had overtaken him at speed and disappeared round
a curve in the road, after which he heard a loud bang. And as he
came round the bend himself, he saw that a car had come off the
road and rolled some way down the hill.' Steve paused. 'And there
was no sign of the other one.'

'You mean they hadn't stopped to help?'

'No. It was Dad who phoned nine-nine-nine and scrambled down
the slope.'

'If it was the car behind that crashed, it's possible the one in
front didn't realize what had happened.'

'But it's my bet it was the *first* car, the one that was presumably
being chased, that went over.'

Rona gazed at him in horror. 'You're not saying you think it was
deliberate?'

Steve shrugged. 'If not, why didn't they either stop or turn back?
And Dad remembered something else. The dying man tried to say
something. He was staring up at him, willing him to understand,
and Dad feels guilty because he couldn't. He thinks he was saying
frenzy, which could be a reference to the way they'd been driving.'

He came to a halt and after a minute's silence Rona said, 'And
that's it?'

Steve nodded. 'I'm worried about him, Rona. He'd been making
steady progress after the accident – if it *was* an accident – but since
these memories started resurfacing he's become stressed again. He
feels he let the driver down, because if the other car *was* responsible
for his going over and then didn't stop, whoever was driving it was
guilty of his death.'

Rona frowned. 'But surely the police looked into it?'

He leant forward urgently. 'Yes, but the point is they didn't know
there'd *been* another car! They examined the scene, including Dad's
car, and concluded that for some unknown reason – possibly the
speed he'd been travelling at – the driver had suddenly lost control.'

'Has your father told them what he's remembered?'

'Of course, but what can they do after all this time? Frankly I'm not even sure they believed him. He couldn't tell them the colour or make of the other car – it had passed him in a flash – and to be fair, without that their hands are pretty well tied. They said they'd look into it, but I think that was just to placate us.'

'Who was the dead man? Do you know anything about him?'

'Only that his name was Brett Sinclair and he was a local reporter.'

There was a silence while they both thought over what had happened. Then Steve said wryly, 'I know I've a cheek coming here, but I wondered if there's the faintest chance you could look at the facts again, come at it from a different angle, as it were.'

'It's an ongoing investigation, Steve. I can't interfere with police work.'

'I very much doubt they're doing anything. That's what worries me.'

Rona said slowly, 'I've a friend who works on the *Stokely Gazette*. It's possible she might have known him.'

He leant forward eagerly. 'Could you ask her?'

'I don't see how it would get us much further.'

'It would be a start. Look, if it gets too time-consuming then please say so. I've no right to ask you this in the first place, but it was just when Catherine was saying how you'd had success when the police hadn't—'

'That was a pure fluke, and they were cold cases. I just got lucky.'

He smiled crookedly. 'Perhaps you'd get lucky again.'

'All right, I'll speak to Tess and see what I can find out. What was the date of the accident?'

'I checked with Dad; it was Sunday the sixteenth of June last year. He'd been to a university reunion.'

'Did you look up the press reports?'

'No, I was abroad at the time and it's only in the last week or so that there's been any doubt about it.'

'Well, I'll see what I can do, but I don't hold out much hope.'

'Thanks so much, Rona. And . . . you won't let Dad know I've seen you, will you?'

'Of course not.'

'I shan't take up any more of your time. If you *do* come up with anything, could you text my mobile and I'll contact you?' He fished a card out of his wallet and handed it to her.

'Don't hold your breath,' Rona warned.

They walked to the front door, and as she opened it Lindsey came hurtling up the path, her face distraught.

'Ro!' she gasped. 'The most terrible thing's happened!' Then, belatedly registering Steve, she broke off with a breathless apology.

'This is Steven Hathaway, Linz,' Rona said above her suddenly pounding heart, and, to Steve, 'My sister, Lindsey.'

They nodded at each other and Steve said quickly, 'Good to meet you, Lindsey. Thanks again, Rona.' And he hurried down the path and out of the gate.

Lindsey promptly burst into tears.

TEN

R ona guided her sister inside and installed her on the sofa Steve had just vacated.

'What *is* it, Linz?' she demanded for the second time. 'Not Mum or Pops?'

Lindsey shook her head and, fumbling for a handkerchief, blew her nose.

'It's Carol,' she said.

'Carol?' Rona stared at her blankly.

'Carol Hurst, Jonathan's wife. She turned up at the office an hour ago and demanded to see him. I was talking to Janet, our receptionist, when she re-emerged. Ro, she looked awful – white face and tears in her eyes – and she walked straight past us out of the door and into the street. Then Jonathan came hurrying after her, saw me and said he'd like a word with me. God knows what Janet thought.'

Lindsey dabbed at her eyes, careful not to smudge her mascara. 'Carol had just accused him of having an affair and said she wanted him out of the house before the children came home from school.'

'Oh, God,' Rona said tonelessly.

'Sod's law, isn't it, that after months of fearing this, it's happened after we've broken up? In fact, this was the first time we've spoken since he abandoned me at the Rendezvous – and that evening, I can tell you, was even more disastrous than I'd thought: a friend of Carol's saw us and "innocently" mentioned it to her next time they met. The only glimmer of light is that instead of demanding who he was with, she's maintaining she's not interested in his "floosies" and doesn't want to know. Whether she'll change her mind – and whether he'll tell her if she does – is anybody's guess.'

'There must be more to it than that,' Rona protested. 'Having dinner with someone doesn't mean you're having an affair. Did you ever give him anything or send him a letter or postcard that could implicate you?'

Lindsey shook her head. 'God, Rona, this could put my whole career at risk!'

'Come on, Linz. It's not an indictable offence.'

'It is to an old-fashioned firm like Chase,' Lindsey said grimly, 'especially between partners. Oh, they wouldn't actually fire me, but things could be made very uncomfortable.' What had she said, four short weeks ago? *If it came out, one of us would be expected to leave, and I'll give you three guesses who it would be.*

'Well, let's not anticipate trouble,' Rona advised.

'Wise words!' Lindsey sighed and straightened her skirt. 'Sorry for the histrionics, Ro; it just suddenly swept over me – not only that we'd been found out and what that might do to my career, but the realization that life's passing me by and I seem totally incapable of finding the right man. I've only ever wanted what you and Max have, but the way I'm going I'll end up a lonely old maid.'

Swallowing the lump in her throat, Rona patted her sister's hand. 'I seriously doubt that, but let's take one thing at a time. All you can do for the moment is keep your head down and hope it blows over. For all we know they might have kissed and made up by now. Incidentally, where are you supposed to be at the moment?'

'Having an early lunch.'

'Then you'd better have one.' She stood up and bent to lift the tray of coffee cups.

Lindsey raised an eyebrow. 'Does Max know you're entertaining attractive men in the middle of the day?'

'I've not had time to tell him; it was only arranged an hour ago.'

'Who did you say he was?'

'Steven Hathaway, the son of the man whose experiences I'm writing about. He wants me to do a spot of investigating for him.'

'So what's new?' Lindsey said.

They went down to the kitchen, Gus brushing past them to the danger of Rona's laden tray.

'What would you like for lunch?' she asked, setting it down on a counter.

'A G&T,' Lindsey said promptly.

'Apart from that.'

'What culinary delights can you offer me, sister dear? A can of soup? Beans on toast?'

'You won't get anything if you go on like that. I might not cook, but I eat well. There are eggs in the fridge and some good cheese and a new loaf.'

'OK, having sprung myself on you I suppose the least I can do is cook us lunch. Cheese omelette?'

'Perfect!' Rona said, and sat down at the kitchen table to await it.

On her return to the office Lindsey learned that Jonathan had requested a few days' leave to settle some family business. Just how it would be settled was a moot point; as Rona had pointed out, Carol must have had more to go on than a meal together, but though anxious to know the outcome, Lindsey was unwilling to contact him herself. In the meantime, at least she didn't have to worry about bumping into him at the office, and she told herself firmly that the speculative glances cast in her direction were a figment of her imagination.

'So it's finally caught up with her,' Max said unsympathetically, pouring out the drinks. 'Well, she's been playing with fire for years.'

'Be fair, Max. Jonathan's the only one who was married.'

'Perhaps this will knock a bit of sense into her.'

'You don't really think she'll lose her job over it, do you? It would break her heart. She worked really hard for that partnership.'

'Then she shouldn't have put it at risk.'

Rona sighed. It was no use pleading Lindsey's case with Max; the two people dearest to her observed an armed truce for her sake and she'd reluctantly given up trying to bring them together. Time to change the subject.

'As it happened Linz wasn't my only visitor today,' she remarked, and went on to tell him about Steve Hathaway.

He groaned. 'You're not going to stir up any hornets' nests, are you? I don't want *you* being pushed off a road somewhere.'

'I'll be careful,' she promised. 'I always am.'

*   *   *

'Bloody marvellous, isn't it?' DS Humphries said disgustedly. 'Over a year of stony silence, then out of the blue two blokes come forward with new info – *two*, mark you. Like waiting for a ruddy bus!'

DCI Turnbull sighed. 'Just what I need to come back to after three weeks' sicko. Remind me, Les: how was the case left before this latest development?'

Humphries glanced at the file in his hand. 'The burned-out car – or what was left of it – was examined for mechanical defects at the time but nothing significant was found. No skid marks, implying he'd no warning he was about to go over and hadn't time to brake. Judging by scraped bark on a tree higher up the slope, together with flakes of paint, he must have hit that first, bounced off and continued to roll downhill till he came up against another tree and tipped over. There was alcohol in his bloodstream which might have slowed his reactions, but he was just within the limit. All in all, the conclusion was that he'd lost control for unknown reasons – possibly falling asleep at the wheel – and the file went to the accident records department, from where I had to retrieve it pronto. There was absolutely no indication of any other car apart from the bloke's who tried to rescue him, and that was clean.'

'So no convenient paint traces?'

Humphries shook his head. 'If there had been, the fire put paid to them.'

'How was he ID'd?'

'His mobile was in his pocket together with his wallet. Traffic had just got them both back up the bank when it rang. His wife on the line, poor soul.'

'Nothing useful on the phone?'

'No, just normal contacts and a lot of photos of a pop concert he'd been covering.'

'Right. Now, update me.'

Humphries looked down at the file. 'Two weeks ago – Monday lunchtime – old Hathaway, the rescuer, arrives at the front desk with his son, claiming his memory has been miraculously restored and he's remembered some important details. The first was that two speeding cars had overtaken him and disappeared round a bend some hundred metres ahead. Seconds later he hears a loud crash, rounds the bend himself and sees signs of a car having gone over the edge.'

'No other in sight?' Turnbull interrupted.

Humphries shook his head. 'And as if that wasn't enough, he also maintains that when he reached the wrecked car the dying man tried to tell him he'd been forced off the road, though how he reached that conclusion when he couldn't make out what was said I don't know. Then, if you please, he phones back a few days later to say he thought he'd been saying "frenzy" – as if that was supposed to help.'

'So we search for dancing dervishes?' Humphries grinned dutifully. 'As you say, bloody marvellous. And how did he account for this long memory lapse?'

'Reckons he'd been suffering from PTSD resulting in selective amnesia. He'd been having flashbacks ever since but this was the first he could pin down. Or so he says.'

'Think there's anything in it?'

'You tell me.'

'So what action was taken?'

'Well, I had a word with Bill Haydock of Traffic, who'd been first on the scene. They'd got there within minutes of receiving the call, and the car burst into flames just as they drew up. It was a close call; they'd only just got the men free and up to the road when the petrol tank exploded.'

'The driver was already dead?'

'Yep; they thought at first they both were – Hathaway was unconscious by the time they reached him. Then, as I said, I retrieved the original investigator's report and made enquiries at local repair shops about any car that might have been touched up in June last year.'

'And?'

'Zilch, as you'd expect. So, in view of the lack of crucial info such as make, colour or reg for the second car, we quietly replaced the file.'

'Until?'

'Exactly a week later – last Monday – when we had another father/son act. A young lad who's a student at Farnbridge Uni comes in with his dad with some story about being with a girl in the trees alongside the road and actually *seeing* one car nudge the other over the edge and then drive off.'

'He was the one who made the three-nines call?'

'No, because just then old Hathaway rounds the bend and

promptly goes to the rescue. So young feller-me-lad leaves him to it and scarpers with his girlfriend.'

'And why, might I ask, didn't he come forward as an eyewitness?'

Humphries gave a derogatory grunt. 'Didn't want to explain what he was up to out there, did he?'

'So why come clean now?'

'Belated conscience. He finally told his parents and his dad marched him in.'

Turnbull ran a hand through his hair. 'All in all we don't seem any further forward. Did you believe either of these accounts?'

Humphries shrugged. 'Hard to say. Could be regarded as supporting evidence, but I can't see it's much help after all this time.'

'Any connection between the two of them?'

'Not that we know of. Hathaway lives in Marsborough, as does the lad's mother, but allegedly they don't know each other.'

'God, what a can of worms! When you get down to it, though, it's circumstantial at best and *if* one car forced the other off the road – and in my opinion it's a big if – he's long gone and we haven't a hope in hell of catching him.'

'So I return the file to accident records?'

'Correct. Until, heaven forbid, someone else recovers his or her memory.'

Later that morning Rona phoned her friend Tess Chadwick, a reporter for the *Stokely Gazette*.

'Found any bodies lately?' Tess enquired cheerfully.

'No, but I'd like your help on an old one.'

'Why am I not surprised? Which had you in mind?'

'Someone you might have known, actually. Brett Sinclair?'

Tess sobered. 'God, yes, that was a shock all round. We had a whip-round at the office for his wife.'

Bingo! 'You knew him personally, then?'

'I'd met him. Bit of a Jack the Lad was Brett.'

'Did he work for the *Gazette*?'

'No, he was freelance but he occasionally gave us copy.'

'I read up the report of the accident in the archives. Did anything more come out later?'

'Now wait a minute! What exactly are you after, Rona Parish?'

Rona hesitated, but she would get nowhere by being overcautious.

'Just your impressions of him, really. If he might have had any enemies,' she ended weakly.

'Plenty, I'd say, the kind of things he dug up. Why are you interested in him all of a sudden? It's over a year since he died.'

Rona said reluctantly, 'There's a possibility that it mightn't have been an accident.'

'Wow!' Tess said on a long, in-drawn breath. 'In that case, I demand an exclusive before I say another word!'

'Granted!' Rona said with a laugh.

'Though actually there's not much I can tell you, except that some of the things he sent in our legal department wouldn't touch with a bargepole.'

'You don't happen to know what he was working on when he died?'

'No, and you won't get anywhere there. He didn't discuss his leads with anyone.'

'Not even his wife?'

'That's possible, I suppose. For all his faults he was a real family man and thought the world of Lottie and the kids. We didn't see him often, but when we did we were always shown the latest photos on his phone – a boy and girl, six and eight at a guess. They live in Farnbridge, of course, so I've never met them – or Lottie for that matter, but I believe she works as a nurse at the local surgery.'

'I suppose her address will be in the phone book,' Rona said reflectively.

'Oh, now look, Rona, you can't go stirring things up for her. It was bad enough first time round.'

'If someone *did* kill her husband, I presume she'd like him caught?'

'How sure are you about this?'

'Not sure at all, to be honest, but it's worth looking into.'

'Wouldn't you be treading on police toes?'

'Apparently they're not that interested; the trail's too cold. Don't worry, Tess,' she added, 'I'll be tact personified.'

'What excuse would you give for contacting her?'

'An article on single mums, perhaps?'

'Just don't upset her.'

'I won't, I promise.'

'Well then,' Tess said grudgingly, 'let me know how you get on. And don't forget – if anything comes of it, the story's mine.'

*   *   *

Actually, Rona thought as she put down the phone, a series on single mothers might not be a bad idea; not the hard-up, hand-to-mouth existence that was often portrayed but a more positive angle: the success they'd made of their lives and bringing up their children, how they balanced their careers if they had one and the challenges of making new friends when you were used to being one of a couple. She thought Barnie would go along with that, and it would appease her conscience when she approached Lottie Sinclair.

'Lining up series now, are you?' he asked jovially when she broached the idea. 'Not content with one on the go and a profile in the pipeline?'

'It could be interesting, don't you think?' Rona pressed. 'It might even show there are advantages to being able to make your own decisions.'

'So what gave you this idea? Not thinking of giving Max the push, I hope?'

'Not at the moment!' she said lightly. 'To be honest, it might help with something I'm looking into.'

'Ah-ha, I thought as much! To do with the current series?'

'In a roundabout sort of way. But you did say there was no hurry.'

'All right, I won't ask questions. And yes, I think the mothers angle would go down well, especially if you stress the positive side.'

Lottie, bless her, was perfectly amenable to being interviewed – even flattered, when she learned it was for the prestigious *Chiltern Life*.

'I've read some of your articles at the dentist, Miss Parish,' she said ingenuously. 'It'll be a pleasure to meet you.'

It was agreed that Rona would call on her at six o'clock the next evening. 'The kids will have had their tea and I can plonk them down with a DVD so we won't be disturbed.'

Farnbridge was a forty-minute drive away, but fortunately Tuesday was not one of Max's 'home' evenings. She could stop for a meal on the way back, she thought with satisfaction, which would save having to order a takeaway.

It didn't occur to Rona till she'd almost reached Farnbridge that the stretch of road she was on was where Brett Sinclair had died, and she shuddered as trees crowded in on either side. Though there was still an hour till sunset the overhanging boughs made the road prematurely dark.

Then an anomaly struck her; she'd assumed that as it had been late at night Brett Sinclair would have been heading for home. But Frank had *left* Farnbridge and was on his way to Marsborough when the speeding cars overtook him, so Sinclair must have been driving *away* from there. Where was he going in such a hurry? Might Lottie know?

Rona's sat nav directed her to a neat little semi half a mile from the town centre. There was a Mini in the drive and the garden was bright with autumn flowers. Her ring was answered promptly and her first impression of Lottie was of a small woman in her thirties whose fair hair was caught back in a ponytail.

She was shown in to what was obviously a dining room, for which Lottie apologized. 'I couldn't expect you to interview me in the kitchen,' she explained, 'and the kids are watching a DVD in the front room. I hope you don't mind.'

Rona assured her that she didn't, though sitting across the table from each other made for a more formal atmosphere than she'd been hoping for.

'Can I get you some tea or coffee?' Lottie offered, but Rona shook her head.

'No, really, I'm fine, thank you.' She took out her recorder. 'OK if I use this?'

Lottie looked a little uncertain, but nodded agreement. 'I wondered,' she began hesitantly as Rona was setting it up, 'how you heard of me? That I was a single mum, I mean?'

Rona took refuge in a half-truth. 'To be honest, I heard about your husband's death from a friend, and she mentioned how well you'd coped with juggling the children and a job and everything. It struck me that it would be good to give a more positive view of single mothers, whether divorced or widowed. Actually you're the first I've approached; I hope you don't mind?'

'Of course, I should have realized. Brett's accident was in all the papers.'

'Would it upset you to talk about it?'

'No, not now. I've had to come to terms with it.'

'So what happened, exactly?'

Lottie looked down at her clasped hands. 'I don't really know; that's the worst part. He'd been up to Heatherby to cover the

open-air pop concert and rang me just as he was leaving, at about
eleven. He should have been home by a quarter to twelve, and when
it got to midnight I began to get worried. I told myself the traffic
would be heavy leaving the concert and that must have delayed him
– though he usually let me know if he was held up – and I didn't
phone myself because he'd broken his hands-free connection and I
didn't want to distract him when he was driving, particularly in the
dark. But after a bit I couldn't wait any longer and I did call him.'

She broke off, biting her lip. Rona waited, and after a pause she
continued, 'It was my worst nightmare. His mobile was answered
by a policeman, who asked who I was and told me there'd been
"an incident". At first he wouldn't say if Brett was alive, but when
he asked if anyone was with me, I knew. All I wanted to do was
go to him, but I didn't feel I could phone my sister in the middle
of the night and ask her to come over. Not when it wouldn't make
any difference to Brett if I was there or not.' She dabbed at her
eyes, murmuring an apology. 'Mind you, she told me off later for
not doing so, but soon after two police officers arrived and broke
the news formally, and the woman stayed with me till the morning.'

Rona thought for a minute, remembering the query that had
occurred to her earlier. 'If he was coming from Heatherby,' she said
gently, 'he must have driven *past* the Farnbridge turning. Have you
any idea why?'

'No, I just don't understand it! When we spoke he was about to
set off for home. I asked about the concert but he said he'd tell me
all about it when he got back. And he never did,' she ended flatly.

'I'm so sorry,' Rona said inadequately.

'An elderly gentleman tried to save him, you know – even risked
his own life trying to drag Brett out of the car and got badly burned
for his pains. I wrote to him in the hospital, to thank him.'

Frank hadn't mentioned that. Perhaps it had been during his
amnesic period.

'Tell me about Brett. He was a reporter, wasn't he?'

Lottie brightened. 'Yes, it was in his blood. He had a nose for a
good story and once he got a hint of one he'd follow it no matter
what. Always after the big scoop, he was.'

'Was he working on anything particular at the time?'

'Oh, he always had something on the go! In fact, he'd had a
phone call the night before that really excited him, but all I could
get out of him was that it had given him a fresh lead on something

he'd been working on.' She smiled a little, shaking her head reminiscently. 'He had to cover some pretty gruesome stories in his line
of work, but he'd never discuss them with me – said it was bad
enough one of us having nightmares.'

She stood up and brought over what was obviously their wedding
photograph. It showed a radiant Lottie and a young man about
average height with a cheeky grin and a cocky air about him.

'He looks quite a character,' Rona said.

'That he was. Bit of a temper, though, if he thought someone
had done him down. There'd been the odd fisticuffs in the pub when
an argument got out of hand, but there was no malice in him. Not
Brett.'

It occurred to Rona that she'd asked Lottie more questions about
her husband and his death than about her single motherhood, the
alleged reason for the interview, and she moved swiftly to redress
the balance.

'You work at the local surgery, don't you? Did you have that job
before?'

'Yes, but I was part-time then. Once Brett was . . . gone . . . I
needed to go full-time.'

'How did that fit in with the children?'

'Fortunately my sister lives close by. They go to her after school
for an hour or two, and during school holidays.' She smiled. 'I
feel guilty, but they think it's great having their cousins to play
with. We've always been a close family and that has helped
enormously.'

They talked for several more minutes but Lottie was starting to
get restless and Rona realized she wanted to check on the children.
She switched off the recorder.

'Thank you for being so frank with me,' she said. 'We won't be
running this for a while as there's another series scheduled first, but
I'll let you know when we're going to publish.' She smiled. 'In fact,
I'll send you a copy of the magazine, so you don't have to go to
the dentist!'

Lottie laughed. 'That'll be great, seeing my name in *Chiltern
Life*!'

There was little more to say, and Rona left soon after. She'd
confine comments about Brett to the tragedy of his early death,
she decided. Most single mothers would neither want nor expect
their ex-husbands to be mentioned, particularly since the whole

point of the series was that they were now out of the picture. But her questions, although giving her a clearer idea of his character, had not solved what she now regarded as the outstanding mystery: why, if returning from Heatherby, he had been on that stretch of road at all.

ELEVEN

The morning after Rona's visit to Lottie Sinclair, she received an unexpected phone call.

'Is that Rona Parish?' a crisp female voice enquired. 'This is Vanda Hathaway. I'm visiting my father and brother and your name has come up several times. I wonder if we could meet?'

'Yes, of course,' Rona stammered, taken aback by the tone of voice.

'Are you free this morning? The Gallery Café in half an hour?'

Rona raised her eyebrows but kept her voice level. 'That would be fine,' she said.

'See you there.' And she ended the call.

Rona had wondered how she'd recognize the unknown Vanda, but in fact had no difficulty and paused in the doorway of the café to assess her. Aged, she judged, in her forties, she was wearing more make-up than was usual in Marsborough at this hour of the day, her blonde hair was cropped close to her head and she wore long, intricately twisted earrings that no doubt she'd designed herself. This, Rona thought as she went to join her, could be interesting.

'Ms Hathaway?'

Vanda, who'd been studying the menu, looked up quickly, and Rona guessed from a slight puckering of her brows that she was surprised by what she saw.

'Ms Parish. Good of you to come.'

As if she'd been given a choice, Rona thought, pulling out a chair. Vanda lifted an imperious hand and, unbelievably at the Gallery where service was notoriously slow, a waitress came hurrying over.

Their order duly taken, Vanda turned back to Rona. 'I hear you're trying to get your hands on my mother's private diaries.'

The unfairness, not to mention the directness, of the accusation took Rona's breath away. 'I can't believe either your father or brother gave you that impression,' she said stiffly.

Vanda waved a hand, displaying an elaborate ring on each finger. 'That doesn't alter the facts. Do you deny you want the diaries? Because even if *they* don't object to a reporter rifling through private family papers, I most certainly do.'

With an effort, Rona kept her temper. 'Firstly, I'm not a reporter. I'm a biographer by profession but I also do some work for a monthly magazine which is running a series on people who've had interesting experiences. My father, who incidentally is an old friend of *your* father, told me he'd be a good candidate and Frank agreed to contribute. It was he who remembered the diaries and dug them out for me. I haven't seen them yet as he's finding them difficult to decipher.'

Vanda's purple eyes raked her face. 'Both my father and my brother are vulnerable in their separate ways,' she said. 'Consequently they can be easily manipulated.'

Rona pushed back her chair and stood up. 'I must ask you to excuse me; we're both wasting our time here.'

She turned away but Vanda half rose, putting out a hand to detain her. 'No, wait. I apologize. Please sit down.'

Rona hesitated.

'Please,' Vanda said again. 'Unfortunately I have a habit of speaking my mind. Some people appreciate cutting to the chase – it saves a lot of time – but others don't. I shouldn't have spoken to you like that.'

'No, you shouldn't.'

'Do please sit down again.'

Slowly Rona did so. 'Didn't Frank tell you how we came to meet?'

'He did mention a Tom Parish – your father, I presume – but talk of the diaries had already sent up warning signals and I was determined to prevent their being exploited.'

'Nothing,' Rona said coldly, 'is further from my mind.'

The waitress arrived with their coffees and a plate of Danish pastries, taking a moment or two to set them out on the table. It was a welcome breathing space. As she moved away, Vanda said, 'Shall we start again? I confess I was surprised when I saw you; you weren't what I was expecting.'

'A hard-nosed reporter with attitude?'

Vanda laughed – a harsh bark. 'Something like that. Look, I really am sorry. Tell me about this series you're doing. It sounds intriguing.'

Reluctantly at first, Rona started to outline her ideas, sketching in some of the interviews she'd already held and the various reminiscences they'd evoked, and Vanda listened with interest, interrupting now again with questions or comments.

'I was hoping Frank's contribution would be about the hijacking and the Kuwait invasion,' Rona finished, 'and that was when he remembered your mother keeping diaries of their time abroad, which he felt would give a clearer and more immediate picture of events.'

'I see.' Vanda stirred her coffee thoughtfully. 'Was there by any chance talk of a more recent . . . experience?'

'The car crash? Yes; Steve told me about that.'

'Well, he shouldn't have,' Vanda said shortly. 'It's taken Pa a long time to get over it and is best forgotten. I came up and spent several months with him after it happened, and I don't mind telling you I was seriously worried about him. He was having nightmares and muttering in his sleep and I really thought he should have counselling, but he wouldn't hear of it. I can't imagine why Steve should have brought it up after all this time. It's hardly something you'd feature in your series.'

Rona, about to explain, stopped herself. It seemed neither Frank nor Steve had told Vanda of the recovered memories, in which case it was not her place to enlighten her. They'd probably guessed she'd be against pursuing the matter.

'Do they know you're meeting me?' she asked instead.

'No. I wanted to present them with a *fait accompli* and announce that I'd got you off their backs. I admit I'd leapt to completely the wrong conclusion – not, I might add, for the first time.'

'So will you tell them when you get back?'

Vanda smiled briefly. 'I think not; it would involve embarrassing explanations. In any case, I'm returning to London this afternoon. This was really a business trip.'

'To see the Tarltons?'

She looked surprised and Rona added, 'I've known Kate most of my life, and when Frank said they stocked your work I went in to have a look. I was most impressed, and I love those rings you're wearing.'

'That's kind of you.' Vanda held out both hands for inspection and Rona noted there was a diamond-shaped watch on her left wrist and a bracelet in three shades of gold on her right.

'A surfeit of bling, admittedly,' she added, reading Rona's thoughts, 'but it's deliberate sales policy. I ring the changes – no pun intended – and people are always asking where they can buy items I'm wearing.'

'I hope you're well insured!' Rona said.

'Well enough.' She glanced at the watch. 'I must be going. Pa's taking me out to lunch before my train.'

She called for the bill, and despite Rona's protestations insisted on paying it. 'I invited you here – if that's the word! – and then subjected you to an unwarranted interrogation. The least I can do is pay for the privilege.'

'So I shouldn't mention this to your family?' Rona reiterated, as they parted on the pavement. 'I hope I don't let it slip!'

'If you do, you could say we ran into each other,' Vanda suggested. 'But I'm glad we did meet, Rona. I'm satisfied that I can safely leave Pa in your hands.'

'That's big of her,' Max commented, when Rona relayed the conversation that evening.

'She was pretty intimidating,' Rona admitted, 'but in a way it's good that although she's a high-powered businesswoman living in London she still looks out for her family.' She glanced round the kitchen, suddenly noticing the absence of carrier bags. 'Are we on a starvation diet this evening?'

Max grinned. 'That would teach you, wouldn't it? No, actually I thought we might go to Dino's. It's a while since I was there and as I'll be chief cook and bottle-washer on Friday, I reckoned I was due a night off.'

'Quite right. Have you decided on Friday's menu?'

'Smoked trout mousse, venison casserole with seasonable vegetables, a cheese board and poached pears in wine. How does that sound?'

'Pretty good. In that case I'll stick to pasta this evening.' The last time she'd been to Dino's, Rona reflected, had been with Lindsey after her row with Jonathan. They hadn't known, then, that her secret was blown.

Dino's was busy as usual, but a quick phone call had ensured that their usual corner table awaited them, and Dino himself greeted them effusively. Rona sat back, letting the warm, familiar ambience flow over her.

'You're quiet this evening, my love,' Max commented as their main course was served. 'Tired?'

'Not particularly.'

'You've taken on quite a bit, haven't you? The unforgettable experiences series, that dress designer chap, and now you're being asked to look into what in my opinion should be a police matter.'

'I don't really see what I can do about that,' Rona admitted. 'I'd hoped to learn more by speaking to the victim's wife, but instead it's muddied the waters still further. If he was returning from Heatherby as she said he should have turned off at the Farnbridge exit, instead of which he was driving *away* from it. He phoned her as he was leaving, so what happened between the time they spoke and his crashing off the road in the woods?'

Max wound his spaghetti round his fork. 'From the Hathaway angle, though, it's immaterial, isn't it? They're not interested in where he was going, just if he was deliberately pushed off the road.' He glanced at her. 'Tell me if I'm speaking out of turn, but just how reliable is this old boy? I mean, it's taken him long enough to come up with this.'

'That's the way amnesia works,' Rona said. 'Something triggers a memory and it comes flooding back. In Frank's case he heard the word *frenzy* and it unlocked something in his mind.'

'OK, but the fact that two speeding cars overtook him minutes before the crash is neither here nor there, particularly as no trace of a second car was found. Personally I think the police are right to be sceptical. They doubtless examined the scene pretty thoroughly at the time.'

Rona nodded, recalling the report in the newspaper archives.

'As to what the poor guy said, he was probably completely out of it and talking gibberish. He could have come out with anything, and you can't hang a murder case on a single word. I appreciate it was a traumatic experience for old Frank and it's obviously been preying on his mind. Perhaps he had a vivid dream which he thinks is real, or is suffering from false memory syndrome – which might be the same thing. Whatever, I certainly don't think it's worth your digging any further, particularly as his daughter would be so against it.'

Rona laid down her fork dispiritedly. 'So what should I do?'

'Tell his son you made enquiries but couldn't come up with

anything, then get back to whatever you were originally going to interview Frank about.'

'I suppose you're right, but I don't like to give up. And I *would* like to know what Brett was doing on that stretch of road.'

They left it there, but the conversation replayed itself in Rona's head hours later as she tried to sleep. What would make a man who, after all the noise and excitement of the concert, was no doubt longing for bed, drive past the turning for home and speed off in the opposite direction? It just didn't make sense. And things that didn't make sense worried her.

'God!' Max exclaimed as he flicked through his diary at the breakfast table. 'It's Father's birthday next week. Cyn sent a reminder and invited us up, and it went right out of my head.'

Roland Allerdyce, Royal Academician, lived in Northumberland and although now a senior member, was still submitting paintings to the Royal Academy Summer Exhibition. Max's sister lived nearby and her daily contact with him added to Max's burden of guilt. An occasional phone call had been his only communication in the last six months, despite his best intentions.

'Of course – the nineteenth, isn't it? Then let's go up for the weekend. It would be good to see him again. If we went on the Friday and came back Sunday you wouldn't need to reschedule any of your classes.'

Max brightened. 'That's an idea. And if we flew, we'd have more time with him as well as sparing ourselves the long drive. I'll get on to Cynthia and let her know we're coming. I must go,' he added, glancing at his watch. 'Ted Bright has a sitting at ten and I didn't tidy up after yesterday's class.' Bright was the principal of the local art school.

'How's the portrait coming along?'

'So-so; I need to check several things, though.' He bent to kiss her. 'If you have a minute, could you book us a Friday afternoon flight and home again Sunday evening? It'll be good to see the old boy again.'

Despite Max's advice, Rona postponed texting Steve Hathaway about her lack of progress. It was less than a week since he'd asked for her help and she felt she should allot him a little longer. As Max had said, the Hathaways weren't concerned with why Brett had been where he was, yet she couldn't help feeling it was pivotal to his death. He'd been speeding away from home in the middle of the night when his wife was expecting him, which surely meant he was in a panic about something – a frenzy, even. But what about? And, crucially, had he been the pursuer or the pursued?

Friday evening, and two sets of friends to be introduced to each other. Fortunately there was an immediate rapport between them, and Rona relaxed. She was fond of both couples, though she knew the Ridgeways much better having been at school with Magda and, pre-Max, been on the point of becoming engaged to Gavin. On the other hand, the Furnesses' house had been rented out for as long as she and Max had lived here and she'd met them only on their brief visits home until the trouble with their tenants the previous year and their permanent return this spring.

Magda turned to Monica. 'I believe you're featuring in Rona's series on ex-pats?'

'She has asked me, yes; I've been rooting out old photo albums to jog my memory.'

'It's not specifically ex-pats,' Rona intervened. 'The brief is unusual experiences, but for most of our readers life abroad would certainly qualify.'

Magda raised an eyebrow in mock indignation. 'Then why haven't you asked me? I grew up in Italy, remember!'

Rona laughed. 'Sorry, Mags, but I don't think that has the same cachet as Hong Kong or Bolivia!'

Max called them to dinner in the kitchen, which smelt appetizingly of the imminent venison. Beyond the table patio doors gave on to the darkness of the garden, where reflected candles hung like a host of fireflies. As the level in the wine bottles went down, conversation became more animated and lively discussions ensued, increasing the enjoyment of the meal.

It was as Rona was serving the dessert that Gavin dropped his bombshell. 'By the way,' he remarked, passing the cream jug to Monica, 'have you heard Dominic Frayne's leaving? Didn't he once have a thing going with Lindsey?'

Rona's hand stilled. 'How do you mean, leaving?'

'Going to live in Paris – end of this month, I believe. I've a friend who's an estate agent and he told me the penthouse is to be let for a year, with a view to a permanent sale.'

Oh, God, Lindsey! Rona thought.

Max touched her elbow and she automatically spooned out the wine-red pears and passed them down the table.

'He does a lot of work on the continent,' Gavin was continuing, 'so I suppose it makes sense.' He turned to Charles. 'This is one of our local entrepreneurs – chauffeur-driven Daimler and private plane, no less. Two marriages behind him and his name's been linked with various daughters of the aristocracy.'

'Sounds like someone to be reckoned with,' remarked Charles.

'Oh, he's that all right. Smooth as they come, from all accounts. Well, ask Rona; she's met him.'

Feeling she should come to Dominic's defence, if not for his own sake then for Lindsey's, she said truthfully, 'Actually, I like him.'

Gavin gave a little laugh and a shrug. 'There you are, then!' he said.

The conversation moved on but Rona's mind lingered on her sister; she still hadn't told her of seeing Dominic with a woman at the Clarendon. Perhaps that was immaterial now, but should she let her know about his leaving, or allow her to find out herself in the fullness of time? Which, she wondered, would cause the less hurt?

'Coffee here or upstairs?' Max asked.

'Oh, here,' Magda replied promptly. 'We're nicely bedded in and moving might break the flow.'

'Forgive my wife's mixed metaphors!' Gavin said, but there was a general consensus of agreement and Max went to plug in the cafetière.

'So who are my fellow interviewees for the series?' Monica enquired, leaning back in her chair.

Rona ticked them off on her fingers. 'One was nanny to the children of a Middle Eastern sheik and had to flee the country with the family; one was in the Falklands war; one was a choirboy at George VI's coronation and one was involved with the London Olympics. Plus Monica here and another ex-pat who's actually a friend of Pops and has had several hair-raising adventures.'

'A motley crew!' Gavin pronounced.

'It was interesting,' Rona said reflectively, 'that several of them remarked on how once they started to look back, memories came flooding in – things they'd totally forgotten about. One man commented that memories have hooks – you recall a particular event and find another memory hanging from it, which in turn leads to another, until an entire episode emerges.'

'Suppose there are things they'd rather *not* remember?' Magda asked. There was a brief, awkward silence, then she turned to Monica and Charles. 'I should explain that I had an unpleasant experience a few months ago when I foolishly volunteered to allow a stage hypnotist to put me under.' She paused, turning her spoon between her fingers. 'And somehow my memory and that of another volunteer became mixed up and for weeks I kept "remembering" things that had happened to him. Including,' she ended in a tight voice, 'murdering his wife.'

Monica and Charles stared at her in horror. 'My *God!*' Charles exclaimed, and Monica, simultaneously, 'What did you do?'

Gavin said smoothly, 'It got sorted out in the end and since it was actually manslaughter rather than murder and there are kids involved, it's my bet when his trial comes up he'll get a fairly lenient sentence. But Magda has a point; there are probably memories most of us wouldn't want resuscitated.'

'In which case,' Charles commented, 'they presumably wouldn't volunteer for Rona's series.'

But the reminiscences she'd contacted Frank about weren't the ones that were troubling him now, and Rona wondered uneasily if Steve had told him that he'd approached her. Somehow, she doubted it.

'Memories are fascinating, though, aren't they?' Charles mused as Max returned with the coffee. 'They're what define us and are unique to each one of us. Even in the unlikely event of two people doing everything together all their lives, they'd remember things differently – which is why eyewitnesses are so unreliable.'

Monica said, 'I read once that memory has to be selective, because if we remembered absolutely everything our brains would be over-loaded and we wouldn't be able to cope. Sadly the result is that we often desperately *want* to remember something – particularly, I suspect, as we get older – and can't, while certain memories that we'd much rather forget lodge in our minds.'

'What's your earliest memory?' Gavin asked. 'Mine is falling off the garden wall when I was about two and landing in a bed of nettles, but my mother swears it never happened!'

'I remember sitting in my pram,' Monica said. 'My gloves were sewn on to each end of a long piece of tape which was threaded up one sleeve of my coat and down the other, so I couldn't lose them!'

'It's false memories that intrigue me,' Max put in, passing

coffee cups down the table. 'Some can be deliberately implanted, but others seem to happen spontaneously and the person is completely convinced they're true.' He glanced at Rona. 'Suppose someone's memory comes back in patches, after a spell of amnesia, say. Is it a true recall of what happened or is the mind playing tricks? And how can one tell? Sometimes it mightn't matter one way or the other, but at others it could be of vital importance.'

'Well, before *I* forget, Monica,' Rona said quickly, unsure what Max might come out with next, 'let's make a definite appointment for your interview. Are you free on Monday?'

'After the school run, yes. Half-term is looming, so it would be as well to get it in before that.'

'Ten o'clock suit you?'

'Perfect. I'll look out those photo albums.'

'I thought you were doing the Mackenzie thing first?' Magda said. She gave a little laugh. 'I mentioned it at work the other day when we were sorting through his collection, and Claudia, one of my assistants, was green with envy! She met him briefly last summer and still hasn't recovered!'

'Met him how?' Rona asked.

'Oh, he was dining at the hotel where she was staying. She plucked up the courage to ask for his autograph and he signed her menu for her.'

'The celebrity culture!' said Gavin dismissively.

'To be fair,' Magda defended him, 'he *is* rather gorgeous, quite apart from being so gifted. At least he's not just famous for being famous.'

Rona answered her original question. 'As to the order I'm working in, Barnie's had to do some rescheduling so there's a bit of leeway.' Not to mention the fact that Ross had slept with her sister.

'Is this the dress designer you're speaking of?' Monica asked with interest. 'The one who was at a fashion show at the Clarendon?'

'That's right,' Magda replied, 'and it's a pity I hadn't met you then, or you'd have received an invitation.'

'Of course – Rona said you're a boutique owner! Sorry, I hadn't made the connection. I might well come in to see you – I'm not equipped for cold British winters!'

'You'd be more than welcome. We pride ourselves on personal service.'

'If you're embarking on a sales spiel, beloved,' Gavin said, pushing back his chair, 'it's probably time we were making tracks. Thanks, guys, for a great evening, and it's good to have met you two.'

Slowly, almost reluctantly, they rose to their feet and made their way up to the hall. Thanks and goodbyes were exchanged and the guests departed, two to drive home across town, two to walk the few metres down the pavement to their own gateway.

Max, closing the front door, stifled a yawn. 'I suppose I'll have to take the pooch round the block,' he said unenthusiastically. Said pooch was wagging an enthusiastic tail at his side.

'No option,' Rona agreed. 'It was a super meal, Max. Well done.'

He bent to attach Gus's lead. 'They all got on well, didn't they? It was a good idea to introduce them; the Furnesses won't know many people around here.'

'They'll soon make friends,' Rona said confidently, 'through the school, if nothing else. But to help things along we could arrange a coffee morning in a week or two, and invite the Grants, the Dawsons and the Kingstons – and Magda and Gavin, of course. It would have to be a Sunday, as most of them are working.'

'Before you plan any more entertaining, there's this lot to clear up,' Max reminded her. 'It's late now, so just stack the dishwasher and we can see to the rest in the morning. Yes, all right, old boy, I'm coming.'

As the door closed behind him Rona returned downstairs to survey the debris. As Max said, it had been a good evening, and furthermore she had a firm date on which to interview Monica. It was time she stopped wavering between tasks and settled down to some serious work. And perhaps she would follow Max's advice and reluctantly tell Steve Hathaway there was nothing she could do.

TWELVE

At five to ten on Monday morning Rona walked up the path of number seventeen Lightbourne Avenue and rang the bell. There was frost on the parked cars, and, not having bothered with a jacket, she shivered as she waited for the door to open.

'Come and get warm!' Monica greeted her. 'There's a fire in the sitting room – the first since we moved in. I hope the chimney sweep did his stuff – I don't fancy a heap of soot in the grate!'

Rona went gratefully into the warm room and held out her hands to the flames. 'I suppose you're not used to this temperature?'

'Not at this time of the year, certainly. It can get cold with the winter monsoons but in October it's usually still in the twenties. Push the albums aside and sit down, and I'll pour you a coffee.'

Rona seated herself on the sofa and accepted a mug, glancing at the pile of albums. 'You certainly took a lot of photos!'

'Some will be surplus to requirements, but you mentioned South America and as I wasn't sure where you wanted to hear about, I played safe and brought the lot down.'

'I'd like to start with Hong Kong, if you're happy with that; it's where you've been for as long as we've known you, but if the series goes well I might come back later for the Bolivian instalment!'

'Fair enough, Hong Kong it is.'

Rona took out her recorder and glanced at Monica enquiringly. 'OK?'

'Of course.'

'So – let's start with your first impressions.'

Monica sipped at her coffee. 'It's hard to think back when we came to know it so well, but to start at the beginning Charles was on a seven-year contract and the company came up trumps with a very generous package which included a housing allowance, health insurance and school fees. The children were five and seven at the time, and we were very lucky to get them into the international school, which really dictated where we decided to live.'

For the next hour or two, prompted by Rona's questions, Monica described the Buddhist temples, the beaches of golden sand and the various festivals, British as well as Chinese, the trams, the 'wet' markets where animals and fish are sold alive and the elevated walkways that form an intricate pattern round the city. 'You can travel round Hong Kong from home to the shops or office without ever setting foot on the ground!' Monica said with a laugh.

They sat side by side on the sofa as she flicked through the album pages, explaining the various photographs or the occasion on which they were taken, and in the process Rona watched Harriet and Giles grow from small children into teenagers.

'This is Ocean Park,' Monica said, pausing at one page. 'It was a favourite outing at weekends, principally to see the pandas. Here they are, all four of them. China presented two to Hong Kong when it was handed back in 1997 and another two in 2007 to mark the tenth anniversary. Believe it or not, when it gets really hot their enclosure is air conditioned!'

She looked up, smiling ruefully. 'It makes me quite homesick, looking through these. We were very happy there.'

'You've certainly brought it alive,' Rona said. 'Thanks so much, Monica; that was fascinating.'

'Do you realize,' Monica remarked, closing the album, 'this is the longest time we've ever spent together, just the two of us? We always seem to meet with our husbands in tow. Incidentally, we liked your friends very much. Thank you so much for introducing us.'

'I was saying to Max we must have a coffee party soon and invite some more people for you to meet. We should have done it before but time goes so quickly; I can't believe it's three months since you moved in.'

'That would be great. And in the meantime perhaps we could have lunch together? I'd love to talk to you about your books.'

'And I about your modelling career,' Rona said. Before her marriage, Monica's face had graced many a magazine cover.

'Right, I'll phone you in a week or two and we can arrange it.'

It had been an interesting and profitable morning, Rona thought as she returned home. She pushed open the front door to find the landline phone ringing, and caught it up.

'Hello?'

'Rona!' A smooth Scottish voice came down the line, and she caught her breath.

'Hello, Ross.'

'Is this a good time to call?'

'I've just come through the front door, but yes, go ahead.' She bent to pat the dog, who had bounded up the stairs to greet her.

'I was wondering what progress you were making on the profile?'

Rona bit her lip. 'I'm afraid the answer is none,' she replied, keeping her voice light. 'I haven't made a start on it yet.'

'Ah.'

She waited for him to continue, but when he didn't, added, 'I did say I couldn't promise when it would come out.'

'Right. No matter, I just thought you might have come up with some points you'd like clarified.'

'If I do, of course I'll be in touch.'

'Can you give me any idea when you'll be starting on it?'

'Probably in the next week or two, but I've various things to clear first.'

'Well, far be it from me to hassle you; as one artist to another, I know how detrimental that can be. However, I was really phoning to ask if, when you *have* written it, I could see it before it goes to press?'

Rona suppressed a sigh of exasperation. 'We don't usually—'

'Please?'

Better to give in than get his back up. 'Very well,' she said reluctantly.

'Thank you.' He paused. 'Lindsey well?' he asked casually.

'She is, thank you.'

'Give her my best. And when you do get down to the profile, let me know if there's info you need.'

'I will,' she promised, and put down the phone with a little thud. Her final reply could have applied either to his request to pass his regards to Lindsey, or to let him know if she needed more information, or both. Well, he could take it whichever way he liked, she told herself as she went downstairs to prepare lunch.

Jonathan was back in the office on the Wednesday. He looked drawn, his mouth tight and shadows under his eyes. Lindsey wondered in some trepidation about the state of play, and when an excuse offered to consult him on some point, she tapped at his door and went in.

'How are things?' she asked quietly.

'Pretty bloody.'

She gave a strained smile. 'Could you be a bit more explicit? Such as does Carol now know the identity of your dinner companion?'

He shook his head. 'She still insists she doesn't want to.'

Lindsey allowed herself a small sigh of relief. Next point of concern: 'And are you . . . living at home?'

He grimaced. 'In a manner of speaking. I spent Friday night at the Lansdowne but after a session on Saturday I was allowed back on condition that I slept in the guestroom. I think you could say a state of armed neutrality exists, but a front of sorts is kept up when the kids are around.' His mouth twisted. 'The guestroom is explained by the fact that my snoring keeps her awake.'

'And was it just our being seen at the Rendezvous that sparked all this?' Lindsey pressed.

He shook his head. 'That started it, but after her so-called friend told her about it she went through my things and found the airline tickets to bloody Paris. Ironic, isn't it, since the trip was never going to happen.'

'I'm sorry,' Lindsey said.

'Oh, don't be. We both know I've been getting away with murder for years. Time I got my comeuppance. And it's shown me how much I value Carol. I don't want to lose her, Lindsey.'

'Then let's hope you don't,' she said.

Frank sat back in his chair, his hands folded on the cover of the diary, his mind still in the past. It had been a strange experience, reading Ruth's accounts of episodes in their lives. Some, vividly described, he couldn't remember at all; others reignited in his brain so that he relived them as he read. He wished uselessly that he knew more about the workings of memory, why so many hovered tantaliz-ingly out of reach, while on hearing certain pieces of music – often the pop songs of yesteryear – others came flooding back, transporting one to a beach or restaurant or a situation previously long forgotten.

Steve put his head round the door. 'Time to light the oven?'

The Hathaways had a daily help who, in addition to keeping the large house clean and tidy, prepared an evening meal three times a week and left it ready in the fridge.

Frank nodded absently and Steve's eyes fell to the book on his lap.

'Is that the last one?'

'Yes; I was just philosophizing on the vagaries of memory.'

Steve gave a short laugh. 'You're not the first, Dad. It can be the very devil, always resurfacing when you least want it and seldom when you do.' He paused. 'About the diaries, though; is there anything you'd rather Rona didn't see?'

His father shook his head. 'They're very innocuous; no family secrets hidden in them. It was the ones relating to Kuwait and Entebbe that she's interested in and with a little judicious editing here and there she's welcome to them. If need be I could enlarge on various points. Thanks for your help in decoding them, Steve; it would have taken me twice as long without your input.'

'I enjoyed it. It'll be interesting to see in due course what Rona makes of them.' He hesitated. 'Shall I tell her they're ready for collection?'

'Yes, if you would.' Frank slapped his hand on the book in a sudden excess of frustration. 'I wish to God I could remember more of what happened in the woods that night.'

'Those last words, you mean?'

'Yes, what else he was saying that I couldn't catch? And what the hell did he mean by "frenzy" anyway? *He* was in one? The occupants of the other car were? Or had it been the cause of something that had happened earlier, instigating the car chase?'

'I do wish you'd stop worrying about it, Dad; even if it does come back to you, it's unlikely to do any good after all this time. For one thing, there's no corroborating evidence there *was* another car.'

'Two had overtaken me just before,' Frank said stubbornly. 'All right, I concede the other one might have had nothing to do with the crash – if it was in front, it mightn't even have known it had happened. But my gut feeling is that it had, and it did.'

Steve relinquished the argument. 'Fair enough, but talking of gut feeling, mine relates to hunger so I'm going to light that oven.'

Frank smiled, accepting the end to the conversation. 'You do that,' he said.

Lindsey came hurrying out of the office the following evening, her mind still churning with the implications of Jonathan's marital affairs. She wouldn't be able to relax till things in the Hurst household returned to a semblance of normality, and that would take time. Why oh why, she asked herself, did she get embroiled in these situations? She'd resumed the affair with her eyes wide open, and if things had gone pear-shaped had only herself to blame. Which was no comfort at all.

She was searching in her bag for her car keys when she heard a voice behind her call 'Rona!' She half-turned, caught her heel in a gap between the paving stones and stumbled forward, aware of a sharp pain in her ankle. The next minute someone had grasped her elbow, steadying her, and she looked up into the face of the man she'd last seen on Rona's doorstep.

'I'm terribly sorry – that was my fault,' he was saying. Then he broke off, searching her face. 'And you're not even Rona, are you?'

'Lindsey,' she managed, biting her lip. She was balancing on one foot, leaning against him for support.

'Of course – we met briefly. Steven Hathaway. Can you put that foot down?'

She tried tentatively but came to a halt, grimacing.

'God, I'm so sorry.' He looked round him helplessly, his eyes coming to rest on the Clarendon Hotel across the road. 'Let me help you over there and you can rest it while I get you a drink.'

'I really don't—' she began.

'You can't drive like that, can you?' Steve pointed out, glancing at the keys in her hand. 'Don't worry, I'll see you get home safely, but in the meantime you need to sit down.' He put an arm round her. 'Hang on to me and we'll get you there.'

Since she'd no option Lindsey did so, and they staggered together across Guild Street and through the familiar doors of the Clarendon, where he seated her in a corner of the bar and pulled a stool over to act as footrest.

'What can I get you? A brandy, perhaps?'

Lindsey took a deep breath and eased her injured foot on to the stool. 'A G&T would be welcome, thanks.'

He returned with two drinks and seated himself opposite her, regarding her anxiously. 'It's not broken it, is it?'

'I don't think so – probably just a sprain.'

'Would you like me to take you to A&E?'

'God, no! I'm sure a cold compress will work wonders. It'll have to – I've a wedding to go to next weekend and I'm determined to wear my new shoes if they kill me!' She smiled wryly. 'I always seem to be in a parlous state when we meet.'

'Well, this time it was down to me. I mistook you for your sister – I suppose that's always happening?'

She nodded. 'What did you want with Rona?'

'To tell her that my mother's diaries are ready for collection. She's using them in one of these articles she's planning.' He studied her face. 'You're not quite identical, are you?'

'Officially we are but of course there are differences, especially below the surface!'

'Really?' He gave an amused laugh. 'I think that requires an explanation.'

Lindsey took a substantial drink of her G&T. 'Well, Rona's the sensible one. She met Max, married him and lived happily ever after. Added to which she has four biographies to her name, quite apart from what she does for *Chiltern Life*.'

'And you?'

'Met Hugh, married him, divorced him, and proceeded to have a number of affairs, some more serious than others. Which, I might add, is as truthful a summary as I've ever given. Put it down to a combination of shock, pain and gin, but at least it explains the state I was in last time we met.'

Steve said quietly, 'I'm sorry things haven't worked out.'

'What about you?' she asked flippantly. 'Life been a bowl of cherries?'

He smiled. 'It's had its ups and downs.'

Lindsey took another sip. 'I was upfront with you,' she prompted.

'Very well; I met and married Ella and we had a son, Luke. Five years later she left me, taking Luke with her, and eventually remarried.'

'I'm sorry,' Lindsey said, taken aback. 'I didn't mean to pry, I was just—'

'And it doesn't end there. A couple of years later she was killed in a car crash. So I reclaimed Luke and escaped with him to the States for a year or two.' Steve took a restorative drink. 'Where I fell in love with someone, which didn't pan out, and I heard last week she's about to be married.'

Lindsey stared at him, appalled. 'God, I'm so sorry; I'd never have asked if . . . My troubles were all of my own making, but yours—'

'Oh, I've a lot to be thankful for,' Steve said lightly. 'Family – father, sister, son – health, adequate funds, a job I enjoy and am good at. Life could be a lot worse. And I'm quite sure there's a more positive side to yours, too. Work, for instance?'

Lindsey closed her mind on thoughts of Jonathan. 'I'm a partner at Chase Mortimer, the solicitors on Guild Street.'

'So you have brains, which is a good starting point.' He paused as she shifted her position, wincing in the process. 'Any painkillers handy?'

'I think there's some paracetamol in my bag.'

'Might be a good idea to take a couple.'

Lindsey did so, washing them down with the last of her gin.

'Another drink?'

'Better not, thanks. Tell me about your son,' she invited, as he continued to look worried.

His face softened. 'He's a great kid. He's been through a lot, but thank God seems relatively unscathed. It's half-term at the end of next week, and I'm trying to fix him up with things to do while I'm working.'

'He must have friends at school he could play with?'

'Probably, yes. I'll have to look into it. You say you've a wedding coming up?'

'Yes, my soon-to-be stepsister's.' She laughed at the expression on his face. 'Don't ask!' Then, abruptly, she sobered. 'Actually, I'm dreading it. Perhaps I could use my ankle as an excuse after all.'

'Dreading it why?'

'Oh, all that stars-in-the-eyes, till-death-us-do-part stuff. It just doesn't wash when I'm divorced and my parents are in the process – which explains the "soon-to-be" clause. Rona and Max are the only survivors in our family.'

'So one of your parents is marrying again?'

'They both are.'

'Then they're willing to give it another try. Good for them.'

Lindsey brushed a hand across her face. 'Sorry to be such a cynic,' she apologized. 'Of course, I'm glad they've both got a second chance.' She glanced at her watch. 'Won't someone be expecting you?'

'Dad will, yes. I'll give him a call and tell him I'm running you home. Where's your car?'

'In the office car park behind the building; the access is round the corner in Alban Road.'

'Well, if you tell me the reg and give me your keys, I'll bring it to the front entrance. I presume your insurance covers that?'

'Yes, but what about your car?'

'I came in by bus; it saves the hassle of parking and there's a stop at our gate. If you're on or near a bus route, fine, otherwise I can walk back.'

'You'd certainly need the bus – I'm out at Fairhaven.'

'Where's that?'

'A fifteen-minute drive away. Actually, though, I think I'll give Rona a call and see if I can spend a couple of nights with her.'

'That sounds a good plan. She'll be able to bandage your ankle for you.'

But there were complications Lindsey hadn't foreseen: Rona and Max would be away over the weekend. 'It's Roland's birthday on

Saturday,' Rona explained, 'and we're flying up tomorrow. You're welcome to come of course, Linz, but after tonight you'd be on your own.'

'Forget it,' Lindsey said quickly, 'it was just a thought. Have a good time and regards to Roland and Cynthia.'

'No good?' Steve enquired.

Lindsey shook her head. 'They're going away tomorrow. If we were a *normal* family,' she added viciously, 'I could have gone to my parents, but I've no intention of planting myself on Mum and Guy, especially with the wedding looming. I'll just have to manage.'

'The obvious answer,' Steve said, 'is for you to come back with me.'

He smiled at her startled expression. 'It'll be perfectly proper – Dad and Luke will be chaperones – and we have more bedrooms than the average B&B, most of them standing empty and one even on the ground floor. It's the perfect solution and if, as seems unlikely, you're up to going to work tomorrow I can run you in.'

Lindsey tried to marshal her thoughts; events were moving too quickly but one fact stood out. 'I can't land on your father's doorstep like a refugee!' she protested. 'Added to which, I've nothing with me – clothes, toiletries and other essentials.'

'Would Rona collect some for you? Pack an overnight bag and drop it off at our house? She could collect the diaries at the same time.'

Since there seemed no alternative, Lindsey made a second phone call.

'You're *what*?' Rona interrupted.

'Going back with Steve,' Lindsey repeated. 'He swears his father won't mind, and it's not so far to come into work tomorrow if my foot's still playing up. Please, Ro. I know it's asking a lot when you're busy packing yourself, but I would be grateful. And the diaries are ready,' she added as an incentive. 'You could collect them while you're there.'

Rona's sigh reached her down the phone. 'All right. Give me about an hour; I have to take Gus to the kennels so I'll go on after that.'

'Bless you,' Lindsey said.

To say that Frank was surprised by Lindsey's sudden appearance would be an understatement, but he welcomed her with his usual courtesy.

'What a rotten thing to have happened,' he sympathized, brushing aside her embarrassed apologies. 'Of course, this is the obvious solution and we're delighted to help. That ankle looks quite swollen but I'm sure we can rustle up a bandage. Luke' – he turned to his grandson who'd been watching the proceedings with some bewilderment – 'look in the bathroom cabinet, will you, and bring down that crêpe bandage.'

The boy nodded, his eyes still on Lindsey. 'Are you Rona?' he asked uncertainly.

Steve smiled. 'Sorry, Luke, you weren't here when I performed the introductions; this is Rona's sister, Lindsey. Lindsey, meet my son.'

'Hello, Luke,' Lindsey said. 'I'm sorry to turn your house upside down like this!'

'It's OK,' he replied. 'I'll get the bandage.'

The downstairs bedroom Steve had mentioned had, when the house was built, been intended for the maid, but at the age of twelve Vanda had taken a fancy to it. It was renovated for her use and the adjoining wash house converted into an en suite; she still slept in it on her visits home. While they awaited Rona's arrival the bed was made, fresh towels produced and Lindsey's ankle firmly bandaged. She was ensconced in the sitting room, her foot resting on a pouffe, when the doorbell rang.

'Thanks so much, Ro,' Lindsey greeted her. 'Sorry to be such a nuisance.'

Rona, who had left her suitcase in the hall, regarded her with some anxiety.

'How bad is it?' she asked.

Lindsey shrugged. 'The bandage is helping and the pills have dulled the pain. It'll probably be OK in the morning.'

Rona doubted that, which made her even less comfortable with the present arrangement. She turned to Frank. 'This is very good of you,' she said. 'I'm so sorry we're not able to step into the breach – we're flying up to Northumberland tomorrow for my father-in-law's birthday. But we'll be back Sunday evening, and if the ankle's still not right we can take over then.'

'It's no trouble at all,' Frank assured her. 'We're delighted to be able to help.'

Luke's voice called from the top of the stairs and Frank excused himself.

'How exactly did this happen?' Rona demanded when they were alone.

'I told you; Steve thought I was you. He called after me; I turned awkwardly and twisted my ankle. He took me to the Clarendon and it progressed from there.'

'Well, mind it doesn't "progress" any further,' Rona said.

Lindsey's eyes narrowed. 'And what exactly does that mean?'

'You know damn well, Linz. You're between men and you've already hinted that you found Steve attractive. But he's not one of your playthings; he's a decent guy who's had a rough deal and his sister told me he's vulnerable. So just leave him alone, right?'

Before Lindsey could reply Steve himself came into the room with a plastic carrier bag. 'Here are the diaries, Rona,' he said, handing them over. 'I hope they prove useful. Where the writing was particularly bad I printed the offending sentences on a separate sheet, but if there's anything you can't decipher just let me know.'

'Thanks so much,' she replied, wrenching her thoughts from her sister. 'Of course, I'll still want to interview your father, but I'll go through these first and let you have them back.'

'No hurry.' He hesitated. 'I suppose . . .?'

'Nothing so far, I'm afraid,' she said quickly, aware of Lindsey's heightened interest. 'Now, if you'll excuse me I must get back. I've still some things to sort out before we leave tomorrow.' She glanced fleetingly at her sister. ''Bye, Linz. Hope the ankle improves quickly.' And without waiting for a reply, she let Steve escort her out of the room.

No doubt Lindsey would sulk, she thought resignedly as she drove out of the gateway, but it had to be said. And she'd also have to think up an explanation for Steve's open-ended question before they met again.

THIRTEEN

C atherine and Tom were having a celebratory supper. Within the last few days they'd received a satisfactory report from the surveyor on the house they were hoping to buy, and that afternoon the contracts had been signed. Moreover, it suited them that the present owners weren't in a hurry to move; they were having a house built and it was not expected to be ready until December.

'So the next thing, my love,' Tom said, 'is to put this bungalow on the market. How do you feel about that?'

Catherine shrugged. 'Resigned, I suppose. I've been very happy here, and had been expecting it to see me out. But that was before I met you! And you're right: it's better that we start married life in a house that's new to both of us. Shall we use the same estate agents, or would that be a conflict of interest?'

'We could, I suppose, but since they're acting for the Summers it would be less complicated if we chose our own. There must be several firms available; we can go into town tomorrow and suss them out. Apart from renting the flat, which doesn't really count, I've not been in the housing market for years.'

The telephone rang in the hall and Catherine went to answer it. When she returned minutes later she was smiling.

'That was Daniel, wondering if they could invite themselves over for Sunday lunch.' Daniel was her married son who lived in Cricklehurst.

'Good – you've not seen them for a while. I'll try to arrange a game of golf.' Tom usually made himself scarce when Catherine's family visited, feeling they'd want her to themselves. However, she was shaking her head.

'He particularly asked if you could be there, as you're almost family now.'

Tom flushed with pleasure. 'That's nice of him.'

'It's no more than the truth. As you well know, I've been telling you for some time that we'd all love to have you with us.'

'In that case, I shall be only too delighted,' he said.

*   *   *

Lindsey had not slept well in the unfamiliar bed, her ankle paining
her every time she moved. As she lay waiting for the sky to lighten,
she acknowledged that, as Steve had guessed, she wasn't up to going
in to work today. Which was embarrassing; she'd no idea of the
routine of the house, nor where Steve worked, but Frank had retired
and would presumably be around. She could only hope she wouldn't
be in his way.

When the alarm clock announced it was seven thirty she hobbled
through to the bathroom, manoeuvred her injured her foot into the
plastic bag Steve had supplied, and by balancing on one leg managed
to keep the bandage dry while she took a shower.

She'd been told to go to the kitchen when she was ready for
breakfast, and had been shown where everything was in case
no one was around. However, all three members of the household were at table, and Frank enquired if she'd had a good
night.

'So-so,' she replied, 'but I'm afraid I was a little optimistic about
going in to work. I'm so sorry.'

Steve pulled out a chair for her. 'No problem,' he assured her.
'Would you prefer tea or coffee? There are eggs if you'd like some,
or cereal and toast if you prefer?'

'Coffee and toast would be great, thanks.'

'Are you watching the time, Luke?' Frank interposed. 'The bus
is almost due.'

The boy nodded, muttered a general goodbye and hurried from
the room. Seconds later the front door banged behind him.

'I hope he's remembered his homework,' Steve commented.

Lindsey took a sip of coffee, savouring it. 'What time do you
leave for work?' she asked Steve as he put a rack of freshly made
toast on the table.

'I don't – or at least, not very often; I mostly work from home.
How about you? I know you have your laptop – is there something
you can do?'

She nodded. 'I'll phone the office to see if there's anything urgent,
otherwise there are several things I can be getting on with. I'll try
to keep out of your way.'

Frank smiled. 'As you might have noticed this is a big house –
plenty of room for everyone to "do their thing" as they say nowadays.
As for myself, I play bowls on Friday mornings so I'll be out for
a while, but we converge for a snack lunch about one, if that's all

right? Oh, and our daily help will be here at nine. Don't worry about her – she'll be doing upstairs today.'

'I'll be working in my office,' Steve added. 'I suggest you make the sitting room your base; you can spread your papers on the coffee table.' He glanced at her foot. 'Is the bandage holding up or would you like it retying?'

'It's fine, thanks. Please don't worry about me; I've caused enough disturbance.'

Frank rose to his feet. 'Then we'll see you at lunch. And if the ankle doesn't improve during the day, I think we should consider a visit either to your doctor or A&E.'

Before leaving the house Rona had texted Lindsey to ask how she was, but had received no reply. Sulk continuing, she supposed, but it didn't ease her sense of guilt.

'I feel awful, abandoning Linz when she's in pain,' she admitted as the plane took off.

'Well, I'm sure you needn't,' Max returned drily. 'With three males dancing in attendance, she'll be in her element!'

'That's hardly fair!' Rona protested, though guiltily aware her own thoughts had been running on similar lines. 'She was very pale, you know; even if her ankle's not broken, she's given it a nasty wrench.'

'She'll survive,' Max said, gazing out of the window at the fields far below, 'and I'd be most grateful if from now on we could have a Lindsey-free weekend.'

Rona smiled in spite of herself. 'It's a deal!'

They were met at the airport by Michael, Cynthia and Paul's elder son.

'Mum sends her greetings,' he reported as they drove away. 'She's not at the farm today; she thought you'd welcome some time with just the three of you – there won't be much chance of private conversation tomorrow. The plan is we descend on you about midday for celebratory drinks and to exchange presents, then a couple of taxis will ferry us to the Deering for the birthday lunch.'

'Sounds an admirable arrangement,' Max commented. 'How *is* your grandfather?'

'Oh, you know RaRa,' Michael said carelessly. He and his brother had coined the nickname from the initials for Roland Allerdyce,

Royal Academician. 'Mum says his last words are likely to be, "Stop fussing, I'm perfectly all right!"'

'Really, though?' Max persisted. There had been a couple of health scares over the last year or two.

'He seems fine. Mrs P keeps a firm eye on him – I think she's the only one who has any influence, principally because she threatens to leave if he doesn't do as she says. Not that she ever would.' The housekeeper had been with the old man for more years than either of them could remember.

The farmhouse where Roland lived was on the fringe of a village some five miles from Tynecastle, and though it was far too big for him, he stubbornly refused to move. He'd sold off the surrounding land when he bought it thirty years ago and converted the large and airy barn into a centrally heated studio where he spent most of his time, whether or not he was engaged in painting.

As they turned into the gateway he came out to meet them, looking, Rona thought fondly, like an Old Testament patriarch: tall and straight, with a mane of white hair and hooded eyes like an old eagle. As she emerged from the car he enveloped her in a bony embrace before turning to shake his son's hand.

'Good to see you both. Coming in for a moment, Michael?'

'No, thanks, I must be getting back. I've an appointment in twenty minutes.' He worked for a firm of accountants in Tynecastle. 'See you all tomorrow.'

'Thanks for meeting us,' Max said, retrieving their cases from the boot, and his nephew waved an acknowledgment as he restarted the car and drove out of the gates.

Roland tucked Rona's arm through his, and as he led her towards the house she resolved to do as she'd promised, put Lindsey out of her mind and concentrate on enjoying the weekend ahead.

That evening on her return from work, Mia phoned her ex-husband.

'I was wondering if you've been in touch with Colin again?' she asked.

'Yes, actually; I saw him last weekend.'

'How did he seem?'

'He was OK. Fairly chatty.'

'Better after seeing the police?'

'I think so. At least he's got it off his conscience, but I get the impression he's still not happy about what he sees as someone getting away with it. But you've spoken to him yourself, haven't you? He mentioned you'd phoned.'

'Yes, but it's not the same as seeing him face-to-face.' She paused. 'Has his appetite improved?'

Ewan gave a short laugh. 'Yes, mother hen, it has. He's looking better than when you saw him. Don't worry, he'll get over it in time – he'll have to, because it's going nowhere.'

'There's an Alan Bennett play at the local rep next week,' Mia said. 'Perhaps he'd like to see it.'

'You'll never know if you don't ask.'

'Then that's what I'll do,' she said.

Although most of the swelling had gone down by Friday evening, Lindsey had been persuaded to stay on with the Hathaways over the weekend.

'It will ensure you continue to rest it,' Frank insisted. 'If you go home you'll be tempted to do too much, which could result in it flaring up again.'

Truth to tell, she was happy enough to be persuaded; the empty flat was an unwelcoming prospect after the family atmosphere in Alban Road, and being waited on hand and foot was an agreeable and unusual experience. In fact, she had slotted more easily into the household than she would have believed possible, considering she'd met them all only the previous day. Even Luke seemed to have accepted her as a matter of course, offering to lend her one of his DVDs, an incontrovertible sign of favour.

Steve reflected on all this as he shaved on Saturday morning. This was the most time he'd spent in a woman's company since his return from the States, and he'd forgotten how pleasant it could be. Perhaps it was time, as his father maintained, that he made more of an effort to socialize, especially now that the episode with Inga was well and truly behind him.

Also, there was no denying that Lindsey herself had intrigued him ever since, within half an hour of meeting, they'd exchanged life stories. He'd not been deceived by her flippancy in describing her life following divorce as a string of affairs, 'some more serious than others'. Her distressed state when she'd come running up Rona's path was proof that, like himself, she'd been bruised by her experiences, and he'd felt an instinctive desire to protect her. From having thought of her as a replica of Rona, he'd quickly come to see how *un*alike they were – particularly, as she'd said, on the inside. Briefly, he wondered what it was like to be a twin, to have begun life, however briefly, as one person, and then to have split into two.

Luke's call reached him through the bathroom door, summoning him to breakfast, and Steve snapped out of his introspection. One thing, however, was certain, he vowed as he reached for his shirt: while he might be ready to enjoy female company again, he'd no intention of laying himself open to the kind of hurt he'd recently been through. From now on his head, rather than his heart, would be engaged.

Roland's birthday was a great success. As arranged, Cynthia, her husband and two sons arrived at the farmhouse laden with parcels and a magnum of champagne. Cynthia was small, round and, according to Max, bossy, and Rona, though she seldom saw her, was very fond of her. Though only in her teens when their mother died, she had helped bring up her younger brother and in some way, Rona suspected, still felt responsible for him. In her own male household, her word was law.

After the presents were opened and the champagne drunk, two taxis arrived to convey them to their lunch at the Deering Park Hotel, a Georgian mansion with a country house atmosphere and peacocks in the grounds. The restaurant was busy as always, but Roland was regarded as a local celebrity and they were conducted with some ceremony to a round table in a window alcove overlooking the grounds.

Rona found herself seated between her father-in-law and Paul Fielding, and realized to her surprise that she'd never really had a conversation with Cynthia's husband. He was a quiet, angular man, content to take a back seat at family gatherings, and all she knew about him was that he worked for the tax office. She determined to rectify that, and started by asking where he and Cynthia had met.

He smiled reminiscently. 'You might find it hard to believe, but at the Young Conservatives. Makes a change from work or the local dance hall, doesn't it? She was only eighteen but she was a leading light.' He glanced across the table at his wife, earnestly chatting to Max.

'For me, it was love at first sight,' he continued, 'but her mother had just died and she wouldn't even consider leaving her father and Max. Added to which, Roland kept insisting we were too young

– as of course we were – but a compromise was eventually reached. We married just after her twentieth birthday and lived with them at the farm for the first few years. And I think I can say without boasting that neither of us has had a moment of regret.'

'That's wonderful,' Rona said warmly.

'How about you and Max?' Paul enquired.

'Oh, much more conventional. We met at a party, just as I was about to become engaged to someone else.'

'So he caught you in the nick of time.' Paul smiled. 'I must say I'm in awe of my illustrious relations – Roland and Max with their painting and you with your writing. Then there's me, just a humble taxman!'

Cynthia called across with a question and the conversation ended, but Rona felt she knew Paul a little better, and consequently liked him a little more.

They were studying the dessert menu when they were approached by a small procession led by the maître d' and followed by the sommelier and a waiter, the latter two bearing a bottle of champagne and a birthday cake respectively.

'With the compliments of the hotel, sir,' the maître d' bowed, 'to wish you many happy returns of the day.'

As Roland, touched, was thanking them, some people at the next table started to sing 'Happy Birthday', which, to his acute embarrassment, was taken up by the rest of those present. As it came to an end with a burst of applause he rose to his feet, turned to face the room, and bowed – which led to some cheering. It was a festive note on which to end the meal.

Tom was warmly greeted by both Daniel and Jenny when they arrived at Willow Crescent on Sunday, and eighteen-month-old Alice made his day by addressing him as 'Ganpa Tom'. Though neither of his own daughters was in a hurry to give him grandchildren, at least he could now share this little girl, and he reflected how lucky he was to have been given this second chance of happiness – the more so since Avril, too, had found someone else to share her life. As a family they had much to be thankful for.

Lunch was finishing when Catherine broke their news. 'We've something exciting to tell you!' she began. 'We've found the perfect house to live in when we're married, and we signed the contract on Thursday!'

Amid a clamour of exclamations and questions Tom went to collect the agents' particulars, which were passed around.

'It looks ideal,' Jenny said, 'though we've been hoping you might move nearer to Cricklehurst.'

'At least we're no farther away,' Catherine said. 'We won't get possession till December, which suits us quite well as we still have to sell this.'

Daniel turned to Tom. 'Isn't that when your divorce comes through?'

'That's right.'

'Then it seems everything is coming together; you and the house will be ready for each other at the same time. So when are you going to name the day?'

Catherine gave a little gasp. 'Hey, not so fast! We haven't discussed it yet; it's always seemed so far ahead.'

'Well, it isn't now!'

'Help me out here, Tom!'

'As far as I'm concerned,' Tom said, 'I'd be only too happy to marry you the day after the decree absolute.'

'So why don't you?' Daniel persisted. 'And have a New Year honeymoon?'

'It seems rather indecent haste,' Catherine demurred.

'Not when you've been waiting two years!'

She waved a dismissive hand. 'Well, you can't expect us to decide on the spur of the moment.'

'But you'll give it some thought?'

'I think we can promise you that!' Tom said.

Sunday afternoon, and Lindsey was at last going home, having turned down Steve's offer to accompany her.

'I'll be fine,' she insisted. 'I can't thank you both enough for your kindness in taking in a total stranger and administering TLC.'

'Not a *total* stranger,' Frank corrected with a twinkle. 'As I reminded Rona, we did meet when you were three.'

'And I was the cause of the accident,' Steve said. 'In the circumstances, it was the least we could do. Mind you go easy for the next few days and rest it when you can.'

'I will,' she promised.

'You're sure you'll be OK driving?'

She nodded. 'Just as well it's my left ankle and the car's an automatic.'

Nonetheless, she felt a twinge of apprehension as she climbed into it while Steve put her suitcase in the boot.

'Give us a ring if you change your mind,' Frank instructed. 'You'd be welcome to come back for a few days if you find you're not up to it.'

Lindsey laughed. 'Enough, already! I'll be fine, and I'm very grateful for all you've done.'

Then, as they stood in a group on the drive, she backed cautiously out on to Alban Road and, with a last wave, turned in the direction of home.

It was seven o'clock on Sunday evening when Rona and Max returned home, and the first thing she did after unpacking was to phone Lindsey. She was never happy when there was any kind of coolness between them, and hoped a phone call would be harder to ignore than a text.

It was a moment or two before Lindsey picked up, and Rona held her breath. Then:

'Hello?'

'Hi, Linz. We're home again, and I was wondering how you are.'

'OK,' Lindsey said.

'*Where* are you?'

'At home.'

'Sorry I couldn't help before, but now we're back how about coming here for a day or two?'

'No, thanks. I only came home myself today and am looking forward to my own bed. In any case I couldn't face all those stairs – *three flights* if I was sleeping in Max's old studio. I hadn't thought it through when I suggested it – I think I had visions of a duvet on the sitting-room sofa.'

'That could still be arranged.' Rona was assimilating the fact that Lindsey had spent the weekend with the Hathaways.

'Really, I'm better here. The swelling's gone down now.'

She made up her mind. 'In that case, the mountain will come to Mohamed in the guise of Gus and me. We'll arrive tomorrow evening with a takeaway and stay overnight. OK?'

Another pause. Then: 'OK. See you then.' And she rang off.

Rona let out her breath in a soundless whistle. Lindsey was a black belt when it came to sulking, but the first defences had been breached and she was convinced once they were face-to-face all would be well.

'How is she?' Max asked as she rejoined him.

'Better, I think. She spent the weekend in Alban Road.'

'Didn't I tell you there was no need to worry? That girl will always land on her feet, even if one of them has a sprained ankle.'

'I've invited myself for the night tomorrow.'

'So my goodnight call should be to your mobile?'

'Please.'

Max glanced at her. 'Have you told her yet about her friend Dominic's departure?'

Rona shook her head.

'Don't you think you should?'

'Probably, but I'll wait till she's over this.'

'For God's sake, Rona, she's not an invalid! If you delay much longer she'll find out from someone else and then you'll be for it.'

'I suppose you're right,' Rona sighed. Which made the prospect of tomorrow's visit even more daunting.

There was a parade of shops about a mile from Fairhaven which included an Indian restaurant among its amenities, and it was from there that Rona purchased their evening meal. Five minutes later she had parked on the gravel outside the flats and, juggling her overnight grip, the carrier bag of food and Gus's lead, pressed Lindsey's intercom. The response came at once.

'Rona?'

'Hi!'

'The door's on the latch. Put it down once you're in.'

Rona manoeuvred herself and her encumbrances inside, almost tripping as the dog wound his lead round her legs, and pushed down the latch as instructed. Lindsey had not, as usual, appeared at the top of the stairs. She bent and released Gus, who went charging up ahead of her, and started more slowly after him hoping that, as on previous occasions, he would have broken the initial ice.

Lindsey was in the kitchen, patting him as he jumped excitedly up at her. She looked up as Rona appeared in the doorway.

'We come in peace bearing offerings,' Rona said.

Lindsey's mouth twitched, and before she could respond Rona

dropped both bags on the floor and went to hug her. After a minute, she felt her sister respond.

'I'm sorry I lectured you,' she said contritely. 'I was in pain and feeling sorry for myself. I expected sympathy, not a moralistic onslaught. And in case you're wondering, I did *not* leap on Steve the minute your back was turned.'

'Ouch!' Rona disengaged herself. 'I suppose I deserved that. I really am sorry, Linz.'

Lindsey nodded to where the dog was sniffing interestedly at the carrier bag. 'You'd better rescue our supper,' she said. 'The oven's on, so it can reheat while we have a drink.'

Rona extracted the foil containers and put them in the oven, where two plates were already warming. 'So how is the ankle, really?'

'Aching, but much better,' Lindsey answered, taking two glasses out of a cupboard. 'As you can see I'm still wearing the bandage, but really just for support.'

'And how was the weekend?'

'Fine. They couldn't have been kinder. I had my laptop with me and the office provided me with work when I rang to explain my absence.' She handed Rona a vodka and tonic and she nodded her thanks.

'Talking of the office, what's the news of Jonathan?'

'He's surviving. He was in on Wednesday and said he's back home, but banished to the guestroom. Which serves him right!' she added with a smile.

'And did you find out what the touch paper was?'

Lindsey motioned her in the direction of the sitting room. 'After being told about the dinner, Carol went through his things and found the airline tickets intended for the weekend.'

'Ah!' Rona settled back in her chair. 'And are you still unrumbled?'

'I was at the last count; she's still insisting she's not interested. If it was me, I'd have had my hands round his throat demanding to be told who it was.'

'So the office still doesn't know either?'

'I think one or two have their suspicions, but staff rather than the other partners.'

Rona took a deep breath. It was now or never. 'Actually, I've some news of another of your exes,' she said.

Lindsey raised an eyebrow. 'Oh? Who?'

'Dominic. He's . . . moving to Paris.'

Lindsey went still, and Rona continued quickly, 'Gavin knows an estate agent who told him the penthouse is being let for a year with a view to possible sale at the end of it.' She paused but Lindsey didn't speak. 'I'm . . . sorry,' she offered lamely.

Lindsey drained her glass. Then she said almost steadily, 'I suppose Bloody Carla's going with him?'

'I've no idea.'

'I'd say you can count on it. Her flat will also be up for let or sale, mark my words.'

Rona was casting around for some soothing comment when Lindsey rose to her feet and said abruptly, 'Top-up?' Without waiting for a reply she picked up Rona's half-full glass and returned to the kitchen.

Rona waited tensely. Please don't let her be too upset, she thought, bracing herself as Lindsey came back with the drinks. Thankfully, there was no sign of tears.

'Well,' she said brightly, 'that's enough of me. Tell me about your weekend. How's Roland?'

Crises successfully negotiated, the conversation resumed on a less personal level which continued throughout the evening. Lindsey made no further mention of her time in Alban Road and Rona dared not ask questions. All that mattered was that peace was restored between them, and it would be a long time before she rocked the boat again.

FOURTEEN

When Rona returned from Lindsey's on Tuesday morning she determined to make a start on the diaries. Whether or not she'd incorporate the hijacking and the invasion into one article depended on how fully Ruth had described both events, added to which Frank might well be able to add details that she'd skimmed over or omitted altogether, his memory having been reactivated by his own reading of them.

The Entebbe crisis, which took place in late June/early July

1976, appeared some way into that particular diary following a detailed account of a holiday Ruth and Frank had spent in Greece, touring the islands and visiting historical sites. It came as a surprise to Rona that the plane, which had begun its flight in Israel, had touched down at Athens en route for Paris, and it was there that the hijackers had boarded along with several passengers, including the Hathaways.

There were in fact two accounts of the event: the first consisted of scribbled notes made while the hijacking was actually taking place and included incoherent messages addressed to the family at home – 'if you ever get this' – poignant indications of the stress Ruth was under and decipherable only thanks to Steve's typed transcription. The second, far more detailed record had been written from the safety of a Paris hotel a week later.

Enthralled, Rona read of the appearance of the four hijackers soon after leaving Athens, one of whom forced his way on to the flight deck. The terrified passengers were informed the hijacking was in support of the Popular Front for the Liberation of Palestine and that the plane was being diverted to Benghazi in Libya, where they would refuel. It wasn't until twenty-four hours after leaving Athens that they touched down at Entebbe, where they were conducted at gunpoint to the old airport terminal that was being used as a warehouse. Several more terrorists appeared, passports and documents were collected and Jewish and Israeli passengers separated from the rest.

There was a little girl of about five on the flight, Ruth had written. *She was unaccompanied and travelling in the care of one of the stewardesses, but it transpired that the stewardess was Jewish and despite her protests the hijackers forcibly removed her from the child, who was crying bitterly. Frank immediately got up and, defying an order to remain in his seat, made his way down the aisle towards her. I was terrified – one of the hijackers had a gun trained on him the whole time – but he remained perfectly calm, picked her up, brought her back to me and put her on my lap. Poor little thing; she clung to us until we landed in Paris and handed her over to her grandmother, who was there to meet her.*

By far the most information – including, incredibly, a visit by Idi Amin – was contained in this second account, and Rona decided to ask Frank's permission to quote large passages verbatim. Nothing she could write all these years later could reproduce the remembered terror, apprehension and overwhelming relief that came across in the words set down so soon after the ordeal.

At eleven o'clock she was interrupted by a phone call from her mother.

'All set for Saturday?' Avril asked brightly, and Rona, still mentally marooned in the desert, took a moment to adjust.

'Saturday?'

'The *wedding*, darling!'

'Oh, sorry. Yes, of course; we're looking forward to it.' She paused. 'Have you heard from Lindsey?'

'Not lately, why?'

'She had an accident on Thursday and sprained her ankle, but it's much—'

'She's still coming?' Avril interrupted anxiously.

'I'm sure she is, but she mightn't want to stand around too much.'

'Well, that's easily arranged. Sarah and Clive were delighted with the coffee service, by the way. Of course you'll be hearing from them, but probably not till after their honeymoon.'

She was speaking of Sarah as though she were her own daughter and Rona felt a faint pang. But perhaps, she reasoned philosophically, that was as it should be; after all, Avril would soon be *step*-mother of the bride.

'It'll seem strange,' she was continuing, 'sitting in the front pew at St Giles again; memories of yours and Lindsey's weddings.'

And with Guy rather than Pops beside her, Rona thought.

'Well, I just wanted to touch base. It seems a while since we spoke.'

'Sorry, Mum, I should have phoned.'

'Oh, that wasn't meant as a reprimand; we're all rushing around these days. Right then, see you at the church, as they say!' And she rang off.

Rona returned to the diaries, eager now to tell their story. But first she needed to speak to Frank and she reached again for the phone.

'Frank Hathaway.'

'Hello, Frank, it's Rona.'

The usual pleasantries followed, after which he asked, 'What can I do for you?'

'Well, first, I'd like to thank you for your kindness to Lindsey.'

'Oh, nonsense! It was a pleasure to have her. How is she?'

'Much better; she went into work yesterday and we spent the evening together.'

'That's good news.'

'The other reason I'm phoning is that I've been reading Ruth's entry about the hijacking. What an experience you had!'

'One we'd happily have done without. We'd been looking forward to three days in Paris to round off the holiday, but it didn't turn out that way.'

Rona hesitated. 'I was wondering whether, after reading her account, it brought anything else back to you – instances that perhaps she hadn't mentioned? You might have seen things from a slightly different angle and it is, after all, *your* experiences I'm supposed to be writing about.'

'I've certainly been reliving it.'

'Then could I come round and we can go through the diary together? I'd also like to discuss quoting from it, if you've no objection? She makes it all sound so . . . immediate, which obviously I can't.'

There was a pause. 'There are parts I *shouldn't* want published,' he said then. 'Messages to the family, and so on.'

'Of course; we'd agree beforehand which, if any, passages I could use.'

'Then yes, I'm happy to give you my personal account, which, after all, was what I agreed to.'

'Would sometime today be convenient?' Rona pressed, aware that resuscitated memories could as quickly fade again.

'I have a Probus lunch, but I'll be home again about three, if that's any good?'

'Great – thanks so much. I'll see you then.'

She seemed to be wearing a track to four-two-seven Alban Road, Rona thought, turning into the gateway and hoping her family wasn't proving too importunate.

As before, Frank was awaiting her in the doorway. 'Come in, the kettle's on the boil.'

More déjà vu; this appointment, she realized, was at exactly the same time as her first visit almost five weeks ago. She went ahead of him into the sitting room and took Ruth's diary out of her briefcase while Frank made the tea, returning minutes later with a tray.

'Between us, my sister and I will be eating you out of house and home!' Rona protested as he passed her a plate of biscuits.

'It's a pleasure to see you.' He poured the tea and came to join her on the sofa, where he picked up the diary and began to leaf through it. 'Now, how do we start?'

'What I'd really like is for you to imagine I know nothing about the hijacking and tell me how you first realized it was in progress, the reaction of the other passengers, the long stopover in Libya which Ruth glosses over, and so on. And if you don't mind, I'll switch on my recorder so I don't forget any of it.'

As Rona had hoped, once Frank started speaking it was apparent that more memories were flooding back: a woman passenger who managed to escape at Benghazi by pretending to have a miscarriage, the female hijacker who was as fanatical as her colleagues, the threat of execution of the hostages if demands for the release of prisoners were not met, the arrival by helicopter of Idi Amin, who insisted on being addressed as 'His Excellency Field Marshal Doctor Idi Amin Dada'.

Each time Frank came to a temporary halt Rona read out passages from the diary, prompting his recollection of that particular section and thereby eliciting more facts. 'One of the episodes that stuck out for me was that poor little girl being separated from the stewardess who was looking after her. It seemed so . . . inhuman, somehow.'

Frank nodded. 'Totally heartless,' he agreed. 'The little thing was terrified. I've often thought of her over the years and wondered what became of her.'

Further memories surfaced, and by the end of the session Rona felt she had doubled the amount of information she'd started with.

'That was great, Frank!' she said at last, switching off the recorder and sitting back.

He gave a short laugh. 'You should be a hypnotherapist!' he said, and she wondered if he was wishing she could stimulate his memory of a more recent trauma. But she'd promised Steve not to refer to that.

'Perhaps we could go through the same procedure with the Kuwait episode in due course,' she suggested, 'but that will need a separate article so there's no hurry.' She glanced at his hand resting gently on the closed book. 'Would you like the Kuwait diary back till I'm ready for it?'

He shook his head. 'There's no need – I know it's in safe hands.'

'I'll return this one anyway, as soon as I've written it up.' As they walked together to the front door she added laughingly, 'When you had lunch with Pops that day, I bet you didn't know what you were letting yourself in for! First me, then Linz, then me again in quick succession!'

Frank smiled. 'And Lindsey again on Sunday!' he said.

'Sunday?'

'Didn't she tell you? She's insisting on taking the three of us to lunch at the Clarendon by way of a thank you. Sweet of her, but totally unnecessary.'

'Well, I hope you all enjoy it, and thanks again for this afternoon.'

As she drove home Rona was aware of both indignation and hurt: why hadn't Lindsey mentioned this during all the hours they'd spent together? Because, Rona wondered uncomfortably, she thought Rona might interpret it as indicative of her pursuit of Steve? And was it?

Mia had discovered to her annoyance that the Darcy Theatre was fully booked for Saturday's performance, which had necessitated a quick call to Colin in the hope that he'd be free Friday evening. Fortunately it transpired that his last lecture was at two o'clock and he could leave as soon as it ended. He had, however, declined her invitation to stay for the weekend, suggesting he leave after lunch on Saturday.

Over a quick pre-theatre supper at home, Mia was reassured by her son's appearance. As Ewan had said, he'd lost the drawn look that had been so noticeable when they met at the pub, and he was certainly doing full justice to the meal she'd prepared.

'You're feeling better, aren't you, darling, now everything's out in the open?'

He nodded, then smiled a little sheepishly. 'And there's another reason I've perked up,' he admitted. 'I've starting see a girl.'

Mia smiled. 'Nothing new there, surely?'

'She's not just any girl, Mum.'

'Oh? Tell me more.'

'Her name's Jessica – Jess – and she's in my year. She's American.'

'Well, that makes a change! Whereabouts does she come from?'

'Colorado. She's going back for Christmas and . . .' He broke eye contact, looking down at his plate. 'She's invited me to spend it with her – or rather, her folks have. There'll be snow and skiing and so on. I know we usually—'

Mia said quickly, 'Time moves on, Colin, and we must move
with it. But I should like to meet this Jess.'

His face broke into a smile. 'Dad thought you might be upset
– about Christmas, I mean – but I said you'd understand. Thanks,
Mum. Actually, that's why I'd like to leave after lunch tomorrow;
there's a party in the evening that we've both been invited to.'

'Just as well the theatre was fully booked, then,' Mia said.

Saturday morning dawned cool and sunny – just the weather for
her new outfit, Rona thought contentedly.

'Mum seems to regard this as a family wedding,' she remarked
as she and Max drove to Belmont, 'but it isn't for us; we've never
met Clive's parents, nor the best man, nor the bridesmaids, and
we'll hardly know any of the guests.'

'Just as well we've got each other, then!' Max said facetiously.
'And Lindsey, of course.'

'She bought some new shoes for the occasion,' Rona remembered.
'I hope she'll be able to wear them without doing her ankle any
further damage.'

The wedding service, as always, brought a lump to Rona's throat.
Hearing the beautiful, familiar words never failed to bring back
memories of her own wedding and her hand reached instinctively
for Max's. She felt his quick glance as his fingers tightened round
hers.

Sarah wore a dress of ivory satin, classical in outline with no frills
or embellishments, its simplicity of line perfectly complementing
her figure, and Rona, burying her reservations, acknowledged that
she made a radiant bride.

It had clouded over by the time they emerged from the church,
and since the exterior was not particularly photogenic and a cool
wind was blowing, it was decided to take only a few photographs
in the doorway and the majority in the more sheltered garden of
Tall Trees.

'I'm not going to hang around,' Lindsey said in an undertone.
She was, Rona had noted, wearing her new shoes. 'My ankle's
starting to play up and the sooner I'm sitting down with a glass of
champagne in my hand, the better. I'm going to drive straight back
and if necessary wait in the car till everyone else arrives. See you

there.' And, one hand anchoring her large-brimmed hat, she started along the pavement in the direction of her car.

Rona had been studying the guests who now milled around, greeting each other and exclaiming on Sarah's dress and the service. As she'd suspected, there was no one she recognized. Avril had told her there was a contingent from Belmont Primary where both the bride and groom worked, but Rona had been to the school only once in the last few years, and on that occasion her mind had been on more serious matters than members of staff. Now her mother and Guy, along with Sarah and Clive, were being marshalled into position by an officious photographer, and since the possibility of speaking to any of them was out of the question, Rona turned to Max. 'Let's go back and join Linz,' she said.

The marquee was pleasantly warm in the sunshine, the meal had been excellent, the champagne flowed freely and the last official photograph – of the bride and groom cutting the cake – had just been taken. There was now a ten-minute comfort break before the speeches and Rona and Lindsey, who'd been given dispensation to use the en-suite facilities, went upstairs together.

'How's the ankle bearing up?' Rona asked.

Lindsey grimaced. 'I'll put the bandage on again when I get home. I knew I shouldn't have worn these shoes but they go so perfectly with the outfit.'

'Better not wear them for your lunch date tomorrow,' Rona advised, nonchalantly taking out her comb.

Lindsey looked at her sharply. 'Where did you hear about that?'

'Not from you, certainly.' Rona eyed her sister's embarrassment with satisfaction. 'Why didn't you mention it, Linz? We talked about the Hathaways – surely the most natural thing would have been to say you planned a thank you?'

'It might come as a surprise, Rona,' Lindsey retorted waspishly, 'to learn that I don't tell you everything. For God's sake, don't let's fall out over this as well.' And she went into the bathroom and locked the door.

Once everyone had reconvened the toastmaster announced that the health of the bride and groom would be proposed by Mr Stewart Nairn, godfather of the bride.

'Why isn't Guy doing it?' Rona whispered to Max, who shrugged in reply.

Stewart Nairn was a distinguished-looking man in his sixties who appeared well accustomed to public speaking and soon had the company laughing, and it wasn't until after both the groom's and the best man's speeches that Guy finally rose to his feet.

Having thanked everyone for coming, he glanced down at Avril. 'Not all of you might be aware,' he continued, 'that this charming lady at my side is not yet my wife, and I hope that at this stage of the proceedings Sarah and Clive will forgive me for stealing a little of their thunder by announcing that we have now fixed the date for our own wedding.'

There was an outburst of applause and Rona and Lindsey exchanged startled glances. This was the first they'd heard of it.

'We shall be tying the knot on the twenty-second of February next year, and I'd like to take this opportunity to thank Avril for all the love, help and support she's given Sarah and myself since she came into our lives. It isn't easy to follow a much-loved wife and mother, and Sally will always be with us. But Avril has made a place for herself with tact and dignity and we're both enormously grateful to her. So though it's a little unusual, could I ask you to stand with me and drink a toast to Avril, soon to be the second Mrs Lacey?'

The company rose as one and raised their glasses. 'Avril!' they repeated obediently, and Rona saw her mother blush prettily and nod her thanks.

As the last of the applause died away and normal conversation resumed, Lindsey leant forward. 'Do you think Sarah knew about this?' she asked Rona.

Rona shook her head. 'She looked as surprised as we were.'

Lindsey nodded and turned to reply to the neighbour on her right. At least the shock of the announcement had smoothed over the latest difference between them, Rona thought thankfully. But she'd love to be a fly on the wall during Sunday lunch at the Clarendon.

Monday was Max's birthday, but as it was a working day with the usual evening class they'd decided to postpone the celebrations till Wednesday, when they'd treat themselves to a meal at the Serendipity, Marsborough's premier restaurant. He did, however, open the cards and presents that had arrived, including the packages Roland and Cynthia had entrusted to Rona during their visit.

'Have a good day,' she instructed as he bent to kiss her goodbye.

'You too.'

'I shall; I'm hoping to finish the Entebbe article today, then I can return the diary to Frank. Though he didn't say so, I had the impression as I was leaving that he'd rather not have parted with it again; it brought Ruth back to life for him.'

'Good luck with it, then. Speak to you later.' And he was gone.

Rona had just reached her study when the phone rang and she swore under her breath. Interruptions were the last thing she wanted and she was tempted to switch it off altogether. She waited, eying the answerphone. Would whoever it was leave a message?

'Rona?' It was Monica's hesitant voice and Rona, sighing, lifted the phone.

'Hi, Monica.'

'Is this a bad time?'

'No,' she lied, 'I've not started work yet.'

'We said we'd have lunch sometime and I wondered how you're fixed today?'

Rona hesitated. She would have much preferred a clear day's writing, but she'd agreed they should meet and, after all, she was entitled to a lunch break. She could work all morning, she reasoned, and what remained of the afternoon on her return.

'That would be great, Monica. I can tell you about the wedding!'

'Where would you recommend? I'm still not au fait with the local hostelries.'

'The Bacchus Wine Bar in Market Street is good value, and we don't need to book at lunchtime.'

'Excellent. Then shall we make our way there about twelve thirty?'

It was an effort, at twelve fifteen, to drag herself away from the hijacking when she'd almost completed the account, but the break would allow her to come back to it with fresh eyes and make any necessary tweaks.

Over lunch, Monica was interested to hear details of Sarah's wedding, especially the announcement of Guy and Avril's plans. 'They always say one wedding leads to another,' she commented.

'And no doubt we'll also have Pops and Catherine's before long,' Rona said. 'It's making Max and me feel like an old married couple!'

She signalled to the waiter and ordered coffee.

'So, how's your magazine series going?' Monica asked as it was served.

'Reasonably well, I think. I've not got round to your story yet.'

'What are you working on at the moment?'

'It's another ex-pat account, but a rather more dramatic one; a friend of Pops was involved in the Entebbe hijacking in 1976.'

Monica's coffee spoon clattered on her saucer. 'My God!' she whispered.

Rona looked at her sharply. 'What is it? Are you OK?'

'Yes – no – I'm not sure!' Monica laughed shakily. 'You're not going to believe this, but so was I – involved, I mean!'

Rona stared at her. 'You? But—'

'Obviously I was only a small child at the time. My father worked at the embassy in Tel Aviv and I was flying to Paris to spend the summer with my grandmother.'

Rona's mouth went dry. 'In the care of an air stewardess?'

'Well, yes. I don't know about nowadays, but then unaccompanied children—'

'Who was separated from you by the hijackers?'

'God, Rona, what is this? How—?'

'Now it's *my* turn to say what you won't believe. It sounds very much as though Pop's friend, Frank Hathaway, was the man who rescued you!'

Monica stared at her. '*No!*'

'It was in his wife's diary – how you were left alone crying and he braved the armed hijackers to go down the aisle to collect you. I was speaking to him only last week, and he said he often wondered what had happened to you.'

Tears were streaming down Monica's cheeks. 'I can't believe – I mean, it just doesn't seem possible . . .'

'Does his name sound familiar – Frank Hathaway?'

'The Frank part, yes; they asked me to call them Uncle Frank and Auntie Ruth. God, Rona—' She blew her nose. 'Sorry!'

'Sadly his wife died, but would you like to see him again?'

'Oh, I would – to thank him. Grandma told my parents about his kindness, but she hadn't thought to ask for his address, and though they tried to trace him they never could.'

'He was probably based overseas himself at the time,' Rona said.

'I just can't *believe* he lives here in Marsborough!'

'Why did you never mention this, when we were talking about your life abroad?'

'It never occurred to me. I was only five at the time and to be honest I've done my best to forget it. Anyway, you were asking about Hong Kong and Bolivia.' She dried her eyes with her hand-kerchief. 'I'd . . . like to get used to the idea a bit before I meet him, though, and I think he should have some warning too.'

'I agree. I'll let him know, give you each other's phone numbers and then it will be up to you.'

Monica said wonderingly, 'Just think, if we hadn't met today, and I hadn't asked what you were working on, this might never have happened.'

'You'd have found out when you read the article,' Rona reminded her. 'But at least this way you'll have time to get over the shock.'

Half an hour later, back at her computer, Rona read again what she'd written that morning. The article would, after all, have to wait a few more days before it could be completed, with an ending she could never have imagined.

FIFTEEN

Rona regaled Max with an account of the lunch when he phoned that evening.

'I'd decided to speak to Steve in the first instance and ask him to tell Frank,' she ended, 'but when I rang their number on a high I was met with the answering service and I still haven't manage to get through.'

'Well, it is half-term, remember; that's what governed the date for the wedding. Perhaps they've gone away for the week.'

'Possibly, though when Steve mentioned it he said he'd be working.'

'He might have decided to take some holiday. It looks as if you'll just have to be patient, love. Surely there's something else you can be getting on with in the meantime?'

'Ross Mackenzie's profile, I suppose,' she said resignedly, 'before he phones again to ask if I've done it. I'll tell Monica I can't get through to save her trying. At least it will give her more time to prepare for their meeting; it's bound to be emotional.'

Wednesday evening, and Max's birthday celebration. There were several features about the Serendipity that made it unusual, one being the knot-garden effect achieved by a continuous waist-high partition snaking in and out around the tables. Another was the counters on either side of the room laden with raw meat and fish, behind which were charcoal grills; customers were invited to make their own selection and, if they wished, watch it being cooked. And lastly there was a table in the centre of the room displaying a giant sculpture carved out of ice. Those booking far enough in advance could request a particular shape, the two most popular being a dolphin and a swan, but this evening the magnificent head of a horse was attracting a lot of admiration.

Max and Rona had just been served with their first course when he exclaimed suddenly, 'OMG!'

'What?' Rona glanced at him, spoon poised over her avocado.

'Look who's being shown in.'

She turned in time to see the maître d' escorting Dominic Frayne to a table further down the room, at his side the woman she'd seen at the Clarendon.

'Wouldn't you know it?' Max commented. '"Of all the gin joints . . ."'

'I thought he'd have left by now,' Rona said.

'Farewell meal, perhaps? But don't let him put us off ours.'

Minutes later Dominic, on his way to the fish counter, paused at their table and, after greeting them, indicated his companion. 'May I introduce Dolores Milan, a business colleague?' And, to the woman: 'This is Rona Parish, the well-known biographer, and her husband, the artist Max Allerdyce.'

Polite nods and smiles were exchanged. Rona, refusing to skate round what was uppermost in her mind, turned back to him. 'I hear you're leaving the country?'

'At the end of the week, yes; which is why I'm particularly glad to have the chance to say goodbye.'

'Is it a permanent move?' asked Max, who had risen for the introductions.

'A little early to tell,' Dominic answered smoothly. 'I'll have a better idea in a month or two. In many ways I'll be sorry to leave Marsborough. However, I'm only across the Channel.'

'And you have your plane,' Rona commented, a subtle reminder of the trips he'd made with Lindsey.

Dominic, well aware of the allusion, met her eye. 'As you say.' He paused. 'But we mustn't hold up your meal. I hope we'll meet again, on one of my visits if not when I return. And in the meantime, please give my regards to Lindsey.'

He shook both their hands and moved on, guiding his companion through the maze of tables.

'Reckon she's the new amour?' Max asked, reseating himself.

'I doubt it,' Rona said dismissively, 'the chemistry wasn't there. Probably, as he said, simply a business colleague tying up loose ends before he leaves the country.'

'Did you ever get round to telling Lindsey he's going?'

'Yes, when I was there that evening.'

'How did she take it?'

'Pretty calmly, to my relief. I think she'd given up hope of them ever getting back together.'

'So no doubt the merry-go-round continues.'

Rona did not reply.

Three hours later Dominic Frayne stood at the window of his penthouse apartment, a glass of whisky in his hand, looking out over the sloping darkness of the park to the lights of the town below. This had become a habit during the eighteen months he'd lived here, a late-night review of the day just over – clients met, contracts signed, women kissed – before retiring to bed. It was a sobering thought that only two such reviews remained to him and by the end of the week he'd have left this apartment, probably for ever.

It had worked well, he reflected; his assistant Carla, whose home when they lived in London had been across town, had moved into the same building and installed herself in a flat two floors below him, an arrangement equally convenient for their working life and for the occasional nights when, in need of physical release, he had taken her to bed.

Looking back, they'd been an eventful eighteen months, some of which had had a lasting effect. Though highly successful on the business front, in his private life he'd faced several crises, among them the messy break-up with Miranda Bellington-Selby and his uncomfortable lunch with her father, Lord Rupert. Then there'd been the trouble with his daughter Olivia wanting to drop out of university in order to marry. And, of course, there was Lindsey.

He frowned and drank some more whisky. Seeing Rona this evening had forced her back into his mind when he'd almost succeeded in erasing her. The fact that he still dreamed of her he dismissed as a sign of weakness, but the truth was that she had lodged in his consciousness as one of the biggest regrets of his life.

With two divorces behind him he had determined never again to allow a woman to come close, and until he met Lindsey none had. He'd behaved badly, there was no denying it, but when she'd stormed out of the apartment that evening he had not for one minute expected it to be for ever. That it had proved to be so was largely due to his pride – an unwillingness to make the first move towards reconciliation. In his arrogance he'd expected her to come back. She hadn't, and now it was too late.

He sighed, finished his drink and turned from the window. He was getting maudlin – a sure sign of tiredness. Tomorrow was another day, and perhaps after all it was as well that he was leaving Marsborough and its memories. Paris, he thought ironically, putting his glass on a table and switching off the lights, here I come.

Rona sat in her study, drumming her fingers on the desk. She'd forwarded the account of the coronation to Barnie and as the Hathaways were still not answering their phone she was unable to complete Frank's article. What's more, since the series was not to be run in consecutive months there was no immediate pressure to start on another. Which, as she'd said to Max, left the Mackenzie profile. She couldn't keep postponing it, she told herself firmly, retrieving the cassette from the storage container into which she'd thankfully dropped it four weeks earlier. With a sigh of resignation, she opened his file and reviewed what she'd written so far. At least during the interval the Lindsey episode had lost its potency and she was able to view him more dispassionately.

Once she had the complete interview on screen she could start editing it into her own words, and to that end she worked steadily for two or three hours. Though more than willing to discuss all aspects of his work, he'd been inclined to gloss over his private life, saying merely that although he'd had several long-term relationships since his divorce, his partners had become jealous of the time he devoted to his work. So now, Rona thought bitterly, he went in for one- or two-night stands with whoever took his fancy.

The last cassette came to an end and she sat back and stretched. It was almost lunchtime, and on this cool autumn day the contents of her fridge – cheese and salad – did little to inspire her. She picked up the phone and called her father.

'Pops, it's me. It's ages since I saw you, and I was wondering if you're free for a pub lunch?'

Tom hesitated. 'Actually, poppet, I'm at Catherine's . . . Just a minute.' Rona could hear voices in the background, then he came back. 'Catherine says you're very welcome to come here for lunch.'

'Are you sure?'

'Certainly; it's even longer since she saw you. Come as soon as you're ready, and bring Gus with you.'

'How did the wedding go?' Catherine asked as they sat round the table eating her delicious fish pie.

'Very well. The weather was a bit iffy but it didn't rain and the marquee was pleasantly warm.' Rona hesitated, glancing from one to the other. 'Added to which, during the speeches Guy announced that he and Mum are getting married on the twenty-second of February.'

'Excellent!' Tom said heartily. 'And to follow that, *our* news is we're in the process of buying a house and hope to be married ourselves in January.'

'Oh, Pops, that's great!'

'I've kept meaning to phone you and Lindsey but hadn't got round to it – sorry!'

'So tell me about the house – where is it?'

'In Lindsey's neck of the woods – between Hollybush Lane and Fairhaven. The present owners are hanging on there till the house they're having built is ready, the most recent date for which is early December. There's very little we'll need to do, so we hope to move in ourselves mid-January as a respectable married couple!'

'It's going to be an expensive winter!'

'That's just what it mustn't be. We have everything we need, but if you feel you have to give us something, a gardening voucher would be more than welcome. So – what else have you been up to since we saw you?'

'Max and I went up to Tynecastle for Roland's birthday. He's in fine form and still ruling the roost up there.'

'I hope I'm as good at his age!' Tom joked. 'What about the work angle? I hear Frank found Ruth's diaries? He and Steve were here for dinner a week or two ago.'

'Yes, Steve told me.' She hesitated. She'd decided that although she longed to tell him about the link between Frank and Monica, it was only fair that he himself should be the first recipient of the news. Instead, she said, 'Actually, he asked me to see if I could find out anything more about that car crash. Frank—'

'Has remembered something. Yes, we know. But what can you possibly do after all this time?'

'The answer, sadly, is very little. I made a few enquiries, went to see the victim's widow and so on, but nothing new came up. Incidentally,' she added drily, 'I have you to thank for Steve approaching me.'

They looked at her enquiringly and she went on, 'At the dinner you were apparently praising my so-called detective skills.'

Catherine smiled. 'Guilty as charged.'

'Well, they haven't been much use this time, and I worry that Frank's going to keep on castigating himself unless something can be proved one way or the other.'

'It's not your responsibility, love,' Tom reassured her.

Which, though doubtless true, brought little comfort.

That evening Rona phoned Lindsey to pass on their father's news.

'God, it's all happening, isn't it?' she said. 'Do you think we'll need a different outfit for each wedding? We've only just splashed out for Sarah's!'

'Well, they say things come in threes!' Rona replied lightly.

'Have you told Mum?'

'No, they're away at the moment, aren't they? When we said goodbye she said they were treating themselves to a hotel break to recover.'

Lindsey gave a short laugh. 'She won't be happy that Pops and Catherine are beating them to it!'

'They're buying a house out near you.'

'Where, exactly?'

'I don't know the address, but between you and Hollybush Lane, where Barnie and Dinah live.' She paused. 'Anything new on Jonathan?'

'No; we're keeping a discreet distance from each other.'

A pity, Rona thought, that they hadn't done so earlier.

She continued to work on the profile and by the weekend had almost finished it. On the Monday morning she again phoned the Hathaways, and this time she was in luck. What's more, it was Steve who answered.

'The diary's ready to be returned,' she told him. 'I phoned last week, but I presume you were away?'

'Sorry, yes; it was a spur-of-the-moment decision. I took a few days' holiday and we went to Center Parcs in Buckford. Luke had a wonderful time; it's his first proper holiday since we returned from the States.'

Rona said carefully, 'Actually, I have a rather incredible piece of news.' And she told him about Monica. 'I thought it might be better if you were the one to break it to your father,' she finished.

'It's . . . unbelievable! After all these years and she's more or less round the corner!'

'It might come as a shock; perhaps I'd better delay coming round?'

'On the contrary, I'm sure he'll want to hear all the details. Come today if you can.'

It was after four when Rona arrived at the house, and it was Frank who opened the door.

'Come in, come in!' he greeted her. 'This is fantastic news, Rona! To think we were only speaking about her last week! Steve's just bringing the tea through, so sit down and tell me all about this Monica – I'd forgotten her name. How long have you known her?'

The next half hour was taken up by a questions and answers session, with Frank breaking off every now and then to exclaim at the coincidence, and when it finally ended Rona took the diary out of her bag. 'Thanks so much for this, Frank. We little thought when you handed it over what it would lead to! And thank *you*, Steve, for the typed translations. They were invaluable.' She stood up. 'I must be getting back if I'm to walk the dog before it's completely dark. He's not too fond of fireworks.'

'Nor am I,' Frank admitted as they escorted her into the hall, 'though Luke's off to a bonfire party tomorrow. So, with this article behind you, what will you work on next?'

'By way of something different I'm doing a profile on the dress designer, Ross Mackenzie. I met him—'

She broke off, turning at Steve's sharp exclamation in time to see Frank stumble and reach out to the hall table to steady himself. The colour had drained from his face and her instant fear was that he was having a heart attack. Steve seized his arm and led him back into the sitting room, Rona following, her own heartbeat quickening.

'Dad, what is it?' Steve was demanding urgently, lowering his father gently into his chair. 'Have you a pain somewhere?'

Frank feebly shook his head, moistening his white lips. 'I'm . . . all right. It was just . . . the shock.'

Steve and Rona stared at him. 'What shock?'

He closed his eyes and passed a trembling hand over his face. 'The name,' he said faintly. 'Not "frenzy", as I thought: *Mackenzie*! Ross *Mackenzie*! *That's* what the dying man was saying.'

'It couldn't have been,' Max said flatly.

'He swears it was. He's absolutely certain.'

'He didn't work on the women's page, did he, this reporter? So what the hell would he have had to do with a . . . what do you call them? Couturier?'

'I don't know, Max.' Rona was still feeling shaky.

'Look, love, step back a moment and consider some salient points. One: why the hell would Ross Mackenzie be speeding through Buckfordshire in the middle of a Sunday night? Two: even if those *were* the words Frank heard – which is highly unlikely – it doesn't mean Mackenzie had anything to do with the accident. The man was probably delirious anyway. And three, which is *most* important: for God's sake don't go telling anyone of your suspicions – and you'd better warn the Hathaways too – or you could all find yourselves in court for defamation of character and God knows what else.'

She remained silent, and he prompted, 'Rona?'

'Yes, Max, I heard you.'

'I know you're anxious to clear this up, but that doesn't mean you can seize on any unlikely possibility that offers itself.'

'It's just that this is the first—'

'It's not the first anything,' Max said firmly. 'Don't forget that Frank had concussion, and the resulting memory loss lasted more than a year. Just because he now thinks he's remembered something, you can't immediately assume he's right. Even the fact that there were two cars is open to question.'

'I know,' she said tiredly.

His voice softened. 'Sorry to pour cold water, darling, but you must be realistic. In all honesty you're not one iota nearer to sorting this out than you were this time yesterday. Now I really must go; the students will be here any minute. I'll ring again at bedtime. In the meantime put it out of your mind and settle down with something on the telly. OK?'

'OK,' she replied, since it was expected.

'Love you,' he said, and rang off.

She stood in front of the Aga, holding out her hands to its warmth. Max was right, she thought, deflated after her initial excitement; she was no nearer a solution than she'd been yesterday. Somewhere close by a firework went off, making her jump. Gus whined and slunk into his basket. With a sigh she picked up the phone again.

After several minutes, Steve answered.

'It's Rona, Steve. I'm calling to see how Frank is.'

'Better, thanks. His colour's come back and he's just had something to eat. I think it was just too much for him – the excitement of hearing about Monica and then this, all within a few hours of each other. A double whammy, you might say.'

'But he still thinks that's what he heard?'

'Yep. Convinced of it.'

'I've been speaking to Max, and he says we must be careful not to voice our suspicions or we'd land ourselves in trouble.'

'I realize that, but thanks for the reminder.'

Rona hesitated. 'Do *you* think he's right?'

'God knows. This is the first I've heard of this designer guy. You said you'd met him; would you say he's capable of pushing someone off the road?'

Despite herself, Max's doubts had given her pause. 'It seems ludicrous,' she admitted. 'I mean, what possible reason could he have had, going after Brett Sinclair of all people? I can't think of any way their paths could even have crossed.'

'So you reckon we should discount the whole thing?' Steve asked flatly.

'That's what Max advises.'

'That's all very well for him, but I have my father to deal with.

He's on a high now, thinking that at last he's getting somewhere. I
can't just slap him down.' There was a pause. 'You never came
back to me on this, Rona; *were* you able to find out anything?'

'I'm afraid not. I saw Lottie Sinclair, but she couldn't shed any
light on why Brett hadn't gone straight home as he'd intended when
he spoke to her, least of all why he'd overshoot the Farnbridge
turning and head off in the opposite direction.'

'You said you had a friend on the *Gazette*?'

'Yes, I did speak to her but he was freelance and she didn't know
him well, though she thought he was a bit of a Jack the Lad.'

Rona came to a halt, suddenly remembering that wasn't all Tess
had told her: when asked if he might have had enemies, she'd replied
it was possible as he was always digging things up, things that the
Gazette's legal department wouldn't touch. *Suppose he'd found out
something about Ross?*

Steve was speaking again and she forced her attention back.
'Well, thanks for trying. God knows what else we can do.'

'Something might yet turn up,' she said and, having ended the
call, phoned Monica to ask her to delay contacting Frank for the
next few days.

After her microwave supper, Rona pulled the old basket chair up
to the Aga and opened her laptop. Gus padded over to join her,
settling down with his head on her feet, her closeness an antidote
to the repeated whistles and bangs that were constantly assailing
them from the celebrations outside.

Her screen came to life and she opened a new document, intending
to list the pros and cons of the possibility of Ross having caused
the accident. The cons were depressingly obvious, and she started
by listing those Max had outlined, adding several of her own. Now
for the more positive argument. She sat back, deep in thought, then
wrote down all she knew about Ross Mackenzie that *hadn't* appeared
in her profile, searching her memory for comments he'd made that
she'd not bothered to reproduce and starting with their first meeting
at Magda's fashion show.

What exactly had he said over supper that evening? She thought
back, concentrating hard. He'd opened their conversation by saying
he'd heard from Magda that she wrote for 'the local glossy' and
went on to ask her to write his profile, claiming he needed some
good publicity because his present collection was 'jinxed'. Yet when

she'd asked him at the interview what he'd meant he'd flushed and looked uncomfortable, saying it must have been the drink talking.

Rona sat back, her heart suddenly pounding. He'd told her that it took anything from eighteen months to two years to produce the collection, which meant he must have been working on it last summer! And if he considered it 'jinxed' something must have gone badly wrong, possibly even inducing the illness he'd referred to that had delayed completion.

Step back, she ordered herself, borrowing Max's words to hold down her sudden excitement. But at the very least she now had a tentative foothold. There were a hundred reasons for the collection not being up to standard and Ross's alleged illness, but perhaps – just perhaps – Brett Sinclair's death could have been one of them.

SIXTEEN

R ona had a restless night. At six o'clock she gave up all hope of further sleep, had a shower and went downstairs for breakfast. Gus, surprised at her early arrival, thumped a sleepy tail but didn't emerge from his warm basket.

Her mind was still churning as she filled the kettle, and she reflected it was as well she'd be walking him before returning to her desk. At this early hour there was a sense of purpose in the air – people setting off to work, children on their way to school – that should help to clear her head, and Furze Hill Park was just the place to blow away the cobwebs.

At the park gates a garish notice advertised a firework display that evening, complete with 'giant bonfire, ginger cake and toffee apples', and minutes later they passed the towering construction, already topped with the limp figure of Guy Fawkes. A park keeper was standing nonchalantly to one side – on guard, Rona surmised as she nodded good morning.

At the top end of the park was a large grassy area where dogs could run free, and Rona, hurling the frisbee she'd brought, watched Gus dashing joyfully after it, her mind circling her problems. Since she'd not known Brett Sinclair she could feel no duty towards him; her sole aim was to remove the haunted look from Frank's eyes and that, she knew, could be achieved only by amassing sufficient evidence to indict *someone*, no matter who, for causing his death.

At the moment Ross Mackenzie was the only remote possibility – and 'remote' was the word. All she had to go on were the alleged words of a dying man and a 'jinxed collection' that was evolving at that time. Her challenge was to bring together all the facts, impressions and rumours she could glean about him – what he'd said, how he'd looked, how he'd acted – and to see if, taken together, it was sufficient to place him on the Farnbridge to Marsborough road on a June night last year. It was a tall order.

Gus returned and triumphantly dropped the frisbee at her feet, panting expectantly. She bent to retrieve it and threw it farther up the slope, her eyes following its flight and alighting on the tall, Dutch-gabled houses of Park Rise, one of which had been Dominic Frayne's home. By now, he and no doubt Carla would be in Paris. Rona had never been to the penthouse, though Lindsey had described it to her. A little sadly, she wondered who was living there now.

She turned away and, mentally dismissing her sister's former lover, walked to a bench where, once, she had sat with a murderess looking over the roofs and steeples of the town, and, seating herself, concentrated on the matter in hand. But after several minutes of discarding one possibility after another, the only person left who might be able to add something was Magda, and the question was how she could bring the conversation round to Ross without – bearing Max's warning in mind – giving rise to any suspicion.

Suddenly coming to a decision, she stood up and called the dog. 'We're going to Magdalena's for coffee,' she told him.

Rona had gambled on Magda being at the Marsborough boutique that day, since it was there that she spent most of her time. And she was in luck. Furthermore, the boutique was empty of customers when she arrived – fortunate for her, if not for the proprietor.

'Rona! Is it too much to hope you're looking for something to wear at one of your parents' weddings?'

'Sorry, Mags, not at the moment. I've been up in the park with Gus; there's a cool wind blowing and I thought I'd treat myself to a coffee and one of your delectable pastries. And it would be even better if you could join me?'

'Delighted. As you see, we're not exactly overwhelmed at the moment.'

They walked down the shop to the little screened-off area that comprised the café. 'Espresso? Latte? Americano? Cappuccino?'

'Latte, I think, and a Viennese slice.'

'Make that two,' Magda told the waitress. 'So tell me, how did the wedding go? Was your outfit admired?'

'I was positively besieged by people wanting to know where I'd bought it!'

'Yeah, yeah, right!'

'Seriously, Mags, it was perfect – just right for the occasion. And yes, I probably shall have to think of something for the other weddings coming up.' Inspiration came and she added jokingly, 'If I wore the same outfit for both parents, I might even stretch to a Ross Mackenzie! Mates' rates, of course!' Ruefully she shook her head. 'Wishful thinking, but when I write my bestseller, yours is the first place I'll make for!'

She paused, anxious to keep Ross in the conversation and wondering how to achieve it. 'How's his collection going?'

The waitress returned with their coffee and pastries. 'Quite well,' Magda said, pushing across Rona's slice, 'considering the economic climate.'

'Will you be interested in his spring offering?'

'I'll decide that when I see it.' She sipped at her latte. 'How are you getting on with the profile?'

'OK, but I'm scratching around for any titbits I can find to eke it out. You've met him several times; any anecdotes you can pass on?'

'Not for publication!'

'Oh?'

Magda smiled and shook her head. 'He has a name for the ladies, but nothing scandalous. No doubt that hard-faced sister of his keeps him in line.'

'You reckon she's the one in charge?'

Magda nodded decisively. 'He has the flair but she runs the show. I suppose, to be fair, artistic people need someone with a business sense to keep their feet on the ground. For example, Claudia noticed that when she saw them that time it was Isobel who chose the wine. It wouldn't surprise me if she even runs his bath!'

'Claudia?'

'The girl I was telling you about, who got his autograph.'

God, how could she have forgotten? 'Perhaps,' Rona said

carefully, 'she might have something I could use? Is she . . . based here?'

'Yes.' Magda beckoned the waitress. 'Ask Claudia to come in, would you, Beth?'

Minutes later a pretty girl aged about eighteen appeared. 'You wanted me, Magda?'

'Yes, come and sit down for a moment.'

'Oh, what a gorgeous dog!' the girl exclaimed, catching sight of Gus beneath the table, and he thumped his tail in response.

'Claudia, this is Rona Parish, who, as I told you, is writing the profile of Ross Mackenzie.'

She turned to Rona and smiled shyly. 'I know who you are; I was on the desk when you bought your wedding outfit.'

Rona returned her smile; she had the feeling of being on the brink of something, something important. 'Magda tells me you met Ross, Claudia; when would that have been?'

Her face lit up. 'Last year – he signed my menu for me! It was Mum's fiftieth and Dad had taken us to the Priory at Narrowland for a long weekend. I couldn't believe it when he came into the restaurant on the Sunday evening.'

Rona tensed. 'When was this, exactly?'

'In June.'

'Can you remember the date?' The girl looked surprised and Rona added unconvincingly, 'I might be able to slot it into the profile if it's in the right timeframe.'

'Well, I can certainly remember, because the Sunday was Mum's birthday. It was the sixteenth.'

A wave of heat washed over Rona and as quickly receded, leaving her cold. The sixteenth of June – the date of the car crash. And what was more, since the Priory Hotel was some forty miles north-west of Farnbridge, Ross must have driven home along that road on his way to the M1. But how could it be proved? Rona thought wildly. She'd only the word of this girl to go on – it would never stand up in court.

'Mum was going to keep the menu as a souvenir,' Claudia was continuing, 'because it had the name of the hotel and the date printed at the top, but when Mr Mackenzie signed it she let me have it.'

'The date was on the menu?' Rona hardly recognized her voice.

'Yes, they printed it on every day.'

'And you still have it?' She realized that both Magda and Claudia were staring at her.

Claudia gave a slightly nervous laugh. 'Of course I have!'

She'd done it! Rona thought exultantly. All right, she still couldn't prove Ross had caused the accident, but she could at least prove he *might* have done. Belatedly she struggled to compose herself.

'That's great, Claudia. It must have been exciting for you.' She paused. 'And well done for recognizing him; I doubt if many people would. Dress designers aren't as high profile as pop stars.'

'But that was the point!' Claudia said excitedly. 'I wouldn't have done if I hadn't seen him on the telly the night before, when I was getting ready for dinner. It was about him being on the Queen's Birthday Honours list! So I congratulated him and asked if he'd got the medal with him, and he laughed and said he'd have to wait till the investiture in September.'

Magda was regarding Rona with a slight frown. 'All right, Claudia, thank you.'

The girl pushed back her chair. 'Nice to see you, Ms Parish,' she said, and with a quick pat for Gus she returned to the shop floor.

'And what the hell,' Magda asked slowly, 'was all that about?'

'I will tell you, Mags, I promise, but not just at the moment.'

'Why on earth is Ross having signed a menu so important?'

'It's not really,' Rona lied. 'As I said, I'm just interested in how he interacts with people.' She forced a laugh. 'He's certainly got a fan in Claudia!'

Magda drank her latte, her eyes still on her friend. 'All right, we'll leave it for the moment, but don't think you're getting away with it.'

Out on the pavement ten minutes later Rona stood hesitating, her heartbeat still fast. If only there was someone she could discuss it with! she thought in frustration. But Max would pooh-pooh the idea, Lindsey was at work – and in any case the Hathaways were still a delicate subject. As for the family themselves, it was too soon to get their hopes up.

The best plan, she decided, was to go home, write down all that she'd learned, and look at it from every conceivable angle. For a start, her pros and cons list was in urgent need of updating. Only then could she decide on her plan of action.

Gus, who, having waited for her to indicate which way they were going, had finally sat down, was jerked to his feet again as Rona started walking quickly towards home.

*   *   *

By lunchtime she had listed everything she knew about Ross Mackenzie, and it was still pitifully little. However, during the morning she'd thought of one person whom she might consult, though she was far from sure what reception she'd have. Detective Sergeant Archie Duncan, who was stationed at Marsborough Police Station, was a student at Max's adult education art classes and had been consulted in the past when Rona ran into trouble. He at least would be able to judge the plausibility of the case against Ross.

Accordingly, after a sketchy lunch of bread, cheese and an apple, she set off again, this time leaving Gus behind. She'd not phoned in advance to make an appointment and it was with fingers mentally crossed that she walked into the foyer of the station.

'Could I have a word with DS Duncan, please?' she asked the man on the desk.

'May I ask in what connection, ma'am?'

Rona hesitated. 'I should like his advice concerning a cold case.'

The desk sergeant's eyebrows went up. 'Perhaps—'

'Please!' she broke in. 'I do know him; I think he'll see me, if he's available.'

'Could I have your name, please, ma'am?'

'Rona Parish.'

The sergeant lifted his phone, turned his back and spoke quietly into it. Then, finishing the call, he faced her again. 'He'll be down in a minute, Ms Parish.'

'Thank you.'

Rona wandered to the far side of the foyer, reading the various notices on the wall and trying to avoid the curious glances of a couple seated on one of the benches.

'Rona!' Archie Duncan was coming towards her, hand outstretched and a smile on his round, rosy face.

'Hello, Archie. Thanks for seeing me.'

'Always a pleasure. There's something you'd like to discuss? Better come in here.'

He opened the door of an interview room, showed her inside and they seated themselves opposite each other across the scarred wooden table.

'Now, what can I do you for?'

'I want to ask you about a cold case from June last year; it took place near Farnbridge, and I know that's not your patch, but I'd be very grateful for some advice.'

'Sounds intriguing. What case is that?'

Rona leant forward earnestly, her clasped hands on the table. 'It concerns a fatal car crash in Farnbridge Woods.'

'Ah!'

'You remember it?'

'I do. Go ahead.'

'Well, Frank Hathaway, an elderly man who's a friend of my father, was the driver who went to the victim's aid and was with him as he died. He was badly injured himself when the car burst into flames and was in hospital for some time with concussion and amnesia. Then, a few weeks ago, he was on a crowded escalator when he overheard something that immediately transported him back to the scene of the crash.'

She glanced at Archie, but his face gave nothing away.

'He didn't know what it was,' she continued, 'but it brought back memories of what had happened immediately before it and immediately after. Just *before* the accident *two* cars had sped past him, either racing each other or one chasing the other, and it seemed pretty obvious it was one of them that had crashed, though there was no sign of the second one. And he also remembered the dying man had been trying to say something.

'Later, he thought the word he'd overheard was "frenzy", and that that was what the man had been saying. He and his son reported this to the police, but they either didn't believe him or thought there was too little to go on after all this time, which is understandable, I suppose, especially as there'd been no sign of any other car at the scene.'

'I think I should stop you there,' Archie said. 'As it happens, I'm pretty au fait with the case because I have a mate who's stationed at Farnbridge and we were discussing it over a pint a week or two ago.' Archie studied his hands. 'What I'm about to tell you must go no further, though I don't actually see what harm it can do. The fact is that this old chap wasn't the only one to come forward recently.'

Rona stared at him. 'What?'

'A young lad from the uni turned up at the station saying he'd actually *seen* one car nudge the other off the road.'

Rona gasped. 'But that's wonderful! Why didn't he come forward before? Surely *he* hadn't lost his memory?'

'Scared of getting into trouble with the authorities, I guess, but his conscience won in the end. With his father's help,' Archie added with a grim smile.

'Well, surely this backs up what Frank says?'

'To a certain extent, but as he couldn't give any details about the second car – reg, make or even colour – it didn't get us much further. Enquiries were made at repair shops and so on in a fairly wide radius, but nothing turned up and quite frankly there was little else they could do. I might say it's really bugging my pal Les; he's a bloke who likes to close a case with all loose ends neatly tied up, though God knows it doesn't always happen that way.'

'Well, what I'm about to tell you just might help him to achieve that.'

Archie's eyes widened. 'There's something else?'

Rona looked down at her clasped hands. 'Yes, but this is the tricky part.'

'Go on.'

'Have you heard of the dress designer, Ross Mackenzie?'

'Can't say I have.'

'Well, I met him at a fashion show and he asked me to write a profile of him for *Chiltern Life*. And when I mentioned this to Frank yesterday, he nearly had a heart attack because he now realizes that's what the dying man was saying – not "frenzy" but "Ross *Mackenzie*".'

Archie was looking sceptical, and Rona determinedly ploughed on. 'Someone on that escalator was probably saying he was due to attend the show at the Clarendon, and that's what Frank half-heard.'

'I hope you're not suggesting we should rush off and arrest him on the strength of that?'

'No, I'm not. For one thing, I couldn't for the life of me see what possible connection there could be between Mackenzie and the dead reporter. Come to that, I still can't. But nor could I imagine what Mackenzie, who lives in London, could be doing in Buckfordshire in the middle of the night.'

Archie's eyes were intent on her face. 'Are you going to tell me you've found out?'

'I think so, yes. In any event, he was having dinner that evening at the Priory Hotel, Narrowland. Which means that to get back to London he'd have to have driven down that stretch of road to reach the M1.'

'How did you discover this?'

'From someone who happened to be staying at the hotel. She went up and asked for his autograph, and he signed her menu. Which,' Rona added with emphasis, 'was printed with the date – June the sixteenth last year. The day of the crash.'

Archie leant back and whistled soundlessly. 'Well, well.'

'Surely you – or at least your colleagues – can do something now?'

'What you haven't explained is your interest in all this. Is it just part of your Miss Marple act?'

'No,' she answered steadily, 'it's because Frank has been consumed with guilt about his faulty memory. Sinclair was trying desperately to communicate with him, and he feels he let him down.'

Archie considered for a moment or two. 'Does Max know you're here?'

She shook head. 'He doesn't know the latest bit either – about the menu – because I only learned that this morning.'

'I hate to tell you this, Rona, but it's all pretty circumstantial. We couldn't go out on a limb with it as it stands.'

'I thought you'd say that, but I have an idea that might work. I know Mackenzie was ill last summer, which held him up for some time, and that he was never satisfied with the collection he was working on, considering it to be "jinxed". Something like causing the crash could account for that.'

'As could a hundred other things.'

'Yes, but the fact that he was ill afterwards – unspecified, but it could have been a breakdown – might mean it's still on his mind.'

'So?'

'Well, I was just wondering how he'd react if he was confronted with Frank.'

'Confronted how?'

'He's anxious to see the profile I've just finished. I thought I could arrange to take it to him at the London hotel where we met for the interview, and that while we were talking Frank Hathaway could just "happen" to come in and I could introduce them. There's just a chance it could throw him.'

'And what exactly would you do if it did?'

'Well, that's where you'd come in. Or your friend Les.'

'How, exactly?'

'He could be at a nearby table and if Mackenzie reacts as I think he might, he could at least arrest him on suspicion.'

'The lad might have ears like a bat but I doubt if over all the chatter in the room he'd catch anything significant.'

Rona thought for a minute, then slapped her hand on the table. 'I know – I could use my recorder! Have it switched on in my open handbag!'

'It's still a wild goose chase . . .' Archie's voice tailed off.

'But your friend likes to have things cleared up and this case has been bugging him. Surely he'd take a chance?'

'It wouldn't be up to him, but I dare say if they've not got a lot on and could spare a couple of bods . . . An unofficial recording wouldn't be admissible in court, but it would at least give us an opening for pursuing the investigation.'

'Then you'll speak to him?'

'Oh, I'll certainly do that.' Archie pushed back his chair. 'Thanks, Rona, you've raised several interesting points. If it's decided to go further and we need your cooperation, I'll be in touch.'

SEVENTEEN

'So what do you think, Guv?' Les Humphries demanded eagerly, later that afternoon. 'I mean, what have we got to lose? If chummie doesn't rise to the bait, or it's the wrong bloke anyway, well, we've had a wasted trip to London but it's no big deal. Let's face it, we've nothing else in the pipeline and it just might turn up trumps. And if you're thinking of manpower, we're not exactly bogged down at the moment.'

DCI Turnbull sighed and ran a hand through his hair. 'All right, Les, you win; we'll give it a go. As you say, we've nothing to lose, but we'll have to contact the Met as a matter of courtesy and fill them in. Check which is the nearest nick to the hotel, will you, and get a contact number in case you need to summon assistance and/ or transport.'

He paused. 'As a matter of interest, given that you won't be able to hear what's going on, how will you know if you're wanted?'

'I'll arrange a signal with Ms Parish – raising her hand or something, but the body language should give us an inkling.'

'He'll be on his own, will he, this designer bloke?'

'I asked about that, and DS Duncan got back to her. There's an off chance his sister might turn up if she gets a whiff of it. Likes to stick her nose in, by all accounts.'

'In which case she's presumably implicated too, by aiding and abetting if nothing more. Which, of course, would complicate things. For a start we'd require separate transport to the local nick. God knows they've had long enough to discuss this if they're guilty, but for court purposes we'd have to follow procedure and keep them apart. And though you could ferry him back here afterwards, she might need a bed overnight till we can get someone down to collect her.' He sighed. 'Not quite such a simple business as you're trying to make out, Les.'

'But worth the effort, eh, Guv?'

Turnbull grunted. 'Who do you propose taking with you?'

'I thought Bob Sanders; he was present at the interviews both with Hathaway and the uni student.'

'Fair enough. So what happens next?'

'Once you've sanctioned it Ms Parish will contact Mackenzie and Hathaway to arrange the meeting, then get back to me.'

Turnbull nodded and, preparing to end the conversation, switched on his computer. 'Very well. Keep me informed,' he said.

'Steve? It's Rona – again!'

'Hello there.'

'I've something to tell you, but first, how's Frank? Has he recovered now?'

'Oh, yes, thanks. It was just the shock, as he said. By this morning he was as right as rain.'

'Then I hate to be a nuisance, but could I pop round to see you? I know I'm always turning up on your doorstep, but I think this should be done face-to-face rather than over the phone.'

'My goodness, that sounds serious!'

'Important, anyway.'

His voice quickened. 'You have some news?'

'Yes; what would be the best time? I don't want to interrupt your meal.'

'Is your husband at home?'

'No, he has evening classes tonight.'

'Then how about eating with us rather than on your own?'

'Oh, now look—'

'Really. Unless you have boeuf bourguignon on the hob, that is?'
She gave a spurt of laughter. 'If you knew me better, you wouldn't
have to ask!'

'Right. As to this news of yours, would you like to impart it
before or after the meal?'

'Before, please.'

'Well, it's five thirty now, and we usually eat around seven, so
come whenever you're ready.'

'Thanks very much; I'll be there in half an hour.'

Waiting to cross rush-hour Guild Street, Rona couldn't believe it
had been only that morning that she'd learned of the dated menu.
From being despondent about her lack of progress, events had moved
with astonishing speed. She could only hope her news wouldn't
have an adverse effect on Frank, and that he'd agree to the proposed
meeting.

Once again she was ushered into the sitting room at four-two-
seven Alban Road, relieved to see no sign of Luke.

'I must apologize for my drama act yesterday,' Frank said with
a wry smile. 'I'm not usually given to such histrionics!'

'You're all right now?'

'Thank you, yes, and prepared for whatever news you have to
impart.'

'Well, a lot has happened in the last twenty-four hours, the most
important being I've discovered that Ross Mackenzie was dining at
the Priory at Narrowland on Sunday evening the sixteenth of June.'
She heard their joint in-drawn breath. 'And on his way home he
would have driven through Farnbridge Woods.'

There was a beat of silence. Then Steve said, 'Can it be proved?
That he was there?'

'Yes; someone at the hotel asked for his autograph and he signed
her menu, which was dated.'

'Then we've got him!' Steve breathed.

'Not exactly; we now know he *could* have been involved. We
still have to prove he was, and if so, why.'

Steve's face fell. 'He's not likely to tell us.'

'Not in the normal way of things, no. But we might be able to
shock him into it.'

Frank frowned. 'How?'

Rona breathed a silent prayer. 'By your confronting him,' she said.

They both stared at her. Then Steve said violently, 'No way!'
Frank held up a hand. 'Let her explain what she means.'

She took a deep breath. 'As I said, I'd agreed to write his profile
and he phoned about three weeks ago to ask if I'd made a start on
it. I hadn't, but I've now finished it and as he made me promise to
let him see it, I propose to suggest we meet again at the Argyll
Hotel in Mayfair, and you just happen to drop in. I could introduce
you and ask you to join us, and could then mention you were
involved in the crash. His reaction should tell us all we need.

'I know it's a huge gamble,' she hurried on when neither of them
spoke, 'but accepting for the moment that it really was him, my
impression is that there'd been repercussions for him too. The
collection he was working on didn't come up to scratch and he had
an unspecified illness. I think – and hope – it's been preying on his
mind, and meeting you might shock him into an admission. He
could even be wanting to get it off his chest.'

'It all sounds very tentative,' Steve objected.

'And even if it did all come spilling out,' Frank said, 'it would
only be our word against his.'

'This is where my recorder comes in. It would be switched on
in my bag throughout our conversation. I've also inveigled a couple
of detectives to be present at a nearby table. *If* we get a confession
– and I appreciate it's a big if – they'll be on hand to arrest him.
It all depends now on whether you're prepared to go ahead.'

Another silence. Then Steve asked, 'Have you arranged to meet
Mackenzie?'

'No; I wanted to check with you first.'

Frank thumped his hand on the arm of his chair. 'Let's go for
it!' he said.

'Dad—'

'No, Steve: this has been on my mind for well over a year,
more so since my memory started coming back. Now I have a
chance to end it, one way or another, and I have to take it or I'll
regret it all my life.' He glanced affectionately at his son. 'Which
doesn't mean it won't be a strain, and I'd be grateful if you could
accompany me.'

'That goes without saying.'

'Then you'll do it?' Rona pressed.

'I'll do it.'

'Thank you.'

'No, thank *you*. God knows how you achieved all this – finding out about the menu, even arranging for police presence – but if it provides an answer one way or the other I'll be eternally grateful.'

'Then I just have to contact Ross.' She paused. 'Shall I phone him now?'

They both nodded and watched as she took out her mobile and pressed the requisite buttons, feeling a little like Judas Iscariot. 'Ross? It's Rona Parish. Just to say I've finished your profile and as promised am phoning to ask when you'd like to see it.'

The two men waited, their eyes on her face. The designer's voice reached them merely as a rumble in the background.

'Yes,' she replied, 'I think I could manage Thursday.' She raised her eyebrows questioningly and they nodded affirmation.

'What time would suit you? Five thirty at the Argyll again? Fine. See you there.' She closed the phone. 'Trap set,' she said.

There was a lot to tell Max when he made his bedtime call.

'You're *what?*'

'It's perfectly safe, Max, and too good an opportunity to miss. And if he *does* get nasty, which is highly unlikely in the middle of a Mayfair hotel, the police will be on hand.'

'But if it's on Thursday I shan't even be able to lurk in the background.'

She smiled. 'Probably just as well!'

'*Why* do you keep getting involved in things like this? Everyone else manages to live normal, everyday lives without continually putting themselves in danger—'

'I've just explained I shan't *be* in danger, and when it's over I'll travel back with the Hathaways.'

'I'm still not clear about how you got on to him.'

'I'll give you a blow-by-blow account when you're home tomorrow. In the meantime don't worry about it – I'll be fine.'

At lunchtime on the Thursday Rona had a phone call from the switchboard at *Chiltern Life*.

'Rona, we've had a Lottie Sinclair on the phone wanting to speak to you. She asked for your number, which of course we didn't give her, but you might want to call her back. She said to tell you she's on her lunch break so she'll be on her mobile.' She read out the number.

'Thanks, Liz; I'll get on to her straight away.'

Mystified as to what Lottie could want with her, Rona made the call. 'It's Rona Parish, Lottie. I believe—'

'Oh, Rona, thank God!' Lottie's voice was shaking. 'Thank you so much for coming back to me. I've been nearly out of my mind, wondering what to do.'

Rona felt a pulse of excitement. 'Something's happened?'

'Yes, yes, it has. At least, I think it might have done. I had a quick word with my sister before leaving for work and she said I should go to the police, but I wanted to speak to you first – less official, if you see what I mean.'

'Not really,' Rona said above the sudden hammering of her heart. 'Suppose you start at the beginning?'

'Sorry, yes, of course.' She gave a nervous little laugh. 'Well, Brett's been on my mind since talking to you, and I decided it was time I pulled myself together and cleared out his clothes and took them to Oxfam, something I've been putting off. So last night I sorted through them and put a pile ready in the hall. Then this morning I went through the pockets one last time in case there was the odd hanky or something in one of them.' She paused and drew a deep breath. 'No hanky, but I did find a crumpled piece of paper stuffed into a corner.'

Rona tried to contain her impatience. 'Yes?'

'He'd torn a strip off a page of newspaper dated Saturday the fifteenth of June last year. He often did that when he was on the phone – jotted down something the other person was saying on the nearest scrap of paper.' Her voice shook. 'And on the bit that had no print he'd scribbled *Sharon recognized RM on telly* and three exclamation marks.'

Rona tensed. 'Have you any idea what that means?' she demanded urgently.

'Well, I don't know any RM but I know Sharon – she's the daughter of a friend of Brett's who was raped in London last year, when she was only thirteen. She'd gone shopping with a friend but they lost each other and the police found her half-dressed and crying in a street at five in the morning. She was pretty traumatized and her description of her attacker would have fitted half of London, Brett said. Her dad Jack begged him to look into it and he worked his socks off for months but didn't get any further than the police.' She paused and when Rona didn't speak, added nervously, 'Do you think I should get on to them?'

Rona's brain was reeling. *Ross* the rapist of a thirteen-year-old?
It didn't seem possible. But even if Brett had decided to pursue the
possibility, he'd only gleaned this scrap of information the night
before the crash and wouldn't have time to plan anything. Of *course*
the police should be informed, but it was too late now to cancel the
meeting that afternoon. Anyway, she couldn't do that to Frank, not
when he was keyed up for the confrontation. Perhaps she could use
this new snippet, unlikely as it was, to shock Ross into a reaction
– in which case the police would already be on hand. And if he
didn't give himself away, Lottie could pass on the information which,
Rona argued with her conscience, would only have been delayed
by one day.

'Rona?' Lottie prompted.

'Lottie, I have an idea about RM but I can't say any more at the
moment. Could you hold on for a couple of days before contacting
the police, and I'll come back to you?'

'Yes, of course, if you think that's best.' She paused. 'I've been
thinking: Brett must have scribbled that note when he had that phone
call the night before he was killed. It must have been from Jack,
telling him Sharon had recognized someone on TV.'

As had Claudia. Another piece of the jigsaw slotting into place!
Rona thought exultantly.

'Should I phone Jack and tell him what I've found?' Lottie asked,
when she didn't speak.

Rona hastily marshalled her thoughts. 'Again, wait till I get back
to you. It's possible I might have some news by then.'

Lottie breathed a sigh of relief. 'OK, thanks, Rona. That's a load
off my mind.'

'I'll be in touch in a couple of days, I promise,' Rona said. And
God willing Ross Mackenzie would by then have belatedly been
brought to justice.

16 June the previous year

Brett's mind wasn't on the concert, and all the time he was photo-
graphing the gyrating youths on stage he was thinking of Jack's
phone call. Could that highfalutin designer really be the brute who'd
attacked Sharon? The bloke had been awarded some gong in the
Birthday Honours and Jack said when his picture came on the screen
Sharon had screamed, 'That's him!' and started crying and shaking

so much Liz had a job holding on to her. Then minutes later she changed her mind, swore she'd been mistaken and refused point blank to accompany her father to the police station.

'She's clammed up because he's famous and she thinks no one would believe her,' Jack had said desperately, 'and after all, what proof do we have? She's no idea where he took her. I just don't know what to do, Brett. No point carting her off to the police if she's not going to make a statement. And supposing it really wasn't him, and it was just his hair or something that looked similar? If we're wrong, he could make mincemeat out of us.'

Then the crunch had come. 'We were wondering,' Jack had continued, 'if now we've got a possible lead you could do a bit of digging and see what you come up with? There's no one else I can ask – it's you or no one, mate, unless we can get Sharon to play ball.'

He'd spent the rest of the evening looking up Mackenzie on the internet, memorizing every detail of that good-looking face, the way his hair was parted, the carefully enigmatic smile, until he was satisfied he'd recognize him once he ran him to earth. And that, he was determined to do.

A blast of even louder music, followed by prolonged screaming, brought him back to the present and the thankful realization that the concert was over. Not his scene at all, being bombarded all evening with mega-decibels, but Bob, the *Gazette*'s showbiz journo, had found himself with a double-booking and since he'd done Brett a favour in the past, he'd agreed to cover for him.

He turned and made his way to the car park, intent on a quick getaway. The beer they served in the tent had left a lot to be desired and he was looking forward to relaxing with a whisky before bed. After giving Lottie a quick call to say he was on his way, he set off for home.

It must have been half an hour later that he first noticed the Bentley behind him, weaving erratically from side to side. Better keep an eye on him, Brett thought apprehensively as it edged up close behind him.

A string of cars coming towards them prevented overtaking, which was obviously fuelling the driver's impatience. Suddenly, without any signal, he swerved out, scraping Brett's wing mirror and sending it rocking back on its hinges before immediately swerving back in again, so that he had to jam on his brakes. He leant on the horn. 'Bloody maniac!' he muttered under his breath. What the hell was he playing at?

A roadside sign came up indicating a petrol station and Little Chef ahead and the Bentley's indicator immediately switched on. Right, Brett decided, he'd follow it and give the driver a piece of his mind – he could have been killed. Accordingly he followed the car up the slope leading to the café and pulled in alongside it under one of the overhead lights.

The passenger door opened and a woman emerged, then, as the driver joined her, Brett froze. It couldn't be! It just couldn't – *far* too much of a coincidence. But he was damn sure it was! Divine justice! he thought exuberantly.

He scrambled out of his car as the couple started to walk towards the café, calling after them, and as they both turned he demanded furiously, 'Are you aware that you damn nearly caused an accident, cutting me up back there?'

Mackenzie said, 'You're the one who tooted? Sorry if I cut it a bit fine.'

The scent of alcohol reached Brett on the still night air. That explained a lot. 'You're Ross Mackenzie, aren't you? The dress designer who's been awarded the MBE?'

The man looked startled, then nodded impatiently, glancing over his shoulder towards the lights of the café. Arrogant bastard! If Lottie were with him she'd recognize the signs of rising temper and advise him to count to ten. But Lottie wasn't here and Brett allowed his anger to boil up, fuelled by thoughts of Sharon.

'Been celebrating, have you, sir?'

The woman caught Mackenzie's arm and tried to urge him towards the café. 'We're very sorry if we drove too close,' she said hurriedly, looking anxiously about her, but no one else was in sight.

'Going for some coffee to sober up?' Brett continued levelly. 'Not before time; the state he's in, he should never have been behind that wheel.'

'Now look here,' Mackenzie blustered, 'we've apologized – can we leave it at that? My sister will drive the rest of the way. Will that satisfy you?'

Brett drew a deep breath. 'No, it won't, as it happens, but it's an amazing coincidence running into you like this. Or rather, you nearly running into me. I work for the local paper and I was planning to—'

The woman said sharply, 'Look, this is neither the time nor place for an interview, but if you'd like to discuss the award, my brother would be happy to speak to you if you make an appointment through the studio. I'll give you our card.' She started fumbling in her bag.

'That would be great,' Brett said, his voice heavy with sarcasm. 'But what I'd *really* like to ask him is if he makes a habit of raping thirteen-year-old girls.' Hell's teeth! Now he really had blown it, shooting off his mouth when he'd no proof, no evidence of any kind since Sharon had retracted her accusation.

But his momentary dismay dissolved when he saw that the shaft had gone home. Mackenzie was swaying as if pole-axed, one hand to his head, and his sister grabbed at him to steady him.

'What the *hell* are you talking about?' she gasped. 'Ross, you can't let him speak to you like that – it's . . . it's slander! Ross!' She shook his arm frenziedly as he continued to sway, his face blank.

Conscious of still being on dangerous ground, Brett shrugged. 'Just as you like, sir. There's more than one way to skin a cat.' He turned back to the car and was getting into it as Mackenzie at last found his voice.

'No – wait!' he shouted hoarsely. But Brett was exultant; in his book, that reaction had been as good as an admission. He switched on the ignition as Mackenzie attempted to open the driver's door, falling back as he accelerated. But a glance in the mirror showed the couple hurrying to their own car. Damn it, they were coming after him – *not* what he'd intended! And if he didn't want them to know where he lived, he'd better lose them before the Farnbridge exit. Putting his foot down, he shot down the slip road at fifty miles an hour.

As the day wore on, Rona became increasingly anxious. Was she guilty of withholding evidence by advising Lottie to delay going to the police? Yet the more she thought about it, the more unlikely it seemed that it could have been Ross who attacked that girl. Magda had said he was fond of the ladies, but not young girls, for God's sake. On the other hand, if Brett had suspected and somehow challenged him, there was a plausible motive for Ross going after him. The flaw in that theory, she reminded herself yet again, was that the timing didn't fit. So by what malicious twist of fate had their paths crossed that Sunday night?

By the time she caught the London train she had decided to ignore the Sharon angle, reckoning it would only complicate things. As far as she knew, the police weren't aware of the connection and it had nothing to do with Frank, who was her main concern. Furthermore, if it had indeed been Ross who'd attacked the girl, she would probably be more ready to come forward once he was in custody.

It had been agreed that she should arrive at the hotel half an hour in advance of the appointment so that she could meet the two detectives, who introduced themselves as DS Humphries and DC Sanders.

'I'm very grateful to you for coming,' she told them. 'I just hope it will be worth your while.'

'Us too,' Humphries replied. 'Archie Duncan made out a strong case for you, so good luck. We recced the lounge bar,' he added, 'and as we're early there shouldn't be any difficulty in nabbing the table next to yours. Even so, it's unlikely we'll hear what's being said, but if it works and he spills the beans, just touch your hair and we'll be over in a flash.'

Rona nodded and they separated to take up their respective positions.

By five thirty her stomach was in knots and she felt slightly sick. Suppose Ross was late and the Hathaways arrived before he did instead of ten minutes after as had been agreed? Suppose he didn't come at all?

And then there he was, coming towards her with a smile, Isobel at his side. Two for the price of one, Rona thought. Would his sister's presence be an asset or a hindrance?

Greetings were exchanged, seats taken and drinks ordered.

'Right,' Ross said jovially, 'let's be seeing it then.'

She opened her bag and took out the article, at the same time surreptitiously switching on the recorder. Her mouth was dry. 'I hope you'll be pleased with it,' she said, and as Ross took it from her, Isobel moved her chair closer to her brother in order to read it with him.

Engrossed as they were, they did not see Frank and Steve appear in the doorway, both looking as tense as Rona felt. *Please let it work out!* she prayed silently as she forced a smile.

'What is it about this hotel?' she asked lightly. 'Last time we met my sister turned up out of the blue, and now here are a couple of my friends.'

Ross and Isobel turned as the Hathaways approached their table, both wearing strained smiles.

'Fancy running into you!' Frank said, as they'd rehearsed. 'We're meeting some friends and thought we'd have a drink while we're waiting.'

'Come and join us till they arrive,' Rona invited and signalled to a waiter, who hurried over to take their order.

Father and son seated themselves and Rona went on, 'Frank, this is Ross Mackenzie, the dress designer, and his sister, Isobel Firth. My friends, Frank and Steven Hathaway.'

Ross's brows drew momentarily together as though the name was familiar. It would, of course, have been in the press after the accident.

'As it happens,' she continued, 'it was an article on Frank that I was working on before your profile. He's had an eventful life; not only did he survive the Entebbe hijack and the Kuwait invasion, he also had a hair-raising experience nearer home.' Please don't let my voice shake, she thought fiercely. 'He was involved in that car crash in Farnbridge Woods last year. You might have read about it?'

Isobel drew in her breath sharply and Ross's hand, in the act of lifting his glass, froze in mid-air.

'He was the driver who went to help and got severely injured for his pains.'

She risked a glance at Ross. His eyes were fixed on the still-suspended glass and there was a pulse beating in his temple. Isobel cleared her throat.

'How appalling for him,' she said hurriedly. 'Thanks for letting us see the profile, Rona, it's absolutely fine. I hope you'll excuse us now – we have a meeting. Ross?' She turned to her brother.

'*Did* you read about it?' Rona asked, as if she'd not spoken. 'The victim was a reporter called Brett Sinclair, a young man with a wife and family. He'd been covering an open-air pop concert in Heatherby and was on his way home.'

'God!' said Ross, barely audibly. 'Oh, God, God, God!'

'Ross!' Isobel's voice was sharp and she pushed back her chair. 'It's time we were going.'

At last he moved, turning a blank face to Rona. 'These people didn't arrive by chance, did they?'

'*Ross!*' Isobel sounded desperate.

'No,' Rona answered simply.

'How did you . . .?'

It was Frank who replied. 'Sinclair said your name as he died.'

'He can't have done – there must be some mistake!' Isobel cried shrilly. 'Ross wasn't anywhere near those woods! How could he have been?'

Rona stole a glance at the nearby table, where the two detectives appeared totally oblivious of them.

'He was on his way home from Narrowland,' she replied. 'And I believe you were with him.'

Ross's glass fell to the table, where it overturned, spilling the small amount of liquid remaining in it. 'What's the use?' he said in a dull voice. 'They know.'

Isobel clutched his arm. 'For God's sake, don't say anything! They can't prove a thing!'

But he slowly shook his head. 'This is it, Izzie. Nemesis. They know the worst; let me at least try to explain.'

Defeated, she covered her face with her hands.

'Were you staying at the hotel?' Rona asked conversationally.

He stared at her. 'How the hell do you know about that?'

'You signed a menu for a friend of mine.'

He shook his head in bewilderment. 'I don't remember.'

'Fortunately she did.' Rona glanced at the Hathaways, neither of whom had touched their drinks but were staring with fascination at Ross's disintegration. 'What I don't understand is how you knew Brett Sinclair?'

'I didn't,' he said flatly. 'I'd never seen him before in my life, and to answer your earlier question, no, we weren't staying at the Priory. We'd been to a fabric trade show near Milton Keynes and went on to spend the weekend with friends in Narrowland. Dinner at the hotel was our thank you before we set off for home.' He paused before adding, 'I'd imbibed pretty freely, but I could do with a top-up now.'

Frank signalled the waiter and between the ordering of the drink and its arrival no one spoke. Ross took a gulp of it, set down the glass and turned to his sister. She was now sitting ramrod straight staring down at the table and refused to meet his eye. He put a hand briefly on her arm, then cleared his throat.

'We were late leaving the hotel so although I'd been drinking I insisted on driving because I go faster than Izzie. I was perfectly capable,' he added defensively, looking round at them, 'though I admit I took chances I wouldn't normally, and that was when I made a literally fatal mistake.'

He paused and moistened his lips. 'It was about half an hour after leaving the hotel and I needed a pee. We hadn't reached the motorway and I'd been looking for somewhere to stop, and just as I was giving up hope there was a notice by the roadside announcing a petrol station a mile ahead.' He took a deep breath. 'I was desperate not to miss the turn-off, and in my haste to get back into the inside lane I inadvertently cut up the car in front of me. I wasn't even aware of it until the driver leant on the horn and kept leaning. I glanced in the mirror and saw this little Mini behind me with a broad white stripe down its roof and bonnet.

'I thought no more of it at the time. The turn-off to the restaurant came up and I drove into it and up into the parking area. There was a Little Chef alongside and Izzie suggested we had a coffee – a tactful attempt to sober me up.'

Another pause. 'But as we were getting out of the car, the Mini came zooming into the space next to ours and the driver got out and started haranguing me for cutting him up. I was prepared to bluff it out, but he . . . smelt my breath and accused me of drink-driving and to my horror addressed me by name. Well, you can imagine how embarrassing this was, especially in view of the recent award announcement, and I was prepared to make some conciliatory gesture when he announced he was a reporter for the local paper.'

Ross's eyes went swiftly round the table, but no one moved. 'That, of course, put a completely different complexion on it,' he continued, 'and while I was still reeling from the implications, he turned and got back into his car, suggesting it would be of interest to his readers. Well, you must see I had to stop him.'

There was an appeal in his voice, but again no one responded, and he went on with increasing desperation: 'I had my hand on the car door when he started the engine and shot out of the car park. So, in the hopes of persuading him not to publicize it, we set off after him.'

He stopped again, his breathing ragged. 'I must stress that all I wanted to do was to speak to him – pay him off if necessary, anything to stave off damage to my reputation.'

It was far more likely, Rona thought privately, that, on recognizing Ross, Brett had accused him not of drink-driving but of raping Sharon, which he'd only just learned about the previous evening. And that was something he'd have gone to any lengths to keep quiet.

'Presumably he'd have had no idea who you were when you cut him up,' Steve reasoned. 'He must only have followed you to demand an apology, but when he recognized you it would have seemed the perfect revenge.'

Ross shrugged. 'We'll never know. What I *do* know is we were both under stress, and that affected our driving, making us take risks. But you must believe I never meant him any harm.' He went to lift his glass and saw it was empty. 'We didn't hear about his death till the next day.'

'You must at least have seen him go over the edge,' Frank insisted. 'Why the hell didn't you stop?'

'But we *didn't* see him!' Ross declared wildly. 'He'd managed to gain on us, and by the time we also rounded the curve in the road he was out of sight. There was another bend a few metres farther on, and we went round that expecting to see him ahead, but again there was no sign. We assumed he must have turned off somewhere, and were forced to give up the chase.'

Rona knew differently; Archie had told her a student had actually seen one car nudge the other off the road, but that was privileged information and she held her tongue, confident that his story wouldn't hold water with the police.

After a minute's reflective silence Ross went on: 'Learning of his death was a total nightmare and haunted us for months. The stress had a detrimental effect on my collection, and eventually I went down with a bug and couldn't work for weeks.' He looked challengingly at the three of them. 'So there you have it; a tragedy all round.'

Frank met his eye unwaveringly. 'Sinclair was desperately trying to communicate with me, and for over a year I failed him because I'd not understood what he said. And when eventually I did under-stand, the fact that he'd struggled with his dying breath to say *your* name rather than his wife's suggested he was accusing you of causing the crash.'

Ross said sombrely, 'I was responsible inasmuch as I was following him, yes, but that's all the guilt I can accept.'

Unnoticed by any of them, Rona pushed back her hair. Simultaneously the two detectives rose from the next table and approached them, producing their ID cards.

'Ross Mackenzie,' intoned Les Humphries, 'I'm arresting you on suspicion of causing death by dangerous driving. You do not have to say anything, but it may harm your defence if you fail to mention when questioned something you later rely on in court. Anything you do say may be given in evidence. Do you understand?'

Isobel's head reared up, her furious eyes switching to Rona. 'You little bitch!' she hissed.

'Do you understand, sir?' Humphries repeated.

'Oh, I understand,' Ross said bitterly.

Humphries turned to Rona. 'If you'll just give us the recording, Ms Parish, we won't detain you any further. You and your friends are free to go.'

She nodded, and, aware of a sudden hush as heads turned all over the room, extracted the cassette from her recorder and handed it to him. Then Frank took her arm and, as the detectives turned their attention to Isobel, the three of them thankfully left the room.

It was an hour later, and they were sitting in a nearby restaurant talking over the events of the evening and Ross's account of the tragedy.

'I must say I thought his reaction a bit excessive,' Frank observed. 'I mean, surely the story of his drink-driving wouldn't have ruined his career?'

Rona shook her head. 'I've not had a chance to tell you, but Brett had something far more serious on him.' And she recounted the story of Sharon, and of Lottie's discovery of the note in his pocket.

'Ross knew he was a reporter, remember, and he'd have realized there was no way he could be dissuaded from publishing the story, which certainly *would* have had a detrimental effect. He'd have known that the only way to kill the story was by killing the reporter.'

'So it was murder after all,' Frank said quietly.

'Without a shadow of a doubt.'

'But he shouldn't get away with the rape, either!' Steve insisted.

'I'm sure he won't. Now all this has come up, Sharon's father's bound to inform the police that he told Brett the night before the crash that she'd recognized Ross, which puts a completely different slant on their confrontation. Also, Sharon's a year older now, and since he's already in the dock, so to speak, she mightn't be so reluctant to come forward. I don't know if there'll be enough evidence to bring a charge but Ross might well be in the mood for making a clean breast of everything.'

Frank took another sip of wine. 'I must say it's a tremendous relief. I felt particularly responsible for that young man, having been the only one to have seen the second car, a fact no one seemed inclined to believe.'

Rona toyed with her glass. 'Actually, Frank, you weren't. The only one, I mean.'

Both men simultaneously dropped their forks, staring at her in amazement. 'I only discovered this when I spoke to Archie the other day,' she continued, 'and he didn't want it broadcast, but I think you have a right to know. A student from the uni was in the woods with his girlfriend and he actually *saw* one car nudge the other off the road.'

'My God!' Frank exclaimed. 'Then if he'd already reported it, why didn't the police say so?'

'He *didn't* report it, till a week after you did. Afraid of repercussions, apparently. But while it corroborated your account, it wasn't any help in following it up, because he didn't see the registration or make of the other car.'

Frank considered this for a moment, then nodded. 'Well, at least poor Sinclair will be avenged, and for that I have you to thank, Rona. Though it's a grim story, it's an incredible weight off my mind.'

'I was just lucky the way it worked out,' Rona said, wondering how the bubbly Claudia would feel when she realized it was her testimony that had helped bring down her idol.

'Will you still publish his profile?' Steve asked curiously.

'It won't be up to me, but knowing Barnie I should say he'll rush it out. Talk about topical!'

'Will you add anything you learned this evening?'

She shook her head. 'It will be *sub judice* anyway.'

'So what will you work on now?' Steve enquired, refilling her glass.

'I'll return to my "unforgettable experiences", though they'll seem pretty tame after this!' Her phone vibrated in her bag. 'Sorry; I thought I'd turned it off.'

'You'd better answer it – someone might want to tell you about being stranded on an iceberg!'

Rona pulled a face at him and glanced at the screen. Max. It was early for him – the art class would only just have started.

'Hi,' she said.

'Hello, love. I couldn't wait till bedtime to hear what happened so I left them painting and sneaked out.'

'Well, he didn't tell the full story, but the police will be able to fill in the gaps. They've arrested him.'

'Thank God for that! And he didn't turn nasty?'

'No, it was Isobel who did the snarling. I'm just having dinner with Frank and Steve, but I'll tell you all about it later.'

'Sorry to interrupt, but I wanted to check you were OK. My salaams to the Hathaways, and tell Frank from me he's already had more than his share of experiences and we don't want to hear about any more!'

She smiled. 'I'll do that,' she said.